The Riddling

and other stories by

David R. Grigg

Rightword

ISBN: 978-0-9872654-9-4
1st Edition

A publication of Rightword Enterprises, Melbourne, Australia.
www.rightword.com.au

Body text set in Adriane Text by Typefolio, headings in
Geomanist by atipo. Cover title in Newston by Gearwright.

Cover design by the author.
Photograph of London street by Sarah on Flickr.

For my mother, with thanks for everything

Contents

Short Stories

Flashes of Inspiration

Credits

"The Riddling" is based on a concept developed by Charles Barouch. It will appear as part of the forthcoming *Reality Breaks* project from HDWPbooks, and is published here with the kind permission of Charles Barouch.

"Enhancement" first appeared in *Theme-Thology: Real World Unreal*, published by HDWP Books 2014.

"We, the Dead" first appeared in *Theme-Thology: Day I Died*, published by HDWP Books 2014.

"On the Cold Hill Side" first appeared in *NovoPulp Anthology Volume I*, published in 2014 by Hermit Press.

"The Miracle Cure" first appeared in *NovoPulp Anthology Volume II*, published in March 2015 by Hermit Press.

"The Golden City" first appeared in *NovoPulp Anthology Volume III*, published in November 2015 by Hermit Press.

"This Too, Too Solid Flesh" first appeared in *Cadavers*, edited by G. P. Stratford, published 2014 by KnightWatch Press.

"No Direction Home" first appeared in *The Art of Losing*, edited by Daniel White, published 2015 by Thinkerbeat.

"The Chisel's Sharp Edge" first appeared in *Short and Twisted 2014*, edited by Kathryn Duncan, published by Celaphene Press 2014.

Flash fiction inspired by prompts from Becket Morgan and Chuck Wendig, with thanks.

Short Stories

The Riddling

BRITONS CALL IT "THE RIDDLING", the day that their world was pierced full of Holes.

Lewis Conway didn't think of it that way at the time, of course. In fact, it took him quite a while before he understood that anything strange was going on. He was writing a complex piece of code, in the zone: his entire world was the varicolored text on the screen immediately in front of him. The code finally compiled without errors and he flicked his glance to the left-hand monitor. He cursed softly. The results were still screwy; there had to be yet another bug.

Before he could address the problem, however, his arm was shaken violently. "What the..." Startled, Conway looked up at his colleague Frank Harris.

"Jesus, Lew, you'd keep working through an earthquake. Haven't you being paying *any* attention to what's going on?"

It took Conway a major effort of will to bring his attention back up out of his focus on the code. "What is it? What's going on?"

"Something weird is going on outside," Frank said. "Everyone else has been at the window for the last twenty minutes. I just came back here to see what the media are saying."

Conway stood up, groaning and stretching. He would need to visit the gym later today to work out some of the kinks in his back. Standing, for the first time he was able to see over the tops of the ranks of cubicle walls to the window. Frank was right – almost the entire firm was standing there looking out. There was a babble of conversation.

"Come and *see*," Frank said impatiently. "I can't describe it.

There's these... bubbles... oh, shit, just come look!" He almost dragged Conway to the window, pushing aside some of the other staff.

Conway looked out over the city of London. They had a great view from up here on the 32nd floor, south across the city to the Thames, with the top of the London Eye peeking above the buildings beyond the bend in the river to his right. It took several moments of staring before Conway saw anything unusual. Then he saw his first 'bubble', which seemed to be resting on Leadenhall Street. Somehow it seemed to be even wider than the roadway. The day was overcast, but the bubble shone brightly as though lit by a spotlight, and inside it was what appeared to be a tangle of greenery. It was like some enormous spherical hothouse. Traffic was banked up on either side of it.

"What is it?" Conway said, frowning. "Some kind of publicity event?"

"Not it," said Frank. "It's not the only one. We've spotted a dozen now. Look!" He pointed over to the west. A bubble even bigger than the one in the street seemed to be hovering high above the tallest buildings. It was black but sprinkled with dots of light. Could they be... stars? Conway felt a little dizzy. It was unreal.

"And over there," said Frank, pointing down to a nearby park, where a hemispherical dome sat amidst the trees. It was somehow *hollow*. Even though he was looking down on it from a steep angle, Conway could see an impossibly-tilted landscape through it, with distant purple hills.

To their left, a woman screamed piercingly. He and Frank turned. Mary Edwards, the firm's Business Manager, was pointing out of the window. Mary was normally the most unflappable person that Conway knew. For her to scream meant something was very wrong.

Mary was pointing with a trembling finger out to the nearby 'Gherkin', one of London's most identifiable buildings. There was another of the bubbles there, seemingly filled with an orange-colored gas. It was drifting slowly, and as it moved away from the Gherkin, Conway realized with horror that it had taken a huge, perfectly circular bite out of the side of the building. Even as he watched, the remaining structure began to fold and collapse towards the bite. Debris, furniture, *people* were falling out towards the street below.

Conway felt sick to his stomach, the way he did when he saw replays of the Twin Towers collapsing. But this was *here* and *now*. And what was worse... "Fuck! It's coming this way!" he said. "We've got to get out of here." Frank had turned a greenish-white. Together they ran for their desks. Everyone was scattering.

Conway grabbed up his phone and his gym bag, paused for an instant and then snatched the framed photograph of his wife and daughter, and then raced for the lift foyer with Frank a few steps behind.

"Stairs!" Conway yelled. "Lifts will be jammed." He dodged aside and pulled open the door to the fire stairs. There were already a few people coming down from the upper floors. Conway started down the stairs, at first taking two steps at a time. But it wasn't long before more and more people crowded in, and he and Frank were reduced to a slow walk. The line was moving, though, and for the moment there was no panic. Surprisingly, there was little conversation. Instead, a kind of shocked hush prevailed, mixed in with a few sobs. London had suffered many terror attacks in the past. *Is that what's going on?* Conway thought, *Some new kind of terrorism?* It was too early to understand any part of this.

Down the stairs and around, down and around, the drab concrete walls with stenciled floor numbers all there was to see. They had gone down perhaps a dozen floors when Conway began to feel an ominous shudder beneath his feet. Before he had the slightest chance to say or do anything, everything changed in an instant. The concrete wall in front of Conway seemed to be wiped away and was replaced with a bright orange light. He faintly registered a chorus of screams and yells around him, but he was struck dumb with astonishment as his brain tried to process what he was seeing.

He was looking out high over an alien world. Distant tangerine hills, a plain dotted with cherry-colored blobs which might be vegetation. In the pale orange sky hung a moon or another planet, seen faintly as through a daylight sky. A bird, or a bat, or... something... flew across his vision. All of this in an instant. Then it all slid away, orange sky, hills, moon and all, and Conway was looking out over London watching the orange bubble drift away. Only, he suddenly realized, it wasn't a bubble filled with gas. It was, incredibly, some kind of a *hole* in the world, opening up somewhere else.

Frank was gripping Conway's arm so tightly that it hurt. Conway shook his head, tried to come to his senses. In front of them, sheared right through the wall and part of the stairwell, was a gap in the building. The edges of glass, concrete and steel were all neatly cut, almost polished, in a perfect gentle curve. Two paces in front of Conway, at the turn of the stair, the steps were sheared through and he could see the streetscape below. Lying on the last step was a human arm, still bizarrely clad in the sleeve of a pinstriped business suit, a fancy watch on the wrist. Blood oozed from the severed end, cut as smoothly and neatly as the concrete of the building.

"Oh God," Frank said, "I'm think I'm going to..."

"No time!" Conway said impatiently. "We have to get out. Grab the handrail, we can still get past." He moved down gingerly. There was just enough of the stairs remaining that he could step gingerly past the gap and its gruesome remains, until he was on the solid stairwell again. Frank followed, making gagging sounds. Others in the stairwell above them were also following, hanging on to the railing for dear life. On the next round below, the wall and stairs were also cut, but less deeply. Another few turns, and the appalling gap in the building was above them.

Out in the street at long last, Conway could hear a symphony of sirens. Police, ambulance, maybe fire engines. He and Frank moved right across the street from their building. He looked up at it. An astonishingly precise bite had been taken out of the structure, but it had been a very shallow one compared to the one which had destroyed the Gherkin, and it didn't seem as though the building was in danger of imminent collapse. Not that there was any chance that he was going back into it. He had an instant's regret about the program code he had left unfinished, but then dismissed the thought angrily. Of all things, that didn't matter now. Besides, it would all be backed up in the cloud.

The street was full of people, and the chatter of speculation now began in earnest. When Conway's phone rang in his pocket, he didn't hear it, only felt its vibration. He pulled it out and looked at the screen. It was his wife Sofia. Answering it, he put the phone to his ear, but could barely hear what she was saying.

"It's OK!" he yelled into the phone. "I'm all right, *cara mia*. But there's too much noise here, I'll call you back!" He put the phone back into his pocket.

He turned to Frank and tugged on his arm, pointing to indicate that they should get away from the building. They pushed through the crowd, which was beginning to thin out as people seemed to be realizing all at the same moment that standing next to a tall building which had been damaged was a very bad idea.

Having seen the Gherkin collapse, Conway knew that the streets in that direction would be in chaos. They had to go the opposite way. They turned the corner into Wormwood Street.

Halfway down the street was an elevated pedestrian bridge between a bank and a car park. Conway had never given it a second's glance. Except that today, the centre of the bridge was enclosed in yet another of the bubbles. Not a bubble, a *Hole*, he corrected himself. The bridge seemed to vanish into it from either side. It was like a great bauble, one of those snowglobe things your parents buy you while on holiday in Europe and which you then throw away the following year. Inside the Hole – *through* the Hole? Conway could see a grey sky and tall towers which seemed to be made of a bluish froth. Were they buildings, or something organic? It was impossible to tell.

"Fuck," Frank said, limply. "What's going on? How many of those things *are* there?"

"I don't know," Conway said, looking about. There was a thought forming in his mind, though. These Holes seemed to be openings into other places, other worlds. Alien worlds.

Shaking his head, he pulled on Frank's arm and led him back from Wormwood Street and into Bishopgate, heading north. He looked back over his shoulder, to see a clear view of the remnants of the Gherkin building. The upper part was missing entirely. Sirens were wailing everywhere. Whatever was going on was going to create a massive problem in the city, and his instinct was to get away from it as soon as he could.

His phone rang again. Sofia. He touched the 'answer' button and said "I'm sorry, love, couldn't talk before. I'm OK, though."

"What do you mean, *you* are OK? Lewis, I'm so frightened. There's this... this thing... in our garden. It's like, it's like..."

"Oh God," he said, a chill running through him. "Like a bubble?"

"*Sì, sì! Una bolla.* It's just, just hanging there. There is a tree inside it, a strange tree. Graziella, she wants to go and climb it. Of course I won't let her out of the house, of course not, but now she's crying and saying crazy stuff... Oh Lewis, I am so afraid!"

"Stay away from it," Conway said. "I've seen what they can do. There's been..." He stopped, deciding not to frighten her any further with what had been happening in the city, about how close he and Frank had just come to death. "The edges are *sharp*, Sofia, they can cut through things. If it looks as if it's moving towards the house, you have to take Graziella and get out, do you understand?"

"Yes... I... yes."

"Look, I'm going to try and get home as soon as I can, but there's been problems here too. I don't know if the Tube is still running."

"*Va bene, va bene.*" Under stress Sofia tended to lapse back into Italian. "But Graziella... she wants to talk to you."

"All right." Conway and Frank had kept walking up Bishopgate, away from the chaos in the City. This wasn't his usual route to the Liverpool Street Tube station, but it wasn't much of a detour.

His three-year-old daughter came on to the phone. "Hello, Daddy."

"Hi, sweetheart. Now you be good for Mamma and do what she says, all right? Don't go outside."

"All right, Daddy. Daddy, I saw a angel."

"An angel?"

"Yes. It was pretty. I liked it."

Bewildered, Conway could only say "OK... look, sweetie, I have to go. I'm going to try and get home as soon as I can. You be a good girl, all right?"

"Yes, Daddy."

Conway hung up the phone. "Frank, I... *look out!*"

Frank had turned to watch Conway as he had been speaking on the phone, but they had both kept on walking. Now his eyes widened in astonishment as Conway grabbed hold of his jacket and hauled him to an abrupt stop.

Inches in front of Frank's chest, a fist-sized bubble was hanging in the air. Conway could see blue sky through it. It drifted slowly from right to left as they stared at it. It reached the stone side of the building to their left and simply kept going, apparently without encountering any resistance at all. They could see through the neat hole it punched, clear through to the storage room on the other side of the wall.

They looked at one another. What would have happened if Frank had kept on walking and hit the thing? Well, it was obvious what would have happened. He would have had a neat hole drilled right through his body.

"If there are more of these things," Conway said, "as small as this... they could cause mayhem. At least you can see the big ones easily. We're going to have to be careful, keep a look out." Frank just nodded, his face pale.

They went on, turning a corner into the narrow Liverpool Street. Conway felt as though he wanted to run, worried more than ever about his family. But after Frank's narrow escape with the small Hole, they didn't dare risk it. Instead, they scanned their eyes back and forth and they hurried along, looking for anything which didn't seem right. Thankfully, they reached the entrance to the Underground without further incident.

Would the trains still be running? Conway had been preparing himself for the worst, but inside the station things seemed to be reasonably normal, at least for the time being.

"We're going opposite ways here, I think," Frank said. "You're in Rickmansworth, is that right? I live on the other side of the city." Conway nodded, and Frank went on, "Look... thanks for grabbing me back there, stopping me walking into that..."

"That hole? That's what they seem to be. Holes in the world. It's just crazy stuff."

"Well, whatever they are, you saved my life." Frank was a little embarrassed, constrained by the still-lingering English reserve he had grown up with. After a pause, he went on. "Look, I'm going to try and catch a train home. I hope you get home safe.

Give my best to Sofia. You're... you're a damn good friend, Lewis."

"Same to you," Conway said, slapping Frank on the shoulder. There was a moment's silence between them, and then he watched his friend head off along the station concourse. He wondered sadly whether he would ever see him again. If these Holes were cropping up everywhere at random, who could tell how things would work out?

He pulled out his phone and rang Sofia. "It's me, love. What's that thing in our back yard doing now? Is it moving?"

She sounded stressed out. "No, it's not moving at all. But it's very strange. A bird... or a kind of bird... flew out of it just now. It's sitting in the apple tree. I've never seen another one like it. And, oh, but Graziella is being so tiring. She's talking about crazy things, about angels, and she wants to go outside so she can climb up into the tree in the bubble. When I wouldn't let her out she threw, how do you say it in English? A tantrum? Yes, a tantrum. I made her go to bed. It's time for her nap anyway. When will you be home, Lewis? I really need you here."

"I'm just going to try getting on a train," he said. "So far they still seem to be running. Have you been watching the news?"

"Yes, it's terrible. The building that was destroyed, that's not far from where you work, is it?"

"No, not far." He refrained from telling her that his own building has been hit as well.

"And they are showing a fire at Kew Gardens. There's *lava* bubbling out of a dome there, lava like a volcano, you understand? It's spreading out and destroying the trees, setting them on fire."

"Jesus," Conway whispered to himself. "All right," he said aloud. "Look, I'll get there as quick as I can. Just pray for me, hey?"

"Of course. I love you, Lewis."

"Love you, too." He hung up.

The platform was unusually crowded for the middle of the day, and there was a pervading nervous feeling which you could almost taste. Conway walked to the farthest end of the platform in order to get into one of the first carriages when the train arrived. They were usually less crowded and he had a chance of getting a seat. Then he stood staring back down the length of the platform and into the black tunnel, willing a train to appear. For the moment, it was empty. The platform displays said that a train was now overdue. Would there be one at all? Conway fidgeted. Getting home without using the Tube would be a nightmare.

A blonde woman wearing the uniform of one of the big banks was standing next to him on the platform, tears streaming down her face, mascara running. Conway felt that he ought to say something to comfort her, but he couldn't think of anything. "It'll be all right" would be empty and meaningless in the circumstances. *Would* it be all right? In the end, he just reached out and put a hand on the woman's shoulder and smiled. In ordinary circumstances she might have reacted with hostility to such a move on his part, but today she just looked at him and nodded gratefully, pulling out a handkerchief to stem her tears.

Before Conway could say or do anything else, he felt the push of wind as a train came through the tunnel and drew up on the platform. Everyone crowded on, though there were already several people having to stand on board the train.

"Mind the gap!" came the recorded announcement advising passengers to be careful to step over the space between train and platform, "Mind the gap!". It was all so ordinary, so every-day, that Conway began to wonder if he hadn't imagined the Holes.

The train started off and entered the blackness of the tunnel. A short while later they pulled into the next station on the line. As it was still the middle of the day, this wouldn't be an express, but would instead be stopping at every station, Conway realized. More people pushed on as the doors closed. No one got off. The crowding on the train was almost as bad as at peak hour.

The stations went by. At each station, more people crowded on. But the further the train went, the more Conway began to relax. Perhaps the Holes were all above ground and the train system would be unaffected. Perhaps they were just a tempo-rary phenomenon and had begun to vanish as swiftly as they had arrived. He could hope, at least. There would certainly be some scientific explanation once the boffins had a chance to figure it all out.

That's when it all went wrong.

They had just passed the Baker Street station. Though of course there were lights on inside the carriage, the outside was completely dark. Until the train abruptly began to slow. Everyone in the carriage was thrown forward violently and it was only the press of bodies around him which prevented Conway from falling. Conway could hear the shriek of brakes and see sparks flying up against the darkness. There was a cry of protest from the passengers at the very front of the carriage, who were being crushed.

A moment later, and they were out in bright daylight. For the briefest of instants, Conway thought that they must have reached the next station on the line, which was above ground. Then there was a violent shock as the train lurched and twisted, bumping hard up and down, finally juddering to a halt, tilted a few degrees away from the vertical. There was total silence for a moment before exclamations of astonishment and some cries of pain could be heard.

Outside the windows of the carriage was another world.

They were in what seemed to be a level, grassy clearing surrounded by squat, ferny trees. Except that the grass and the leaves of the trees were all a dark purple color.

Inside the carriage, there was still an astonished silence, interrupted only by someone sobbing in pain. Then a burly-looking man in workman's gear standing next to a set of carriage doors started to prize them open. They slid back with a grinding noise and he jumped out. Someone in the carriage called out "Mind the gap!" and there was a scattering of hysterical laughter. Then more people began to jump out.

Conway pushed towards the doorway, too. Wanting to get out of the wreck was a compelling, instinctive response. He reached the opening and jumped down – it was only about four feet even with the tilt on the train. His feet sank into squishy, maroon-colored mud.

He looked around in wonder. Here and there in the midst of the dark purple grass were dots of bright orange and lime-green – some kind of flowers? The sky was almost paper-white near the horizon, shading into a perfect pale blue near the zenith. The air smelled strange, an unpleasant mixture of peppermint, rotten eggs and gasoline. It felt thick and wet as he breathed it in. Some of the passengers were already beginning to cough.

Conway turned and looked back along the length of the train. Three carriages were lying at varying angles of tilt in the purple clearing, their wheels sunk into the muddy surface, The fourth... for an instant, Conway thought that he was simply looking back into the Tube tunnel, but then his brain started to sort out what he was seeing. Strange tricks of perspective were throwing him off at first; then everything came into mental focus. The fourth carriage was sitting inside a dark sphere more than twice as high as the carriage itself. It was a Hole. He was looking into another of those damned Holes. But this time, he was looking at it from the other side, from within an alien world.

A few of the passengers were helping the shocked train driver out of his cab. "I tried to stop," he was saying. "But it was just there, in front of me. I couldn't stop us, I couldn't..."

"It's all right," Conway said to him. "It wasn't your fault. These sodding Holes have been cropping up all over. We ran into one, underground."

"Holes?" said the man, still bewildered and confused. He was in his fifties, Conway estimated, balding, with a white stubble on his face and chin. His eyes were unfocused. "Was it a sink-hole, then? I seen some pictures on the TV, in America. Swallowed a whole house."

"Something like that," Conway said. Others were helping the man away. Conway looked around at the crowd of people now out on the weird purple grass. Fortunately, there seemed to be few injuries. The swift action of the driver in slowing the train, together with the soft surface into which the train had plowed, had meant that the crash was far less traumatic than it might have been.

Conway was still holding his gym bag. He threw its strap over his shoulder now and started to walk down along the length of the train, towards the black sphere. As he neared it, he could see that an increasing number of the passengers were starting to walk *into* the sphere, apparently without injury. Several people were standing within it, beckoning others to follow them. As he neared, Conway realized that he was now looking back into the Tube tunnel, and that the fourth carriage, though tilted a little, was still essentially on the rails, which ended abruptly at the surface of the sphere.

"Come on," a middle-aged woman in a floral dress said to

Conway as he came closer. "It's safe. We're all going to walk back to Baker Street, let them know what's happened."

Baker Street? Conway thought. That would be a long distance to walk on foot back along the tracks. And it was in the wrong direction. He needed to get home to Sofia and Graziella. He stopped walking and looked up at the huge black sphere. "No," he said to the woman. "Thanks, but I'm going in the other direction. I need to get home."

"Other direction?" she said, puzzled, but Conway hardly heard her. He had begun to walk around the perimeter of the Hole, making sure that he kept a couple of yards distant from its surface. He felt certain from what he had seen, that moving *sideways* at any speed while in contact with the surface would be like pressing yourself up against a diabolically sharp knife.

Underfoot, the dark mud squished up around his shoes. His feet were getting wet, and his business shoes would be ruined. But he had his gym shoes in the bag, and he could always change once he was on dry ground.

A quarter of the way around the sphere, he stopped and looked closely at it. It was now not so dark, its surface illuminated by the sun. *The Sun?* he couldn't help thinking. *No, probably some other star.* The sphere seemed to be filled mostly with dark soil, though when he looked harder, he could see the ends of pipes and polished sections of concrete. It was precisely as though something had taken a huge bite out of the Underground, shearing through everything which crossed the boundary.

Looking back towards the wrecked train, he could see that most of the passengers were now going back along its length and returning to the Tube tunnel out of which the train had come. But there was one other person who seemed to be following his own example and walking around the sphere. He hoped that he wasn't making a terrible mistake in doing what he was doing, but he had lived his whole professional life based on his mastery of logic, and logic said that he was right.

He went on, and within a few minutes he was rewarded by knowing that his thinking had been correct. There was a dark circular opening into the sphere on this side, too. The other side of the Tube tunnel. Going in the direction *away* from Baker Street and in the direction of his home. Gingerly, he stepped across the boundary. He dropped down about a foot as he entered the tunnel, and then was standing on the tracks.

The air here now seemed startlingly dry and cold, the surface underfoot uncomfortably hard. Conway walked a few steps forward into the tunnel mouth, his wet shoes squishing. Then he turned to look back. He could see the alien world clearly, inside a sphere which now curved *away* from him. It was disorienting, so he turned his back on it and started walking along the train tracks. There was enough light coming in from the alien world to guide his steps for the first couple of hundred yards. He had been prepared to use the flashlight function on his phone if necessary, but before he needed to do that he began to see light up ahead. The next Tube station, he knew, was above ground.

"Hi! Wait up, man!" came a voice from behind. Conway turned back. It was the person who had followed him in walking around the Hole in the alien world, a dark-skinned young man barely out of his teens, wearing a black woolen cap and a loose khaki jacket.

Conway patiently waited for him to catch up. "Lewis Conway," he said, extending his hand. After the experience they had shared, he felt a great feeling of companionship with this fellow sufferer. The young man shook his hand. "I'm Billy. Billy Gayle. Saw you coming this way, figured you was right. Didn't want to walk all the way back to the last station, figured we must be close to Finchley Road. Got my car parked there."

"All right. Let's go, then," Conway said, and they began to stride along together. "I have to get back home. My wife rang and told me there's one of these Holes in our back garden. I have a young daughter... I'm really worried about them."

"Holes? That's what you call them?" Billy asked. "Pretty damn strange, hey? I was in Trafalgar Square, been working in the Gallery. Whole top of the column was poking up through one of those things. Poor old Nelson, he's now looking out on Mars or somewhere, hey?"

Conway laughed. It felt good. "Yes, I guess so."

They went another few yards. Up ahead, Conway could now see the opening of the tunnel onto the station platform. But he put a hand on Billy's arm and stopped him as a glowing globe about a yard across drifted down through the tunnel roof not far ahead of them. Another Hole, scattering the daylight from some other world. It kept drifting, down, and then sank down through the tracks. Above, where it had passed, was now a circular skylight, and Conway heard the screeching of brakes and then a crash. He realized that the Hole must have drilled a... well, a hole, in the surface of the roadway above.

Staying well clear of the pothole the globe had made between the tracks, they went on and emerged into the bright light of the station. They climbed up a short ladder and were on the platform. An angry station official was yelling at them, trying to reprimand them for walking on the tracks. Clearly, the other passengers hadn't yet reached the previous station with their report.

Conway was terse with the man. He didn't have time for this. "There's been a crash," he said simply. "The train hit a Hole. There'll be more people walking out, lots of them are going back to Baker Street. They'll give the authorities the details. Excuse me."

He and Billy walked off quickly before the man could delay them any further. In a few moments they were on the street. Conway looked about nervously, but he couldn't see any obvious Holes appearing.

"Where you going, Lewis?" Billy asked. "I can give you a lift if you like."

"I'm in Rickmansworth. Thanks for the offer, but it will be well out of your way, I expect. It's about a half-hour's drive from here. I'll get a taxi... if I can find one." He knew that there was no hope of expecting any more Tube trains.

"No man, I'll drive you, sure thing. You were the one who thought about walking round that Hole thing to get to the other side of the line. Would have taken me a lot longer than half an hour to get back to my car if I'd gone the other way."

"Well, you're very generous, but..." Conway's reserve was holding him back. He didn't know this young man from Adam. But on the other hand, these were extraordinary times. "Look... thanks, yes, I would be very grateful. Let me pay you..." He stopped as Billy held up a hand.

"Now you are insulting me, Lewis. I am offended." But Billy was grinning. "You can chip in five pounds for the petrol, if you like."

"It's a deal," Conway said, and followed Billy as he led the way to the multistory car park. Conway insisted on paying for the parking cost, too, putting his credit card into the pay machine.

The banking network was still up and running, it seemed. For the moment, at least. It wouldn't take too many more Holes, though, and things would start to break down.

Billy's car was an ancient red Ford Fiesta. The floor was covered in discarded chocolate-bar wrappers. Billy tossed a handful of books and folders off the passenger seat, and Conway climbed in, his gym bag on his lap. He realized that he still hadn't changed out of his wet and muddy business shoes. Oh well, he could do that later.

They set off, and Conway excused himself to ring Sofia.

"Are you both OK?" he asked. "What's happening with the Hole in our garden? It hasn't moved towards the house?"

"The Hole? Do you mean the bubble? It's still there, but not it's not moving. We are both all right. Graziella is still having her nap, thank goodness. She was a torment this morning, wanting to go outside and babbling about angels."

"Thank God for that. Don't forget, if the Hole moves, you'll need to get out in a hurry."

"OK. But Lewis, there have been awful reports on the news. They say a Tube train went *into* one of these things."

"Yes." Conway hesitated. "I was on it, Sofia. But I wasn't hurt, I'm fine. It's just that there won't be any more trains along the line for a while." *Quite a while*, he thought. "A friend is giving me a lift. I should be home soon." Beside him, Billy gave a big grin.

After he had hung up, Billy said "You want me to take the motorway?"

It would be the quickest way, but on the other hand if they encountered any problems – another Hole blocking the road, for example – they would be stuck on it, unable to get off. "No," Conway said. "We'll be better off on smaller roads, I think. The M1's probably already jammed with traffic trying to get out of London."

Billy dutifully navigated the car through the traffic and eventually they were on the A40. Traffic was moving reasonably well, and there were no signs of the disruption caused by the Holes. They drove without incident for about twenty minutes along a dual highway, until the traffic on their side suddenly slowed to a crawl. Billy said "Something going on up ahead. Maybe a burst water main?"

Conway could see that water was pouring in a torrent along the roadside. Billy's car came to a complete halt, but he was careful to leave a considerable gap from the car in front. Conway got out of the car and stood up. There was indeed a huge fountain of water up ahead. But the water didn't seem to be spouting out of the road. Billy leaned across and said "Here, man." He handed Conway a small pair of binoculars.

Through the binoculars, Conway could now see that the water was erupting from a point in the air some twenty feet or so above the roadway. Out of a sphere. Out of a Hole, he realized. Perhaps the other end of this Hole came out under the sea on some alien world. He looked down at the water now racing around his feet and he was glad that he hadn't changed into his gym shoes. In the stream of water he saw a bright green fish swim by, its scales glistening. Conway couldn't recognize the species.

"Get in!" Billy said. "Quick, now!" Conway climbed back in and before he even had time to do up his seat-belt, Billy was swerving the car out of the line of traffic and bumping it hard over the low kerb at their left onto the sidewalk. Then he reversed at speed, throwing up a huge wave of water, ignoring the honking horns of other cars, looking back over his shoulder to keep the car going straight. He reached a side-street, reversed far enough past it until he could turn the car and then set off down the street. Weaving past suburban houses, Billy said "I'm going to get lost here now. You got GPS on your phone?"

"Yes, of course." Conway quickly pulled up the maps app and found their location. He gave Billy directions and after ten minutes or so of threading their way through small winding streets they came back onto another major road. Billy didn't stay on it for long, finding another turn-off onto yet another smaller road. "You're right, Lewis, small roads are best."

They wound for a long time through the narrow streets, but eventually they found themselves on a long stretch of road going through a pretty piece of countryside, a big golf course on their right. They had been on the road for nearly an hour and a half, a trip which in normal circumstances should have taken a third of that. But it wasn't far now to his home. Relaxing a little, Conway asked "What do you do for a living, Billy?"

"Me? I'm still studying. Camberwell College. Fine Art, though

I'll probably end up working as a photographer, I think. How about you?"

"I'm a software developer, working for one of the big financial firms. Data mining, that kind of thing." Somehow all of that no longer seemed very important. It certainly didn't seem like something he could be proud of, though it had tested his skills to the limit.

"What do you think is going to happen about all these Holes, Lewis? You think the Government is going to fix it all up?"

Conway frowned. He hadn't been thinking very far ahead. "I don't see what they can do about it, not yet. We have to figure out what's causing the Holes to appear. Maybe they'll just vanish away again. I don't know, Billy."

"I... oh shit!" Billy slammed his foot on the brake and yanked on the steering wheel. The car slewed almost to a right-angle but kept on heading down the road, sliding, tipping up on two wheels. There was a strange 'pock' sound and Billy screamed with pain. The car rocked, and for a moment Conway, gripping on to his seat-belt in desperation, thought that it would roll over. But then it dropped back heavily onto all four wheels, still turned across the line of traffic.

There was now a clean hole about the size of a basketball drilled through the door on Billy's side of the car. The hole passed through the steering column and continued at an angle through the dashboard and into the engine compartment. What was left of the engine was making mechanical sounds of distress.

Blood was flowing freely from a deep gash in Billy's leg. He put his hands over it and swore loudly. The Hole they had struck must have grazed his leg, taking off a strip of jeans material and by the looks of it, at least a quarter-inch of his flesh.

Conway, in shock, looked at Billy's wound stupidly for a moment, then fumbled in his gym bag and handed Billy a clean towel. "Wrap it up in this," he said. He looked back out of the car. The culprit, a small Hole, was drifting across the road. Through it he could see a dark sky filled with lightning. The car had struck it at an angle thanks to Billy's prompt reaction. The damage would have been a lot worse if they had hit it straight on. But nevertheless the car was wrecked.

Conway pulled out his phone and rang 999 for the emergency

services. Only an engaged signal came back. "Shit!" Now that he looked around, he could see several plumes of smoke rising up out of the town ahead. Caused by more Holes? Impossible to tell. But the emergency services probably already had their hands full.

"Look," he said to Billy, who was still wincing in pain, "we're not far now from my house. I could walk there in ten minutes. My wife used to work as an ambulance paramedic before she took time off to have our daughter. If you can manage it, we're probably best trying to get there, she'll fix you up as best she can."

Billy nodded and managed a weak grin. "Lucky, hey? Could have lost my whole leg. Or my balls, hey?"

Conway helped him out. Without the help of the police, there wasn't much they could do about the car blocking most of the road. Nor was there much he could do to warn other drivers. Still, it was a quiet road and the car could be seen easily from the nearest bend. They would just have to leave it. Conway threw the strap of his gym bag over his shoulder again, and put an arm around the young man to help him limp along. Billy had tied the towel tight around his leg, but it was already soaked in blood. Conway hoped that he wouldn't lose too much before they reached Sofia.

It took a lot longer than ten minutes, and by the time they turned into the short cul-de-sac street where Conway lived, Billy was starting to sag and put more and more of his weight on Conway. But they reached his door at last. Before he could ring the bell, the door opened and Sofia looked out in horror. "Lewis!"

"This is Billy Gayle," Conway said. "He's got a bad cut on his leg. Can you help him?"

"Of course, of course. But shouldn't I ring an ambulance?"

"You can try. I've tried a few times over the last twenty minutes, but all I get is the engaged signal."

Shaking her head in dismay, Sofia set Billy down on a couch and went to fetch her medical kit.

Conway's daughter Graziella ran down the stairs from her room. "Daddy, daddy, daddy!" She ran up to Conway and threw her arms around his legs. She was dressed in a khaki-colored T-shirt and dark, short pants. For some reason she despised the color pink. Then she noticed Billy and was silent, looking at him solemnly. "Hello?" she said uncertainly.

"This is Billy," Conway said. "Billy, Graziella."

"Pleased to meet you," Billy said gravely. Now that he was able to rest on the couch he was looking a little better. Sofia bustled in with her kit, all professional now, took off the towel and handed it to Conway. Blood began to flow again from Billy's leg.

"It's a wide cut," she said dubiously. "It really needs stitches. I can sew it up for you myself – I have a sterile needle and suture thread here in my kit – but I can't do as neat a job as a doctor would do. You'll end up with an awful scar."

"A scar don't matter, Mrs Conway," Billy said, and Sofia started preparations. She looked up at her husband. "It's not good for Graziella to see this," she said. He nodded, and led the child out of the room into the kitchen at the back. As he left, he heard Sofia say "I'm sorry, Mr Gayle, this is going to hurt."

Graziella was pulling at Conway's trouser-leg. "Daddy, there's a tree growed up in our garden, but Mamma says I can't go out. I wants to play in it, Daddy!" She pronounced 'Mamma' the Italian way, with the stress on the first syllable.

"Well," he said gently, "it might be too dangerous to play in. But if you promise to keep tight hold of my hand and not let go, we'll go and have a look at it."

Conway and Graziella went to the sliding glass door that looked out into their back garden. It was quite a big area compared to some of the neighboring house blocks, forming a wedge shape at the end of the street. Conway slid the door open and stepped out with the little girl.

As Sofia had said, there was a Hole here, and there was a tree in it. What she hadn't mentioned on the phone was that it was sitting three or four feet above the ground, and that a perfect spherical section of earth, like an inverted dome, was at the Hole's base, seemingly floating above Conway's lawn. The tree was growing out of the centre of the elevated chunk of earth. It had pure white bark, and orange leaves with crimson veins sprouted from the ends of its twigs. There was something odd about the way it branched but it did indeed look like an easy tree to climb. Beyond it was a greenish sky filled with ochre clouds. He looked at the Hole anxiously for a few minutes, trying to determine if it was moving. By keeping his head very still and looking along the edge of the spherical surface, he was able at last to see that it *was* drifting, very slowly, from left to right across his vision, moving on the order of a fraction of an inch every minute. But, thank God, it definitely wasn't coming any closer to the house.

Something red flew out of the tree inside the Hole, circled above Conway's head, then returned to the alien tree. It seemed to have long delicate fronds rather than feathers, but Graziella called out happily: "See the pretty parrot, Daddy!"

"Yes, honey, I see it. Thank you for showing it to me. Now, we have to go back inside. Mamma is right, we can't climb up into the new tree. It belongs to someone else and it's just here on a visit."

"Oh!" she said. "All right. Mamma didn't tell me that. I didn't know that trees could come visit."

"Well, it is very unusual," he said with a slight smile.

"The angel in my room came visiting, too," she said. "Does the tree belong to him?"

"I... I don't know, sweetie. Perhaps it does."

As he turned to go back inside, however, he noticed something which gave him a stab of alarm. There was a dense column of smoke rising from not far away. He thought about the damage that the smaller Holes might do – all it would take is for one to cut through someone's gas supply pipe, or shear through electrical cables, and it would be easy for a fire to start. He still had his phone in his pocket. He pulled it out and rang the emergency number again. Still engaged. That really wasn't good.

Inside, Sofia had finished her work. Billy's leg now featured a neat bandage. She and Billy were watching the television. There were more and more reports coming in of the appearance of Holes, and some awful examples of the death and destruction that a few of them had caused already. London Bridge was gone, and in a 'breaking news' bulletin they saw footage of the London Eye collapsing after a car-sized Hole passed through its hub. Fortunately it had already been emptied of tourists. The Government was calling for calm, but seemed to have no answers.

Then the screen went black. Conway glanced across at his hi-fi system. No lights. The power was out. "That's torn it," he said.

With all the chaos caused by the Holes, who could tell what had gone wrong, or how long it might take to fix?

Sofia got up and hugged him. "I'm so afraid," she whispered. "What can we do? How can we keep Graziella safe, Lewis?"

"I don't know," he admitted. "Did it seem from the news that most of the damage was in the city?"

"Yes. But Lewis, if there are Holes popping up in the country-side, too, they are less likely to be reported there."

He bit his lip. "I was wondering if we should try to get out, maybe drive to my parents farm in Wales. But Billy and I had such a terrible time trying to get here in his car, less than thirty miles. We almost didn't make it."

Graziella was tugging at Conway's trouser-leg again. "Not now, *principessa*," he said to her.

"But Daddy..."

"Mamma and Daddy are talking right now, honey. Just wait for a bit."

Graziella put on what Sofia called her 'stubborn face' and kept tugging. "Daddy, you gots to come and see the angel."

"Graziella, no!" he said impatiently. "Not now." The little girl's face puckered and she started to cry. Conway hardly ever spoke harshly to her, and if he ever did she was distraught. With a small sigh, Conway picked her up and hugged her until her tears dried.

He looked across at Sofia. "I don't have any answers, *mia cara*. Maybe we're safest staying here until we find out more." She nodded sadly.

"Daddy, come and see the angel, he wants to talk with you."

"All right," he said with a sigh, putting her down. "Just for a bit. But after that Daddy is going to be very busy, OK?"

"*Va bene!*" she said, racing off. "*Andiamo!*" she called over her shoulder as she pounded up the stairs. Graziella mixed Italian and English freely and apparently without confusion. Conway reluctantly followed her, his mind full of worry about the situation outside. A big city like London was fragile. Hold up food deliveries for a week, disrupt the water supply for even a couple of days, and chaos would ensue. People would die. They might be better off out in the country, however hard it was to get there.

Graziella's room was painted in bright, cheerful colors, with deep red predominating. It was full of stuffed toys and dolls from a number of over-generous relatives, particularly her Italian grandmother. Conway was expecting to be shown one of these as his daughter's "Angel" and be forced to carry on an imaginary conversation with it. But instead, Graziella ran to her wardrobe, which had a sliding mirror door. She pulled the door open in triumph.

Conway had a sudden lurching instant of vertigo as he found himself unexpectedly looking into a space far greater than could be contained within the wardrobe. He was looking into yet another Hole. A Hole which must be embedded into the outer wall of the house, intersecting with Graziella's room.

There was an angel inside the Hole, looking at him with huge, grave eyes.

Well, no. After a long moment of shock, Conway realized that the creature he was looking at was no heavenly visitor. It was white, and it had wings, and its eyes were grey and somehow wise beyond all measure. But those weren't feathers on its wings, rather they were loose folds of white skin, rippling and overlapping. The creature's face was long and horselike, with three rows of slit-like openings which reminded Conway of gills rather than nostrils.

Then, to his horror, Graziella ran right in to the Hole and directly up to the creature. It was kneeling or crouching, Conway now realized. Graziella leapt up at the alien and... hugged it. The creature's forearms were surprisingly short, but enough to wrap around the little girl. It didn't look down at her, but continued to gaze calmly at Conway, and Conway gazed back, his heart pounding.

"Graziella, honey," he said, "come back out of there. Please. Right now."

"But Daddy, the angel wants to talk to you. I like him, he's my friend."

Conway could not take his eyes away from the creature holding on to his precious child, but he started to absorb a little of its surroundings. There was a blue sky with white clouds which could have been anywhere on Earth. Beyond the creature, perhaps a mile away, over a lime-green field, were tall oddly-shaped buildings, around which he could glimpse flying white figures. What would a city of angels be like? You wouldn't need roads or even sidewalks.

"Graziella..." he said hopelessly. "Please..." He knelt down and held his arms wide to her, imploring her with his eyes.

Graziella said happily. "It's nice, here, Daddy." But to his huge relief, she let go of the alien, dropped down to the ground and ran back into his own arms.

Then the angel spoke, a liquid burbling of musical notes. It beckoned to Conway. *Come.* It was as clear a communication as if it had spoken in English.

"I... I can't," Conway said helplessly. "Not yet. Just... just stay there, and I'll come back."

He scooped Graziella up and carried her protesting down the stairs to the living room. Sofia was talking animatedly to Billy, making considerable use of her hands for emphasis as she talked. They were now on first-name terms, it appeared.

Before Conway could speak, she was on her feet. "Lewis, we have to get out of here. There's a fire in a house just down the street, but I don't see a fire engine. I tried ringing 999, but as you said, there's no answer. If the fire spreads this way.... Oh, I'm so afraid!" Tears sprang into her eyes.

"Mamma, mamma! Daddy saw the angel, too! Come see!" Graziella was bouncing around her parents' feet, excited.

Conway hesitated. The world was going crazy, falling apart. "I did see it," Conway confirmed. "It's not exactly an angel, Sofia. It's inside a Hole, a Hole behind the wardrobe in Graziella's room. It... it seems like it wants to help us."

Sofia's hand was over her mouth in shock. "Help us? How? How could it help us?"

Billy Gayle sat up on the couch, wincing a little at the pain in his leg. "You saying there's some kind of Martian in the little girl's room?"

"I guess I am," Conway said. "But it's not Mars. It's not too different from Earth. I think we could live there, at least for a while."

"You mean go through?" asked Sofia, horrified. "Go through the Hole into the other world?"

"I don't know that we have much choice. Let me have a look down the street for a moment. Even if we stay here on Earth we're going to have to leave the house. Get out our tent and all the camping gear, will you, sweetheart? And your medical kit, of course. I'll be back in a moment."

Without waiting for an answer, he went out into their front yard and looked down the street. The house on the corner was well ablaze, flames rising high and black smoke pouring up. As Sofia had said, there was no sign of anyone trying to put it out. Worse still, he could see yet another Hole, about four yards across, floating about six feet above the roadway. Through it he could see a volcanic landscape, with streams of bright orange-red lava running down distant mountains. It *might* be possible to drive safely around the Hole, but if it drifted downwards they would be trapped in this dead-end street.

He went back inside. Sofia had begun piling things in the centre of the living room. On the carpet were their two aluminum-framed packs, standing upright while Sofia stuffed them with sleeping bags, their compact three-man tent, a gas stove and cylinder, and a selection of clothes. They had both been keen hikers when they were younger: in fact that was how Conway had met Sofia, hiking in the foothills of the Alps in Italy.

"Food!" she called out to Conway. "Take everything in the pantry!" He hurried to comply. In a few minutes he was back with a heavy box of tinned food.

Sofia was helping Billy on to his feet. "You really shouldn't be walking," she said, fretting. "The stitches might tear. But..."

"Don't you worry, Sofia, I'll be OK." He hopped towards the stairs. "I've got to see this Martian for myself."

A few minutes later all four of them stood in Graziella's bedroom, looking into the Hole.

There were now two angels beyond the Hole in the wardrobe. A smaller one had joined the first, its wings a delicate shade of cream. Was it a female? Impossible to know. Standing there facing the pair of creatures, holding on to the cardboard box from Tesco's, Conway felt absurd. This was all so unreal. But the larger angel was beckoning again. *Come, come, and hurry*, it seemed to be saying.

What if it were all a trick? What if these aliens *ate* people? All of the pulp-fiction horror stories about aliens came flooding back to Conway in a flash. But then he dismissed the thought.

Why would an alien species develop a taste for human flesh, even if it could digest it? And besides... he remembered Graziella hugging the creature tenderly, and it hugging back. Surely you had to trust your instincts sometimes?

It seemed a pleasant enough world through there. It wasn't their world, but at least it offered hope.

"Come on, Daddy!" Graziella said, tugging at his trousers.

"All right then, honey," Conway said to her, starting forwards. "Let's go visiting."

Enhancement

"E-GLASSES, SIGNORINA? You must see the Forum through a headset. *Una meravigliosa esperienza!* Only fifty euros for an hour. Program included!"

The young boy hiring out the e-glasses on the outskirts of the Roman Forum was only about 12 years old, Donna thought. His face was eager, his teeth flashing white in the bright sunlight as he smiled. She was sorry to have to disappoint him. "*Mi dispiace*," she said, an attempt to practice at least a little of the Italian she had been trying to learn. "But I already have my own system." And she touched her finger to her own special glasses, the lenses now dark in adaptation to the sunlight.

"Ah!" the boy said, sitting up straighter and looking at her almost with awe. "Is that the new Tiang Model X5, *signorina*? You have the contact lenses and the audio implants? May I see?"

Smiling, Donna took off the glasses and showed him the shining gold-traced contact lenses in her eyes. Then she tilted her head and pulled her long blonde hair aside to show the tiny plastic-coated disc magnetically attached to the implant behind her ear.

"Surely you must be very rich!" the boy said. His voice was excited, eager.

Donna laughed, trying not to look too smug. "Not rich, no." Though no doubt by the standards of this poor urchin she was rich indeed. "My grandfather left me a little money a few years ago, and I spent it on this. Just a little indulgence." Then, realizing that she was being too open with her personal information to a stranger (a continuing bad habit), she started to move on.

The boy quickly put up a hand as if to restrain her. He all but held her back. "Don't go, *signorina*! Today is your lucky day! I have a version of the Forum program suited to your e-glasses.

You can download it in a moment. It is not to be missed, it makes the Forum come alive!"

Donna said, "Well, it depends. How much?"

"Thirty euros only, *signorina*." Then, as she hesitated, "But for you, pretty lady, twenty euros only. Special deal for today!" His eagerness was almost disturbing. He must be very poor to be so concerned not to lose a sale.

She laughed. "Oh, very well. Do you have the code?"

He nodded and opened a small bag at his side and, hands trembling a little with excitement, he selected a card and held it up to her view. It was printed with a complex 2D barcode. She saw it briefly highlighted by her augmented vision, and green text running along the bottom of her sight told her that the boy's program was ready to be downloaded. It would have been checked for malware by the Tiang servers, of course, before any purchase or download was permitted. "All right," she said, in the low soft voice she used to command the e-glasses, "authorized." The payment went through and a moment later the 'success' icon flashed up.

"Thank you," she said, and moved on past the boy and began to walk into the ruins. But he called after her:

"*Signorina!* If you have friends, tell them to come to me for their headsets or programs! Tell them to ask for Claudio!"

She just smiled and went on.

Before her were the magnificent ruins of the old forum, a few columns and arches still standing, broken columns and carved blocks of stone everywhere. She commanded the downloaded program to begin. A sudden bright flurry of static filled her vision for a second, and then was gone. Puzzling. That didn't usually happen. She blinked a few times and looked around again.

Now labels were cropping up as her gaze shifted from point to point, and the audio commentary began. Her e-glasses had automatically selected the English language from the options provided.

You are looking at the Temple of Saturn, of which only the columns of the front portico now remain. This is the third incarnation of the building, replacing the second version which was destroyed by fire in 283 CE...

Interesting enough, Donna thought, but a bit dry. She'd hated having to learn facts and dates in her history lessons at school.

She was here in Rome to enjoy herself, after all, not to qualify for a degree or write a book.

To the left of her vision, two choices were presented. "Forum History" was the current selection. The second choice was "Simulation".

"Let's have the simulation," she said, and her view began to change quickly. In an engaging animation, all of the gaps of the buildings rapidly filled in, stone by stone, walls and columns sprouting up from the earth. Collapsed roofs were restored in a flash, murals painted themselves and tiles were laid out on the ground. In a matter of moments, it was as if she had been whisked backwards in time 2000 years. Even the other tourists in the Forum were painted over in her vision so that they appeared to be re-clothed in togas and gowns, their sunglasses, smartphones and tablets erased from Donna's sight. She looked down at her own body and saw that her designer slacks and fashionable, top-brand sneakers seemed to have been replaced with an elaborately decorated robe and sandals. *Now this is more like it!* Donna thought.

The audio commentary shifted. *You are seeing the Forum as it would have appeared in approximately 20 BCE...*

"Mute commentary," she commanded. The commentary was still boring. Much more fun just to wander around and pretend that she was some proud Roman lady, the wife of a senator, perhaps.

The simulation was really very good. Young Claudio's family must be leasing the software from some much bigger organization which had put a lot of effort and money into the production values. The illusion was almost seamless. There was no lag at all in what she saw as her eyes moved around. Cheaper e-glasses like the ones Claudio was hiring out often caused a degree of motion-sickness if you moved your head too quickly.

That was the benefit of her own state-of-the-art system. The frames of the glasses she wore incorporated tiny but powerful processors which communicated with her special contact lenses and audio implants via high-capacity short-range wireless signal. The images she saw were generated by the processors and projected onto her retinas by the contacts. Similarly the sound she heard was generated by the direct stimulation of her audio system by the embedded chips near her ears. It was only really necessary for her to actually wear the glasses so that she could give voice commands, and communicate via tweets, phone calls or email. She could take the glasses off and the visual and audible simulation would still be there, provided the frames weren't too far away.

Through this miraculous device, she looked in wonder around the reincarnated Roman Forum.

The simulation wasn't perfect in every respect, of course. As an experiment, she approached the solid wall of a temple, and reached out to touch it. But her hand felt nothing, and it appeared to sink into the stone. The wall wasn't really there, must have collapsed thousands of years ago. She pulled her hand back and moved it to a column. This, by contrast, was solid, and she could feel the texture of the stone, which must still be here in modern times. What fun!

She turned back and began to walk idly around the busy plaza of the forum, weaving her way through the crowd of people, all apparently dressed in a variety of what she assumed were authentic Roman costumes. Now she could even hear snatches of conversation in what she thought must be Latin. Was it doing an actual real-time translation of what she heard? Today's software was astounding, so perhaps it was possible.

Part-way across, a tall young man approached her, dressed as a Roman soldier. He was very handsome, with dark, curly hair, and he wore the uniform as if born to it, his hairless arms muscled and bronzed. He had good legs, too, she noted, below the short skirt of the uniform.

He said something to her in what she presumed was Latin. In any case, she didn't understand it. "Turn Latin translation off," she said. It worked. At once she heard the voices of the crowd around her return to the babble of the many different languages being spoken by the tourists: German, English, Japanese, Chinese.

"I'm sorry," she said to the handsome soldier. "Could you say that again?"

"Certainly, *signorina*. I hope I am not disturbing you." His voice was resonant, with a slight but charming Italian accent. "I am with the local Tourist Bureau." He flashed her an identity card and her e-glasses snapped its image. "I saw you wandering here, and wondered if I could be of any assistance."

"Oh! No, no, I'm fine. I'm using my e-glasses, you understand." She reached up and touched the frame. "It's running a simulation I bought. Everything around me looks just as it did in Roman times." She laughed. "In fact, I see you dressed as a Roman soldier."

He grinned. "Ah yes. I have used that simulation myself, though I don't think the e-glasses I hired were as good as yours. It made me feel a little dizzy, to be honest. Have you been long in Rome?"

"No, not really. I arrived here two days ago with my mother. We couldn't do much yesterday, though. She seems to have caught some kind of stomach bug, or eaten something which disagreed with her."

"*Ah, poverina!* That is unfortunate. And she is still unwell today?"

"A little better, thank you. But she still wasn't up to coming out for a long time today, so she told me to go ahead and explore by myself."

"A generous lady. But being a tourist here all on your own is a little sad, I think. Perhaps I could accompany you around the Forum and show you the most interesting parts. Unless you wish to continue using the simulation?"

Donna hesitated, thinking of her mother's admonitions about not trusting Italian men. But that kind of thinking was so last-century. This man seemed kind and helpful, and he was from the Tourist Bureau. Besides, he *was* very handsome.

Though perhaps that was just the simulation? "Excuse me a moment," she said to the man and then addressed her e-glasses. "Simulation off. End running program and return to default menu."

The scenes of Ancient Rome vanished and now she saw the Forum again in its ruined state. The crowd lost their Roman attire and she saw they were dressed in a variety of modern clothes. Her companion was dressed in a very well-fitting, stylish dark Italian suit. Armani? Versace? One of those top designers, anyway. His face was the same, but now he looked very elegant and assured.

"All right," she said. "Why not? My name is Donna, by the way."

He laughed. "You must know that *donna* is just the Italian for 'woman'. I do not feel I can call you that, it seems so disrespectful. Perhaps I may call you *belladonna* instead? That means..."

Donna blushed. "It means 'beautiful woman'. Well, all right. And you are...?"

"My name is Franco. Franco Mangiamele, at your service." He bowed slightly.

He was *so* charming! "Well, then, lead the way," she said. And he did, taking her around the ruins, pointing out features and describing their history. To be honest, Donna found his commentary suspiciously similar to that of the program she had downloaded into her e-glasses. But it was so much more interesting to have the words spoken in a delightful Italian accent by this handsome man at her side.

More than an hour later she said, "Thank you so much, but I'm exhausted! And I should get back to see how my mother is getting on. I've been terribly selfish, I'm sure."

"A lovely young woman like yourself deserves the occasional indulgence," Franco said with a smile. "But I must let you go, I see. You are here in Rome for a little longer, I hope?"

"Yes, for a couple of weeks."

"Excellent. Then let me give you my card. I would be more than happy to show you around the sights of the Eternal City. Tomorrow, perhaps? We could visit the Coliseum, for example. I can bring you another program for your glasses, which will bring it to life in all its terrible glory."

"Not tomorrow. I really must spend some time with my mother. But the next day, yes. Thursday. She is going to have lunch with a friend she knows in our Embassy here. That afternoon..."

"Then I shall meet you outside the Coliseum. At two o'clock, perhaps?"

"But surely you must be busy with other tourists...?"

He held up his exquisitely manicured hand. "Not another word. It will be my pleasure." And she saw that it would be. Charmed, she smiled and agreed.

꘏

Donna spent the next day pleasantly enough with her mother, who had recovered from her stomach upset.

She had said very little to her mother about meeting the handsome young man from the Tourism Bureau. She would just get another tedious lecture. So she had simply told her mother that she'd been guided around the Forum by a helpful attendant. That wasn't a lie.

Together, Donna and her mother spent a long time that day in the Capitoline Museums on the Palatine Hill overlooking the Forum. Her e-glasses were useful there too, but less so. She was relying on the software provided by the museum management. It was really very stilted and not very interesting, with no simulation features. She might have done as well with a printed brochure.

At the end of the day, her feet ached again. Donna felt as if they were going to be worn down to the ankle-bones if she kept up this amount of walking every day over the next two weeks.

It was on the way back to the hotel with her mother that Donna first thought there might be something wrong with her augmented vision. As they walked to the hotel from where the taxi had dropped them, there was a sudden shift in what she was seeing. Everything became a little less bright, as though a shadow of a cloud had passed over; yet paradoxically everything she saw became a little sharper and clearer. It was very odd, and she stumbled a little. Her mother caught her arm before she could fall. Then her vision cleared again and was as normal.

"Are you all right, dear?" her mother asked.

"Yes, I'm fine. Just something went wrong with my lenses for a moment, I think."

"I wish you wouldn't wear those things all the time. I'm sure it's not natural."

"Oh, Mother! There's not much we do that's natural these days. Ordinary sunglasses aren't natural, are they?"

Still, Donna was a little concerned. She took off the frames and examined them, touching the slight bulge on each side which contained the processors. Did they feel a little warmer than usual? Perhaps. But that could just be the Italian sun.

There was a tiny on-off switch on one arm of the frames, there to help conserve battery when the glasses weren't being worn. She flicked it off, waited a moment, and then turned it back on again. Wasn't that what technical people always asked you to do? To her relief, everything in her vision seemed normal now. In any case, the system was still under warranty. She'd upgraded the frames just a few months ago to the latest model processors. There shouldn't be any problem in having the system replaced if it stopped working entirely. Still, it would be annoying.

⋘⋙

Donna lay awake that night, smiling as she contemplated her forthcoming meeting with Franco at the Coliseum. The next morning she spent longer than usual at the mirror, applying her makeup with special care, and took ages to decide what she would wear.

The weather, though, was a little disappointing. A dense cloud covered the sky, although the weather app in her e-glasses told her there was no real prospect of rain. It was dull, though, and the lenses adjusted to allow as much light in as possible to her eyes.

Reaching the entrance, she stood looking around for Franco, but he wasn't there yet. She realized that she was a touch early for their appointment.

Nearby, a group of men dressed up as gladiators and Roman guards were posing with a couple to have their photographs taken. A little altercation began after the shot was taken, as the tourists took umbrage at the fee demanded by the costumed men. Donna smiled, checked the time, and looked around for Franco. He still wasn't to be seen, and she began to be a little anxious that he might have forgotten about meeting her.

Just then, the brightness of her view shifted once more. Dimmer, but somehow sharper. She suddenly became much more aware of the litter on the ground, and the streaks of dirt on the walls of the ancient building. Puzzled, she took off the glasses and felt the processors again. Were they any hotter than usual? She couldn't tell. She was definitely going to have the system looked at. She flicked off the power switch, deciding to wait a little longer this time before turning it back on.

As she waited, she noticed a middle-aged man across the way, wearing a grey, rather crumpled suit, his hair starting to recede. He seemed to be staring – leering – at her. Annoyed, she frowned and turned away. Still, it wasn't the first time she had been ogled by an Italian man in Italy, and she was sure it wouldn't be the last.

Still no sign of Franco. Then she realized that she had Franco's business card in her purse. In fact, she didn't even need to pull it out. Her e-glasses had automatically scanned it already. She could give him a call and see where he was, if necessary remind him of their appointment. She flicked the power switch, put the frames back on and made the call.

The phone was picked up instantly. "I'm here, *belladonna*. Just arrived, so sorry to be late. Look to your left."

There he was, phone in hand, waving at her. Just as tall and handsome as she remembered. He came towards her smiling, putting away his phone in the inside pocket of his immaculate dark suit jacket.

"Well, here I am," he said unnecessarily. "I have the software for the Coliseum for you." He pulled out a card bearing another complex barcode and held it up to her. Her e-glasses scanned it instantly and began the download.

Donna was surprised that she wasn't asked for the authorization of a payment. "No charge?" she asked. "The program I bought from that boy on Tuesday cost me 20 euros!"

"Ah, you were cheated, I think. A common problem. These programs are supplied free by the Tourism Bureau, a service to those visiting our great city."

"Oh, I see. That's wonderful. What a great service."

"I could perhaps try to find that boy and get your money back."

"Oh, no, no, that's all right. He seemed like a nice boy, really. And I can afford it."

"Well then, let us go visit the *colosseo*. Its real name, you should know, is the *Anfiteatro Flavio* – the Flavian Amphitheatre. But your glasses will tell you that."

She smiled. "Yes, but it's nicer to hear you say it." He bowed slightly, with a smile, and led her in through the gate. They climbed up a couple of levels to where Franco told her she would get the best view. She was surprised to hear him panting when they reached the top, and wheezing a little. "Are you all right?" she asked, concerned.

"Fine, fine," he said. "A little *asma*, how do you say it?"

"Asthma?" It seemed odd for such a fit young man to suffer from such a condition. But then children got it, so perhaps it wasn't so strange after all.

He straightened up and seemed to have recovered. They stood looking out over the ruins and she commanded her e-glasses to run the simulation Franco had given her.

She gave a gasp as the confusing jumble of broken walls below were covered over in a moment by a layer of wooden boards, creating a huge floor. This was then liberally covered with a deep layer of sand. Around her, the broken walls of the Coliseum seemed to be being rebuilt in every detail, stone by stone. Above them, wooden masts sprang up at the top of the walls, and were then strung with a net of ropes and sheets of canvas to create a vast awning which covered two-thirds of the arena.

"Oh my goodness," Donna said. "I never imagined it would look like this."

"The program we make is good, yes?"

"Yes!"

Now, through the e-glasses, the stands were filling with virtual spectators, and she heard yelling and cheering. On the floor of the stadium, groups of gladiators fought bloody battles. She saw one man fall to a stab wound, and then another lose his head to the swing of a sword. Blood spurted up amazingly high from the stump before his body fell to the ground. Wincing, Donna was forced to look away. "Ugh, that wasn't very nice. Too realistic by far. I think I'll turn off the simulation." She quickly issued the commands to do that, and her vision returned to normal. The Coliseum, even in ruins, was still just as impressive.

"How about you just tell me about it, Franco?" she said. "I... I love to hear your voice."

And so he did. He told amusing little anecdotes as they strolled around. He joked about the number of tourists holding up their smartphones or tablets in front of their faces, apparently preferring to record what their cameras saw rather than to experience the place first hand. Donna, who had done a little recording herself through her e-glasses, though rather more discreetly, had to laugh and agree.

She found herself liking Franco more and more. He was charming and witty. To hell with what her mother would think.

Towards the end of their visit, Franco's phone rang and he

answered. "*Pronto! Sì?*" A pause. "*All'ospedale? Sì, sì, vengo subito.*" He put it down, looking grave.

"What's the matter? Did I hear you mention a hospital?"

He hesitated for a long moment before speaking. "Yes. My mother. She has an illness. Sometimes it is worse than others. Today, unfortunately it is worse and she has been taken to the hospital for treatment. I should go see her."

"Oh! That's terrible, I'm so sorry."

"Thank you. She has a rare cancer, and the best drug to treat it... well, it is very expensive, I am afraid. We are trying, my sister and I, to save up. But my salary is not a large one. She works as a school teacher, which is also not a very well paid job. Still, we are trying. We hope to have enough soon."

"Oh... well I could..." Donna stopped herself. This could be *precisely* the kind of thing her mother warned her about so often. Franco hadn't actually asked her to help with money, and he seemed quite genuine. Nevertheless, she restrained her first generous impulse. "Well, I hope that you can get there," she said, honestly enough.

He nodded, his face clearing. "Enough of this gloomy talk. Are you free tomorrow? I could take you to see the Basilica of St. Peter's, the greatest church in the world. Not to be missed."

"Yes, that would be wonderful. But you're spending so much time with me. Don't you have other tourists to look after?"

He laughed. "I will be honest with you, *belladonna*. Tomorrow is my day off. But I would love to see you again."

❧❀❧

Donna had to lie to her mother on the following day, saying that she felt unwell.

"I might have a touch of that bug you had earlier in the week," she said. "But I'll be fine here. It's your turn to do some exploring by yourself."

"Well, dear, I don't much like wandering by myself. But I might catch up with Clara again. She wanted to show me the Villa Borghese. That's a huge park, I understand. We'll go see that."

"Yes, you do that. I'll be fine. If I feel better later, I might stroll down the street. Don't worry if you don't find me here when you get back."

"All right, dear. You call the hotel reception if you feel really sick, you hear? Or give me a call, and I will come right back."

"OK. See you later."

As soon as her mother had gone, Donna made herself ready. She put on a pretty new lemon-yellow dress she had bought in Milan and checked that her makeup was perfect. Then she went down to reception and had them order her a taxi.

A surprisingly large number of people were walking down the narrow street toward St. Peter's from the point where the taxi dropped her off; many of them nuns, but lots of other people too. She worried that she wouldn't be able to find Franco in the crowd.

But she needn't have worried. Franco was standing on the raised plinth of one of the columns which ring St. Peter's Square. He waved as he saw her and came forward to hold her shoulders and kiss her on both cheeks. But he looked embarrassed, as he waved towards the piazza. To her surprise, it seemed to be full of chairs, and between each column a security gate had been set up, with *carabinieri* officers checking the people entering.

"*Belladonna*, I am so sorry. A Papal audience. I should have known, I am so stupid. There is no access to the Basilica this morning."

"Oh. Well, never mind. *Non fa niente*, isn't that what you say in Italian?"

"Yes, you are right. Very good. But what shall we do? It will be several hours before the Basilica opens to the public again. I would suggest the Vatican Museums, but the queue is always so very long – that is the only way to visit the Sistine Chapel, you understand?"

"Well, perhaps we could have a coffee or something. Or go visit something else? Though I must say my feet are quite sore from all of the sightseeing that I've done already."

"*Allora*, there is another possibility. Perhaps... perhaps I am being too forward, but..."

"But what?" she said, half-suspecting, half-hoping what he might propose. He was *so* good looking, so charming in his manners.

"Well, my apartment is not too far from here. A quick taxi ride only. I could offer you coffee there..."

"That sounds wonderful. Let's go."

On the taxi-ride, which proved to be not as short as Franco had suggested, Donna's e-glasses glitched again. Just as the taxi pulled into a street lined with expensive-looking apartment blocks, her vision blurred, or shifted somehow. Again there came a slight darkening to what she saw, and the colors changed. It was as if the streetscape had suddenly been painted over in grey, drab colors, and the tops of some of the buildings seemed to have been erased. Then it was gone and she could see clearly again.

"Damn," she said.

Franco put a hand on her arm, looking concerned. "Are you all right? Is there a problem?"

"These e-glasses are acting up. Something wrong with the processors. Or it could be some kind of software glitch. I'll have to take them back to the store. But that's back home, of course." She explained to him the trouble she had been having with the system over the last few days.

His brow furrowed. "That's a pity. But don't worry, I know someone who is an expert with these devices. I'm sure I can get him..." He stopped speaking abruptly, puzzling Donna. "Yes, yes, he could probably help," he finished in a rather vague voice, looking out of the window as though thinking.

They pulled up outside one of the tall apartment blocks, a beautifully designed building clad in a creamy stone. Franco paid the driver and they got out.

Inside, he led her through an elegant foyer, though it seemed very small for such a grand building. Donna did wonder in passing how he managed to afford such a place on his small salary from the Tourism Bureau. Or, for that matter, how he had been able to pay for his elegant suit. But then, she reflected, he would need to keep up appearances in his job, and she'd read that creating *la bella figura* was extremely important to Italians.

They reached the lift. A sign was hanging on it, and Franco gave a small curse. "I'm sorry," he said, "the lift is out of order. But it is only three flights up to my apartment. Can you walk it?"

"Of course I can," she said. They climbed up the narrow stairs and Franco, breathing a little heavily again, opened the door to his apartment

Should I be doing this? Donna thought. *No. But damn it, I'm going to anyway!*

The apartment seemed rather small, but it was very neat and clean, with white painted walls, some nice artwork, and modern-looking furniture.

Donna noticed a slightly odd smell, and she wrinkled her nose. Franco noticed her involuntary reaction. "Ah, the drains here are not so good. What can you do? The city is three thousand years old. Now, did you really want some coffee, or...?"

He reached out a hand and stroked her ear with his finger, ever so lightly. Donna felt a shiver run through her. She smiled and shook her head.

Just at that moment, though, Franco's phone rang. He swore colorfully in Italian. Donna laughed. "That's OK," she said, "go ahead and answer it." There was plenty of time, after all.

He held the phone to his ear. "*Pronto.*" A silence followed, then he said, "*Sì? Allora... Sì, va bene.*" He hung up. "So sorry," he said to Donna. "A little problem again with my mother, not too serious. I will see her tonight at the hospital."

"She's still there? Listen, Franco, you must let me help."

"No, no."

Donna persisted. "I can afford to help you with a little money. A gift, that's all. You've been so kind."

Franco frowned, but then said. "Well, if you are sure... it would be a great help."

Feeling triumphant, she said "It will be my pleasure. Now, speaking of pleasure, where were we?"

Beaming with happiness, Franco leaned in and kissed her on the neck, pulling her close and running his hand down her spine. She sank into the warmth of his body, feeling absurdly happy.

"Should we take this somewhere else?" she murmured. Franco smiled and they moved into the bedroom.

Once there, Franco kissed her on the lips, her face and her neck again. He began to fondle her breasts, sending a thrill through her. She was surprised to find his face so rough, though he appeared to be clean-shaven. And his breath... well, it smelt rather strongly of garlic. *Well, this is Italy,* she thought, putting these distractions aside.

She stepped back from him and began to unfasten the buttons at the back of her dress. They were tiny, and she felt clumsy as she fought to undo them.

Meanwhile, Franco took off his jacket and shirt, revealing a well-muscled, hairless chest. Then he slipped out of his trousers and his underwear. He was well-endowed down there, and *very* ready.

She finally had the dress unbuttoned and quickly slid it off. She kicked off her shoes and removed her glasses, putting them on the bedside table. Then she reached up to remove the audio discs, which could sometimes be uncomfortable when she lay down. But Franco quickly seized her hand. "No, no," he murmured, "don't fuss." He began to kiss her neck once more and reached behind her to expertly unhook her bra, dropping it to the floor.

That was when the vision system glitched again. As she looked over Franco's shoulder the lighting gave another sudden shift. The room dimmed considerably and she jerked away from him in surprise. Then it all came back again, bright and clean. "Damn, I'm really going to have to..." she began.

"What's the matter, *belladonna*?" he asked, stepping back, his face creased with concern.

The device failed once more, this time for much, much longer.

It took an instant for Donna to react. And then she cried out in alarm. She looked around in panic. It was as though she had been abruptly whisked away from Franco's modern apartment and been dumped in a dingy, dirty room. Plaster was beginning to peel from the wall in one corner. Worse still, she turned back to Franco, and he wasn't there. That was when she began to scream.

Instead of Franco, a middle-aged man stood before her, naked. His hair was receding, he had stubble on his chin, and his flesh was pale, with black hairs on his chest. With his nakedness full-frontal to her horrified gaze, she saw his slight pot-belly and his still-aroused genitals.

She put up her hands to cover her breasts. "Who are you? Get out, get out!" A second later, she recognized the stranger. He was the man who had stared at her outside the Coliseum. Her legs seemed to give way beneath her, and she slumped down to sit on the bed.

Then, just as suddenly as it had failed, her system fixed itself again. The room lit up with bright light, and she saw Franco standing there once more, beautiful and bronzed.

Donna had a moment's realization. She grabbed the frames of her glasses from the bedside table and flicked off the power. The room dimmed instantly and the handsome young man was gone, changed back into the gross older one.

She stared down at the frames in her hand. "What have you done to them? What have you done to *me*?" she screamed at the man. His mouth opened and closed but for now no sound came out. She scrambled off the bed. Her clothes were scattered on the grimy floor, on a carpet which clearly needed cleaning.

"Where am I? Who..." But then she stopped. She knew, really. She just didn't want to admit it to herself. She threw on her dress, not bothering with her underwear. Then she turned to glare at the man, her heart racing at what seemed to be hundreds of beats per minute.

The man bent his head and looked down, ashamed. "*Belladonna*, I'm so sorry..." His voice had lost the rich resonance that it had had when she was wearing the processor, but it was still recognizably Franco's voice.

"You're him, aren't you? You're really him? You're Franco?"

He nodded, his arms slack, resigned. "Your e-glasses... they have stopped working." It was a statement rather than a question. "A bug. He told me there might be bugs."

"And we were going to... You were going to...," she said, her voice cracking with disbelief and anger. "You fucking *bastard*!" She picked up a heavy lamp from the table – an ugly pottery thing – and threw it hard at Franco. He tried to dodge, but it struck him on the hip and he yelped with pain. The lamp shattered on the wall behind him.

"How did you do it?" Her voice was full of fury. "Oh, for God's sake put your pants on, I can't stand to look at you." He bent and pulled them on – grey suit pants, a little baggy.

"How?" she repeated. "Tell me!"

He turned his hands away from his sides, palms uppermost, and shrugged, a very Italian gesture. "*Allora*, it was the software. The software Claudio gave you at the Forum. We..."

She was bewildered. "The boy? How do you know him? How could...?"

Franco, or the man Franco had become, shrugged again. "He is my son. He is a genius, I think. Very, very clever. He knows all about the software for your system. That model, with the contact lenses, is becoming very popular now among rich young... among young women like yourself. He hacked... is that the word?"

"Hacked? Hacked!" her nostrils flaring, "Claudio is your *son*?"

"Yes, yes," he said, looking ashamed. "He subverted the simulation software. It really is from the Tourism Bureau. But Claudio found a way to forge the authentication... add his own content to the simulation and force it to run always in the background. He is, as I say, very clever..." His voice trailed off.

She bent to pick up the last of her things and slipped her shoes back on in two angry movements. "You *bastard!*" she repeated. "All that business about your mother... You were trying to steal money from me, apart from everything else. I don't believe you have a mother, let alone that she is ill. You're a thief and a liar, and I *hate* you."

He straightened up then. "Yes, it is true. I wish we hadn't tried that, now. But we truly needed that money. Claudio needs it. He should go to a good university, become a great engineer, not be forced to sell stuff on the street. It was my plan, I admit. I... I am sorry."

"I do not forgive you. I'll never forgive you," she said, heading for the bedroom door.

"Donna, please don't go!" he said. "This was the first time we tried it, I swear. You were the first. I would have paid your money back, taken it as a loan, only. Over the last few days I have grown to truly feel for you. I feel... you are not like any other woman. I honestly have come to have real affection for you. We could... once your device is mended, once the bugs are fixed... we could..."

"What?!?" She was astounded by his effrontery.

He reached out his arms, pleading. "What is reality but what we see and hear? Even now, if you were to turn your glasses back on, the software bug has surely cleared up for the moment. You would see the Franco you knew back again. After all, the simulation is just a kind of enhancement. You wear makeup, don't you, to make yourself look more beautiful? Is this so very different? And were you not attracted by our talks, by my words? Everything I said to you was mine, truly mine. Or did you only like me for how you thought I looked?"

She gaped at him for a silent moment. Then in answer she threw the glasses down to the floor, followed by the audio discs. If she could have done so easily, she would have torn out her contact lenses as well. She stamped hard on the delicate devices, grinding them savagely into the floor and crushing the processors.

Not giving him a backward glance, Donna marched out. Without the system, she felt newly naked, stripped of something vital. But she went on.

Outside, reality waited. It was grubby and decrepit and miserable and *dull*.

She was going to have to get used to it.

The Book That He Stole

WHO WOULD HAVE THOUGHT, of all the things in the world Willie Taylor could steal, that he would steal a book? For Willie lived his life surrounded by books of every variety, and they made his life a misery.

Yet Willie Taylor stole a book, and it changed his life forever.

His day had begun like any other. Up before dawn in the chilly attic above the shop. A hurried breakfast of bread and cheese. Down past Mr Farley's office and into the storeroom. At work there since then. Now at midday his arms and legs felt as though they were strung with red-hot wires.

"Willie! Willie! Where *is* that idiot boy?"

"Here, Mr Farley!" he called out. "In the storeroom." *Now where else would I be likely to be?* he wondered. But he knew that Mr Farley was just putting on a front for his customers. Swiftly, he jumped to his feet off the wooden crate he had been sitting on to take a moment's rest. He began prying at the crate with a crowbar before Farley opened the shop door and glared in at him.

"Haven't you got that crate unloaded yet?" Farley asked. "There's customers out here asking for the latest Macaulay. I won't have you lazing about, do you hear me?"

George Farley was a short, wiry man in his late fifties, with hair greying at the temples, a long bony face and half-spectacles perched on his nose.

"I'm sorry, Mr Farley. I'll have it done soon, though," Willie said, and levered up the lid of the crate with a sharp cracking sound.

"See that you do. When you're done, I've got another job for you."

"Yes, Mr Farley," Willie said with a sigh.

"You don't need to sigh at me, young man. If your father hadn't left me with all his debts I'd be able to employ more staff. As it is, you owe me, Willie Taylor. You should thank your lucky stars I'm so good as to give you honest work."

"Yes, Mr Farley," Willie said, his gaze cast down.

"Young Simmonds isn't here today, damn him. I had a note to say he's ill. So I'm forced to stay behind the counter. Bring in all the Macaulay books when you get them out. And for goodness' sake clean yourself up before you come into the shop, I don't want you bringing down the tone of the place." Farley slammed the door behind him and returned to the shop.

Willie lifted off the lid of the crate and began lifting out the clothwrapped bundles of books and taking them to the sorting bench. He unfolded the cloth from each bundle and spelled out the title and the name embossed on the leather spines, reading slowly and mouthing out the sounds.

Willie's education had been abruptly cut short in boyhood when his father had died, leaving behind a struggling business and a devastated widow. Willie's mother had died shortly afterwards, of a broken heart, Willie had always thought.

George Farley had been Willie's father's business partner, who, as he often told Willie, had managed to stave off bankruptcy and set the bookshop on a secure footing. Since his father's death, Willie had been working for Farley. He knew that he should be grateful – many a homeless orphan died on the cold streets of London – but he couldn't help feeling a yearning to be free.

The fourth bundle he unpacked contained copies of the latest volumes from the popular lady novelist Mrs Macaulay, as did the next. He took off his work apron and brushed the dust and splinters as best he could from his trousers. He polished his shoes a little by rubbing them against his trouser legs. Then he picked up the heavy bundles and carried them, one under each arm, into the shop.

Coming from the dim, dusty storeroom into the shop was like stepping from night to day. Here everything was bright. Glints of sunlight through the large street windows reflected from the polished wood of the counters and bookshelves, from the brass of the ladders and from the bannister which followed the spiral stairs up to the mezzanine landing running around three sides of the shop. The shop was crowded: mostly ladies in fine dresses, their maids a step behind them. A few bearded gentlemen in frock coats were also staring up at the shelves. Looking at them, Willie wondered what made the shop's customers pay good money for books. Reading was such hard work!

Farley nodded acknowledgement as Willie handed him the books. He set them down prominently on the counter. "Mrs Macaulay's latest novel!" he called out, laying a hand on Willie's arm to tell him to wait. It took a while, as the counter was immediately mobbed by eager customers. Farley nodded and smiled and rubbed his dry hands together as he served the ladies. Finally, though, there was a moment's respite, and Farley turned to Willie, the false smile vanishing on the instant.

"Listen," his employer said. "Without Simmonds here, I'm hampered, I can't get away. I need you to take the hand-cart to this address and look over a collection from a deceased estate. Second-hand books don't make the profit of new ones, but there's still a demand for some out-of-print titles. I've written down what I'm looking for. Heaven knows I'd rather not trust a fool like you with the job, but if I don't get in quick, she'll sell to MacIntyre's instead. Here's the list. Do you understand?"

"Yes, Mr Farley."

Farley put his hand into his pocket, but hesitated before removing it. He sighed, as though debating whether to go on. Then he pulled four half-crowns from his pocket and one by one counted them into Willie's palm. "Damn it, here's a pound. Take care of it, now. Try and get all of the books on that list for less, do you hear? In good condition. Bring back all the change, or I'll tan your hide so raw you won't sit down for a fortnight. Understand?"

Willie had grown to be a head taller than his employer, but remained as afraid of Farley as when he had been a child. "Yes, sir."

"All right, then, be off with you. I've got customers to serve."

Willie took the two-wheeled hand-cart from the storeroom, put on a cap, and set off down the back lane. After a while, he began whistling, his heart light. Being allowed away from the shop during business hours was a rare freedom. He turned into the main street and trundled along the cobbled road-way, keeping out of the way of the carriages and carts and steering clear of the many horse-droppings as best he could.

He looked at the paper Farley had given him, his lips moving as he spelled out the address: The Nettle Residence, 30 Collier Street, Pentonville. He knew the general area, but might need to ask for directions when he was closer. He set off again, and soon left behind the prosperous shopping district. Gradually, he found himself walking through shabbier streets. Once owned by wealthy families, many of the houses here had now been sub-divided into small tenements. Paint peeled; windows were broken; half-naked, dirty children ran in the streets.

At last, Willie found the address. It was a three-storey terrace house, in slightly better condition than those on either side. The green paint on the door was only just beginning to flake, and the windows, though barred, were as yet whole. The bell-push, though, was broken. Willie knocked hard on the door. He waited for a long minute, then knocked again, hoping that he hadn't wasted his time on the trip. Farley would blame any problems on Willie.

Eventually, though, he heard steps inside, and the door opened a crack. A woman's delicate face looked out. "Yes?"

Willie took off his cap. "I'm from Farley's Bookshop, Miss. You have some books you're selling?"

"Oh. Yes." The young woman seemed to be thinking as she looked Willie up and down. But after a moment, she opened the door wider. "I suppose you'd better come in, then."

As the door closed behind Willie and his eyes adjusted to the dimmer light inside, he was surprised by the young woman's appearance. A few inches shorter than he, she was about his own age or a little older; slim, and wearing a modest dress of such a dark green that it had appeared black at first glance. It was her hair, though, which was startling. Falling to her waist, it was straight and deep black – except for a streak of pure while about three fingers wide which ran down on the right side of her head. It must be natural, he thought. No woman would dye or bleach her head in that odd, off-centre way.

She looked up at him with a direct, rather unsettling gaze. It was very different to the demure, glancing looks which the female customers of the shop sometimes gave him, giggling to their maids.

"In better times, we would have someone to introduce us," she said. "But those times are gone, and I'll have to do it myself. My name is Florence. Florence Nettle," she said. "And you are?"

"Willie Taylor, Miss. From Farley's."

"Yes. Very well. My father's study is this way."

"Your father, Miss? He's not here?"

She paused and looked back at him, assessing why he was asking the question. "My father passed away last month."

Willie felt a sudden flush of embarrassment. He'd forgotten that Mr Farley had told him it was a deceased estate.

"Here we are," she said, as they reached a door at the end of the passage. She unlocked the door.

As they went in, Willie felt a strange, prickling feeling running through him, and he shivered, though the house was warm enough. It felt as though... he couldn't work it out, but it felt as though this room had been waiting for him to arrive. Puzzled, but trying to throw off the odd feeling, he looked around.

The room was long and narrow. Two small barred windows looked out onto an enclosed yard with a spindly tree struggling up at its centre. Inside, a wooden bench ran along the length of the windowed wall, half a dozen books and other items scattered along it. One huge book lay open in the best light, a notebook with pen and ink-stand close by. All of the other walls were lined with glass-fronted bookcases, each crammed with leather-bound volumes.

Florence placed her hand on the bookcase nearest the door. "These are the books I'm prepared to sell," she said. "I need the others to help me carry on my father's work. Are you interested in purchasing these as a job lot?"

"No, Miss. Just the ones on this list." He held out the paper Farley had given him.

Glancing at the short list, her face fell. "So few? But I was hoping..." She sighed. "Oh very well, every little helps. Read them out to me while I look." She gave him back the list.

Willie began to sound out the words. "Pa... me... la... or... vir... tue... re..."

Florence looked back at him in surprise. "Can't you read? You work in a bookshop, and you can't read?"

Embarrassed, Willie shrugged. "I can read well enough, Miss. I'm just a bit slow."

"A bit...! Well, what a pity. To be always surrounded by wonderful books and not be able to enjoy them."

He shrugged again. 'Wonderful' was not a word he associated with the heavy objects he spent his days moving about and arranging. Pulling them out of crates, stacking them neatly in the storeroom, carrying them up ladders, hauling them from place to place in the shop after closing time, depending on Farley's whims. Their desirability to customers made as little sense to him as did rich people's fondness for cheese veined with blue mould.

"Let me see that list again," Florence commanded. She read through it, frowning.

"Most of these are novels," she said. "I have some of them upstairs on my own bookshelf. But my father was a scholar of the arcane, a collector of unusual volumes. I always understood that his books were very valuable, even these less rare ones that I'm prepared to sell."

"Dunno, Miss. Mr Farley just gave me the list. He said I was to spend no more than a pound."

"A pound! But I need..." She sank down into a wooden chair and gazed out of the window silently. Willie felt uncomfortable, hoping the young lady wasn't going to start to cry. But her face showed anger rather than grief.

"I don't want to deal with MacIntyre's," she said, almost to herself. "My father told me how Joseph MacIntyre cheated him some years ago. But I must raise some money soon, or I'll have to sell this house."

"Perhaps, Miss..." he ventured after a long silent pause, "... perhaps I could take some of your books on commission, like. Mr Farley's done that a few times, I think."

She turned to him, her face brightening. "Yes. It's worth a try at least. Look, I'll take your list upstairs and see how many of the novels I have. I'll sell those to you for the pound. God knows I need all I can right now. And then I'll pick out a dozen of father's books for you to sell on commission. I'm sure they'll find a discerning customer."

She stood up. "Please stay here," she said. "I'll be back as soon as I can. And... for goodness sake don't touch anything."

She went to the door and closed it behind her. He heard her turn the key in the lock, locking him in. That was surprising, but he understood. She didn't trust Willie enough not to leave the study and steal something valuable from another room.

As soon as she had gone, the strange feeling returned. This time it felt as though someone was calling to him, calling silently, though that made no sense. He walked around for a couple of minutes, trying to throw off the feeling. But it just grew stronger. It made him turn his back on the bookcases and go over to the bench beneath the windows. He glanced without much interest at the huge open book, whose pages were crowded with tiny type. That wasn't what was calling him. He felt drawn further down the bench. Frowning, a little afraid, he moved along.

In the dimmer light between the windows lay a small book not much bigger than his hand. It was closed, and on its leather cover was embossed a complex spiral design.

Willie couldn't read very well, but he did enjoy looking at the illustrations in some of the books Farley sold, like the sketches in many of Mr Dickens' novels. Ignoring Florence's prohibition, he wiped his hands on his trousers and reached out to open the book.

The moment his hand touched the cover, a peculiar sensation ran up his arm, like a million sharp little pin-pricks, just for a moment, and then it was gone. He jerked back his hand as though he had been burned. Tentatively, he reached out again. The thrill was repeated, but much less strongly. Fascinated, he picked up the book and opened it part-way.

The pages were filled with type, but the left-hand page, apparently the beginning of a chapter, began with an elaborate decorated capital. Peering closer, Willie saw that the small engraving crudely depicted a tree, with a sword plunged into its trunk mid-way up. The trunk, a branch and the sword together made up the shape of the letter 'F'.

Willie looked at the remaining text. The letters were very strangely formed. He began to sound out the words as best he could. As always, he had to speak the syllables out aloud. "Fo... sh... tor... a..." That made no sense. Perhaps it was a name. Try the next word: "ca... da... la...". He continued, trying to squeeze some sense out of the page. Completing the sentence, he went back and read it aloud again, at a slightly quicker pace. An instant later, everything changed.

She is running, in a forest. Her breath is coming hard, her heart beating wildly within her breast, but she is determined to reach her goal. Branches catch at her white dress, stones painful underfoot. Behind her, the panting and growling of the beast which pursues her, coming ever closer. Ahead lies the tree she has been searching for, the tree pierced by the sword of legend. With that sword in hand, she can kill the beast.

He gave a gasp and dropped the book, his heart pounding. He had *been* in that forest! He had been that desperate young woman! He couldn't help glancing back over his shoulder to make sure some dreadful monster was not there. And something was caught in his jacket sleeve, irritating his skin beneath. Bewildered he looked and saw that it was a twig which had torn through the cloth. A twig from a tree. But how...?

Just then, he heard the key turning in the lock of the study door.

It was at that moment that Willie did something he could never have dreamed he could do. He snatched up the mysterious book from the bench and shoved it into the inner pocket of his ragged jacket. Trying to remove the guilty look from his face, he turned to the door as Florence came in.

"Here are the novels," she said, holding out a stack of books. "I had most of the ones on your list. I hate to let them go, but I see that I must. Now... that pound?"

Willie had to clear his throat before he spoke. His heart was still running at a faster rate than usual. "Here you are, Miss," he said, pulling out the half-crowns.

She looked intently at him as she took the money, as though she knew something was wrong. But she continued, "Now, the books on commission. Do you have a cart to carry them? Yes? We'll need to make a couple of trips to the front door."

Together, they transported the books outside. At every moment, Willie was certain that Florence would see the shape of the stolen book moving within his jacket. Willie had never in his life stolen anything of any value. He felt faint-headed, inwardly astonished at what he had done.

The dozen books which Florence had selected for sale by

commission were all large, thick volumes, dwarfing the small collection of novels.

She looked at the heavily laden cart with concern. "Will you be all right to push these all the way back?" she asked.

Willie nodded. "Yes, Miss. Thanks, Miss."

Quickly, so as not to risk discovery of his crime, he turned away and pushed at the cart. It took a great deal of effort to get it moving, but once it was going it was a lot easier.

His reception by Mr Farley an hour later, once the shop had closed its doors, was a painful one.

Farley was livid. "No change out of a whole pound? And what's all this rubbish?" he said, picking up one of the large volumes. "These weren't on the list, you oaf!"

"I thought..." Willie began.

"You? You don't have a thought in your head, you fool. You're as bad as your father. It's his debts I've been paying off all these years. If I were to add in the cost of the board and lodging I've given you over the years out of the goodness of my heart..."

"Please, sir, I thought you could sell these on commission. The young lady said..."

"Young lady! What would a woman know about the value of books? Rubbish, I say. No one wants these ancient things. You'll have to take them back. Not now, there's too much else for you to do. Tomorrow, though, first thing. And I'll be docking your pay for the wasted time."

Stung as he was by his master's criticism, Willie's heart was actually lifted by this instruction. The truth was, his guilt over taking the magical book had been growing without bound ever since he had left Florence Nettle. What had he been thinking? What if she noticed the book was missing and reported him to the police? In his grandfather's time, men had been hung or transported for less. He needed to return the book, and soon. He would just hide it among the books Farley had rejected. Florence would probably assume that she had given it to him in error, and he would be safe.

But first...

That night, sitting on his bed, Willie lit one of his precious candles, and with a trembling hand reached into his jacket pocket and pulled out the book. There was that electric thrill again, but he barely noticed it now.

By the flickering light, Willie opened the book once more. A new chapter. The decorated initial here was very dark with cross-hatching, but something like a snake curled through it to depict the letter 'S'.

Bending low over the book and squinting in the uncertain light, Willie tried to fathom the words. As before, he spoke the syllables aloud: "So... na... dus... al... da..." and on to the end of the sentence. He read it again, a little faster. And then it happened.

Deep in the darkness, awakening, he breathes in deeply, sniffing the dank scents of the cavern. He stirs, his huge wings rubbing against each other with a husky, leathery sound. Above, there is a light growing brighter with each beat of his great heart. His long imprisonment is coming to an end. Unfolding his wings, he stretches them to their limits, easing their stiffness, and begins to beat them in long, slow, sweeps. Tentatively at first, then with growing strength, he begins to lift. The light above is now blazing. Rising, he welcomes it with his flaming breath...

Willie's bed was on fire, dark clouds of smoke billowing up from the straw-filled mattress and the flimsy blanket. With a cry of alarm, Willie dropped the book, grabbed up the piss-pot and threw its contents over the flames. Foul-smelling steam hissed up. He grabbed the mattress and turned it over and stomped on it. Gradually, the smoke grew less and was eventually reduced to a few wisps.

Staring at the smoking and steaming mess of straw and cloth on the floor, Willie tried to convince himself that the fire hadn't been the result of the vision conjured up by the book. But he couldn't do it. His candle, though now guttering low, was still upright. No. He had dreamed of a dragon, and somehow its fiery breath had escaped from the dream and set fire to his bed.

A bed which was now ruined. It hadn't been much to begin with, but now Willie would have to spend some of his hoarded pennies to replace it, or else be forced to sleep on the hard floor without a blanket. And winter was only a few months away.

Shivering, he put on his work jacket and squatted in a corner of the attic with a scrap of the burned blanket. It took him a long while to go back to sleep. But then he fell into such a deep slumber that he was woken only by the roaring of Farley at the bottom of the ladder. "Willie! Willie Taylor, you lazy oaf! I don't pay you to sleep!"

Willie stumbled up, half-dazed. He looked down at the magical book. His mind was still full of the vision of the dragon. The feeling was not of fear; no, he had *been* the dragon. What remained was the sensation of invincible power. He almost felt as if he could flex his leathery wings and fly away from London to somewhere... he wasn't sure where, but somewhere better.

For a long moment – longer than he could afford with Farley yelling below – he longed to keep the book and not return it, despite the destruction of his bed. But no, he couldn't risk it. He picked it up and stuffed it once more into his jacket. Then he scrambled down the ladder to face Farley's renewed scolding.

"You'll remember that I'm docking your pay while you return those useless books, young man," Farley said. "Given your laziness this morning, I'm docking you the whole day. And don't think you've time for breakfast, because you don't."

"Yes, Mr Farley," Willie mumbled, feeling a pang of guilt. The fact was, guilt was Willie Taylor's abiding emotion. He felt guilt for every mistake he had ever made in the shop, and above all, guilt for the terrible financial state in which his father had left Mr Farley.

On the way back to Florence's house, Willie stopped and tucked the special book between two of the books he was returning. He looked at the pile dubiously. If he was being honest, the small book looked obviously out of place with the larger volumes. Still, it was the best he could do. Sighing, he started the cart forward again.

Florence Nettle was standing in the doorway of her house when he reached it. Her face was grave and her arms were crossed, the white streak in her hair startling in the bright sunlight.

Willie stopped the cart and looked up at her in dismay.

"I think there's something you have to tell me, Willie," she said.

"Um... Mr Farley didn't agree..." he began.

"Not that. Quickly now!"

He hung his head, ashamed. She knew. He wondered if she had already sent for a policeman to arrest him as a thief. "I'm very sorry, Miss. I took a book I shouldn't have. But I brought it back, Miss. See, it's here," he said. She took it silently. "I knew it was wrong, Miss. But the book, it..."

Florence looked at him with narrowed eyes. "Why *this* book, Willie? Of all the books in my father's study?"

He shook his head, not knowing how answer her.

"Come in, Willie. Bring all of the books. I want to talk to you."

It took two trips. As he put the last pile down on the bench in the study, Florence said. "Now, Willie, tell me what made you steal this book."

"Miss... it gave me a shock, like, when I touched it. And then I read it and..."

"You read it?" she asked, incredulous. "But it's written in an ancient language no one now speaks."

"I mean, I mean..." he stammered. "I *tried* to read it. I sounded out the words like I always do, and when I did, something happened. It was like... like being inside the book."

Florence's face showed her scepticism. Impatient, she handed him the book. "Open it. Sit down. Read it. I want to see."

Obediently, he sat, took the book and opened it again at a random page. Again there was an elaborate initial. A snowy mountain peak, with a slanting road: the letter 'A'. Concentrating on the words, Willie began: "A... ma... sa... ca...".

> *The old woman wearily puts one foot in front of the other, each clothwrapped boot sinking into the snow. On her back, she feels the weight of the bundle containing the tools and materials of her craft. Up ahead now she can see the village, and she half-fancies she can hear the groaning of the young woman in labour she has been sent to help. The clouds are dark, and even now snow begins to fall again. But determined to press on, she puts down another foot.*

"Willie!" Florence spoke urgently at his side. She was squatting so as to be on a level with him. Bewildered, he looked at her, his gaze unfocused.

Her eyes were wide, and her face excited. "Look!" she said, pointing to the floor. Patterned over the carpet was a thick scattering of snowflakes, now beginning to melt.

"Quickly now," she said. "Tell me what you saw. Your eyes were rolled back and your body was trembling. I thought perhaps you were having a seizure and I would have to call a doctor. But after about ten minutes you came out of it and then the snow started to fall. Tell me!"

Hesitantly, he described the vision, still feeling the weight of the old woman's bundle on his back, her determination to forge on still in his mind. "Then there was happened last night, Miss." He told her about the vision of the dragon, and how on waking, his bed had been on fire. "It's like a dream, Miss, but not a dream. And then when I wake up some of the story comes with me, like."

"You are the key," she said in a wondering tone. "The key my father tried to find for many years. Listen, Willie. My father collected and studied some very unusual books during his lifetime. This particular book came from the collection of a scholar living in Krakow, and it always intrigued my father. He felt it might contain the secret to a great treasure. It is written in an unknown language, a language my father was unable to even identify, let alone translate."

"But what did you mean, Miss, about me being the key?"

"My father had a theory that certain arcane books can only be read and understood by particular individuals. Such a book is like a locked safe, only able to be unlocked by one or two people. The words in such books are not the words of a language but..."

"But what, Miss?"

Florence was clearly reluctant to go on. "It sounds absurd here in our modern world, a world of commerce driven by steam power and with marvels like the electric telegraph. Yet... my father came to believe that these books contain not ordinary words but rather... *incantations*. Spells, if you like."

"Spells... like magic, you mean?"

"It sounds ridiculous, doesn't it? But how else do you explain these intense visions you experience? Or explain the snow, and the fire? I don't even understand how you can read the words at all. The alphabet isn't our usual one, the one you would have been taught in school."

To Willie, all letters were strange forms he had to struggle to identify. The letters in the book, though, had somehow fallen quickly into place in his mind. He looked down at the strange book, his thoughts troubled.

"But why me? What does it all mean, Miss?"

"It means that this book found you, drew you to it. You are its key. If only my father were still here, he would be overjoyed to have found you. Tell me about yourself, about your circumstances. I need to know."

Though he felt very uncomfortable, under this intense young woman's gaze he felt compelled to tell her about his father's death and the subsequent death of his mother. About his father's debts and how he was helping to pay them off by working for Mr Farley.

Florence frowned. "But that's not right. You shouldn't have to be responsible for your father's business debts, Willie."

Willie shrugged and squirmed on the chair. "Miss, I need to get back to the shop. Mr Farley will be furious if I take too long."

"But I need..." She stopped herself, stood up and folded her arms. "I think it's about time I met your Mr Farley. I have a few things I'd like to say to him. Go and hail a cab, Willie. I can still afford that, at least."

It took some time for Willie to hail a cab in this now impoverished area of London. Finally, though, he found one and brought it back to Florence's house. The cabby grumbled excessively about having to strap Willie's hand-cart to the back, but Florence tipped him well.

Travelling back in the cab, sitting next to Florence Nettle and smelling her perfume, Willie felt very uncomfortable indeed, wondering what Mr Farley would say and how he would react to Florence herself.

The reaction was certainly interesting. Florence marched into the shop with Willie trailing hesitantly behind. Several elegant women were at the counter, where Mrs Macaulay's latest was still selling briskly. Bob Simmonds, newly returned from his illness, was at the counter serving them, Mr Farley at his elbow. Florence strode boldly past the customers and spoke directly to the older man. "Mr Farley?"

Startled, Willie's employer nodded, his eyes wide, staring at the white streak in Florence's hair. "I need to speak to you privately, Mr Farley," she said. "It's about this young man."

Farley glared at Willie. "Why, what's he done?" he growled.

"*Privately*, Mr Farley, if you please," Florence said.

Farley gave a slight shrug and led them up the stairs to his office, which overlooked the street. He sat down behind his desk, indicating the visitor's chair to Florence with poor grace.

"Now, madam," he said. "Whatever he's done, he'll pay for it, I assure you. He's a lazy, good-for-nothing..."

"Willie has done nothing wrong, Mr Farley. On the contrary, he has been of considerable help to me. If fact, I wish to hire his services for a period of a week, perhaps longer."

George Farley had never been more astonished in his life. "Hire him?" he repeated, his mouth agape.

"Yes. Now what do you pay him per week?"

Farley shifted in his chair. "You have to understand, madam," he said. "I only employ the lad out of respect to his father, my deceased business partner. I provide him with his board and lodging, that's not cheap."

"I shall provide for his meals," Florence said. "Now, how much do you pay him?"

Farley, clearly annoyed, hesitated a long time before replying. But, knowing Willie could contradict him if he lied, said at last, "I pay him a penny a day."

It was Florence's turn to be astonished. "A penny? Not even the meanest labourer is paid so little!"

His face starting to shade towards beetroot, Farley snapped "It's a halfpenny too much, if you ask me. What with the debts his father left me, he's lucky he's paid anything."

"But he's not a slave, or an indentured servant. He shouldn't have to..."

Farley interrupted, "I've had enough of this. This interview is at an end. I won't be questioned in my own office by a... by a..."

Florence stood up. "Be careful, Mr Farley. There are laws against slander."

Farley began to speak, but controlled himself with an obvious effort. When he was calm, he said, "I won't hire out the lad. I need him working here."

Fists clenched, Florence seemed about to argue the point, but then relaxed slightly. "Very well," she said in a cold voice. "Goodbye, Willie. Perhaps we may meet again one day." She stalked out.

Farley, his face still red, gestured to Willie. "Get back to work, you fool. Damn you for bringing back that... that shameless jade! It's the last time I'll send you out of the shop to deal with anyone."

The rest of the day was miserable, as Willie struggled to catch up with the work which had accumulated in his absence. After the shop was closed, there was still more labour to restock the shelves, with Farley scolding him constantly. Only well after dark was Willie able to creep back up to the attic with a hunk of dry bread for his supper.

He had forgotten the state of his bed. He gathered together the worst of the burnt, damp straw and dumped it outside in the lane. With what remained, he did his best to stay warm enough to sleep.

Late in the afternoon of the following day, he was unloading a cart which had brought fresh volumes to be sold, when he saw a familiar figure picking her way cautiously through the mud and horse-droppings in the lane. It was Florence Nettle.

The driver of the cart, sitting idly behind his horse smoking a pipe, made a coarse remark and laughed. Florence glared at the man with such a fierce expression that he shrugged and looked away.

"Miss Florence, what are you doing here?" Willie asked. "You shouldn't..."

"Is Mr Farley there? No? Good. Help me up," she said, and he reached out to help her up the short wooden ladder to the delivery dock.

"I had to find a way to talk to you without your employer being aware of it," she said. Glancing back to where the carter sat smoking, she said, "Can you get rid of that man?"

"I'll unload the last couple of boxes," Willie said. "That's all he's waiting for." He did so. The driver shook the reins and the cart moved off, but not without another leer at Florence and a knowing wink at Willie.

"Miss, you really shouldn't be here. People will..."

She stamped her foot, impatient. "Willie, I don't care a scrap for my reputation. What I care about is what we can find out from this book." She drew the small volume out of her bag.

Willie was frightened by the book. Frightened, if truth be told, by Florence herself. But then he thought of the visions he had seen. The young woman in the forest had been frightened, too, but she had also been brave.

He straightened. "All right, Miss, I'll look at the book again. But not when I'm by myself. What if it's a dragon again, and this time I can't put out the fire?"

"I'll stay with you while you read it, Willie."

"But, Miss, we can't let Mr Farley see you here. He'll be in soon, just before he locks up the shop." He stopped, looked about. "You'll need to hide. I'll close the doors to the lane to make it darker, and pile up a few boxes. He won't know you're behind them if you're quiet."

Soon enough, Farley came in. "This storeroom is a mess," were his first words. "Tidy it up and sweep before you go to bed. I'll be checking in the morning."

"Yes, Mr Farley," Willie said, with his usual outward submissiveness. But inside he felt the dragon stirring its mighty wings.

When Farley was gone, Willie called to Florence.

"Now," she said. "Where shall we do this? It's hardly comfortable here. And I want you to try reading several passages in the book. Can we go to your room?"

Willie was alarmed. "No, Miss. It's just an attic, not very comfortable." And it smelled of burnt straw and urine, he didn't add. "Maybe... we could go up to Mr Farley's office. We can get there through the shop."

Once he and Florence were in Farley's office, Willie lit just one of the gas lamps on the wall, to give him enough light to read. He didn't want to make it too bright in the office, to avoid attracting the attention of anyone walking outside.

Florence picked up a carafe of water from Farley's desk. "I am equipped, you see, for the dragon," she said with a smile. "Now, sit on that couch, and open the book where I've placed the bookmark."

The marked spot was close to the end of the book. The decorated initial here was for the letter 'O', a glowing ball. Inside the letter was the faint, sketchy outline of an opened box or chest. "That little illustration has always intrigued me," Florence said. "It was one reason my father thought the book could be a guide to the location of a treasure. We may as well start with it. Please read."

The illumination was poor. Willie tilted the book to gain the best light and began. "Or... da... so... ro..." Though he still needed to speak the syllables aloud, the process was becoming easier each time. "Ordasoro caratamas lamendani..." he read.

He sits at his bench, weary with age, surrounded by his precious library, an open book to one side. In front of him the ball he has laboriously shaped from a crystalline rock and ground to the smoothest of surfaces. Into the crystal he gazes, stroking it all the while and muttering an incantation. Gradually, very slowly, the vision appears...

"Willie! Willie!" Florence was shaking him hard. Dazed, struggling to escape from the vision, Willie gradually realised that he was lying on the hard wooden floor. He must have rolled off the couch. With Florence's help, he slowly sat up. The dizziness persisted, and he was forced to support himself against the side of the couch.

"Are you all right?" Florence asked, her face creased with anxiety. "You were out such a long time..."

Willie felt as though he was seeing double. At the edges of his vision were the ranks of ancient books in the scholar's study. And a glowing ball still seemed to hover in the air in front of him.

Florence, kneeling by his side, said, "Can you get up, Willie? I think I should call for a doctor, but we can't be found here. If you could try to walk..."

"No, I'll be all right, Miss. Just give me a minute."

She was silent a moment. "You could call me Florence, you know," she said. "We haven't known each other for long, Willie, but I feel as though we've been through a great deal together."

He was uncomfortable. "I don't know, Miss. It doesn't seem right."

"All right, let it go," she sighed. "If you're feeling better, can you tell me what you saw? Did you see the treasure?"

"No, not really." He could still feel the presence of the scholar in his mind. The old man seemed to be observing him, amused. "But... can you see something over there?" he said, pointing to where the glowing ball still hovered.

She turned and gave a gasp as saw it too, hovering in the centre of the office. It was about a handspan in size and brighter than any gas lamp. As they watched, it moved towards one wall, where a large map of London was hung.

Willie climbed to his feet, still a little unsteady. "Is it telling us where to go to find the treasure?" he asked. With Florence's help, he approached the map. But the light from the glowing sphere was diffuse, illuminating the whole of the engraving equally. No single spot could be said to be marked out by the light. Florence made a disappointed sound.

Willie narrowed his eyes, concentrating. Then he stepped to one side and lifted the back of the frame away from the wall to peer behind it. A moment later, and he had lifted the frame from the suspension wire and set it on the floor. Revealed was the face of a small metal safe set flush into the wall.

Florence was frowning. "Do you think this is where Mr Farley keeps his money? We can't just steal it, Willie, that wouldn't be right."

"No, Miss, we can't. Besides, he keeps the takings in that big strong box near his desk. I'm not sure why he needs this one as well."

"Yet see how the light from the book is still here. It's trying to tell us something. Can we open this safe and have a look inside, at least? But surely Mr Farley has the key?"

They heard the office door slammed open behind them. "What are you doing here?" came a harsh, slurred voice.

They turned. George Farley was standing there, a look of anger and alarm on his face. Indeed, he looked almost frightened. "Thieves!" he cried out in a loud voice. He turned to the street window. "Robbers!" he yelled as he fought to get it opened. He was unsteady on his feet, and Willie could tell that he had been drinking heavily.

Florence ran quickly over to him. "Mr Farley, it's not like that. We're not here to steal anything from you."

Farley whirled and, ignoring what she was saying, smashed his fist hard into Florence's face. With a cry, she fell to the floor and lay dazed, her hair a disordered black and white halo around her head.

"Hussy! Whore! Thief!" Farley shouted. "You've seduced this stupid boy, I have no doubt. If I hadn't needed to return..." He drew back his foot to kick at Florence as she lay helpless.

All of his life Willie had been afraid of George Farley. The frequent beatings he had suffered, the daily cuffs and constant insults, had made a deep impact on his character. But now

Willie felt the dragon stir within him and everything changed. He ran over and pulled Farley away, so that his kick merely skimmed Florence's head. Turning, the man threw a wild punch at Willie, who had to let go in order to defend himself. Farley, off balance, lost his footing completely and toppled to the floor, striking his head lightly against the window-sill as he fell. He lay unmoving.

Panting, Willie went over to Florence, who was beginning to push herself up, wiping blood away from her mouth with one hand. "Are you all right, Florence?"

She looked with a bewildered air at the blood on her fingers. "Yes, Willie," she said after a moment, "I think so." With his help, she sat up and rested her back against the desk. Her face, though still pale, was beginning to regain signs of colour. She looked over to Farley and whispered "Have you killed him? Oh, say he's not dead!"

Willie looked at his prone employer, his heart racing with passion. "If he is, I'm not sorry," he said. He went over to Farley, knelt down and turned him over so that he lay on his back. "No, listen to him snore. I think he's more drunk than anything else, I can smell the brandy on his breath."

Willie felt inside Farley's jacket pockets. He came up with a bunch of keys. "I'm going to see what's inside that safe," he said. Over near the safe, the soft sphere of light still hung in the air, as though waiting.

"Willie, we can't steal his valuables," Florence said. "I'm not a thief, no matter what... what that man said."

"No. But I want to know what he keeps in there that's so important."

It took him several minutes to find the right key, but then he had it and the door was opened. He reached in and brought out a sheaf of papers. He looked at them in puzzlement for a moment, and then brought them over to Florence, who had now recovered enough to lift herself up to sit on the chair at the desk. As he did so, the glowing ball slowly began to fade.

"Can you read these, Miss?"

"Florence," she insisted.

"Florence. Would you read them for me, please?"

She began to look through the papers as Willie stood and watched her, thinking hard.

He knew that his time working for Mr Farley was at an end, and he had no idea what the future held. But he was old enough now, and strong enough, to find some kind of labouring work. Why had he never thought of that before? Years of being subject to Farley had drained all of his self-esteem. But now... he could feel the steely determination of the midwife as she plodded through the snow; could feel the wisdom of the scholar; the courage of the maiden in the forest; and the power of the dragon. He was a different person now. All because of that book.

Florence spent a long time leafing through the papers, reading one or two briefly, frowning, and then moving on. Finally, she looked up at Willie with a startled expression, her mouth opening as if to say something. Then her face changed and instead she screamed "Willie! Look out!"

Willie turned. Farley was there, brandishing a knife. Willie reached out to grab for it but not quickly enough. Farley lunged at him. He felt a searing pain in his shoulder and sank to his knees, crying out at the pain. Farley now waved the bloodied blade at Florence. "Give me those papers," Farley said. "Now!"

Florence pulled them away from Farley and dropped them on the desk behind her. "No," she said. "I've seen enough to..."

Growling, Farley stabbed forward with the knife. Grim-faced, Florence grabbed his hand and fought to keep the blade away from her chest.

Willie shoulder was an agony and he could feel a warm wetness spreading down his front, but nevertheless he struggled back up to his feet and seized the older man. "Mr Farley, stop!," he gasped out.

Farley's face showed pure fear. Wrenching himself away from Willie and Florence, still holding the knife, he ran to the window and threw it open. "Police!" he yelled. "Police! I'm being robbed! Help!" There must have been a constable patrolling the street just outside, because they heard the sound of a police whistle, followed by the sound of running feet.

Farley turned, his face set in a snarl, the knife held out in front of him as a barrier. "Now I have you," he said. "You'll go to jail for this, Willie Taylor, which is where you belong. And as for you," he said to Florence with a leer, "I'll see you get what you deserve, too. Do you know what the guards do to women prisoners? A pretty face like yours is just what they're waiting for."

Running steps on the stairs. In came the red-faced policeman, his stovepipe hat a little askew. He looked at the scene in bewilderment, his truncheon raised.

"Now then," he said. "What's on going on here?"

"I'm being robbed," Farley yelled. "Arrest these people. I'm the owner of this shop. They are stealing my property. That woman has taken..."

Florence faced the constable. "I have taken nothing from this man, constable," she said in a quiet voice. The policeman was obviously bewildered by her calm demeanour.

"My papers!" protested Farley, but his voice was strangely weak.

Florence reached back to the desk and picked up the scattered papers. "These documents include the title deeds to the shop and the establishment papers for the associated business," she said. Farley made an inarticulate sound, but she went on, remorseless.

"They show that Mr Farley here does *not* own this business. We will be happy to go with you to the police station, constable, where the papers can be examined by a competent legal authority. But by my reading, they show that the true owner of this business is William Taylor, Junior, the heir to the original owner. That is this young man here, who has just been grievously attacked and wounded by George Farley. Willie owns everything."

"Lies!" Farley almost sobbed. "The debts..."

Florence glanced down at the papers and picked out another of the sheets. The policeman was transfixed by puzzlement, but his truncheon had dropped to his side.

"The debts," Florence said, "were your own, George Farley. The papers show that you were taken on as an employee of the business as an act of charity by your friend William Taylor Senior, when your own enterprise failed and you were forced to declare bankruptcy."

She glared at Farley, who had turned completely white. He dropped the knife, which clattered on the wooden floor.

Willie stood leaning against the wall, his hand pressed hard against the wound in his shoulder. The pain was still severe, and this was all bewildering. "But, Florence," he said, "my mother told me..."

Ignoring him, Florence went on, still looking fiercely at Farley, who had now sagged down to sit on the window-sill. "When Willie's father died suddenly, you took advantage of that fact and represented to Willie's mother that you had been a full partner in the business. Poor woman, she must not have understood either the legal situation or your willingness to steal what was not yours."

"I built the business up," Farley said, his voice petulant. "I made it prosperous."

"Yes. But all the while paying Willie here the merest pittance for doing all of the hard work behind the scenes. Constable, let us go. A judge must see these papers. Willie needs that wound seen to by a doctor. He may want to register a charge of assault against this man. And what Farley has done surely constitutes fraud."

The constable scratched his head, but seemed impressed by Florence's confident presentation. Farley, on the other hand, was now weaving and groaning, his face in his hands. "All right, Miss," the policeman said. "I dunno what all this is about, but my sergeant will know what to do." Hesitating only a moment, he stepped forward and seized Farley's unresisting arm.

Florence stood and went over to Willie, who had been gazing at her with wonder.

"Willie," she said. "My father was right about the book, though not in the way he imagined. You've found your fortune. Everything has changed."

"Thanks to you, Mi..." he began, then straightened up and started again. "Thanks to you, Florence," he said. "But I can't run a business like this shop. Not by myself. Only if you can help me."

She smiled. "I will, if you'll have me."

He took her hand in his. "And I'll need to learn to read and write properly," he said, considering.

"I'll teach you," she said.

The Miracle Cure

GETTING OUT OF THE LAST TOWN HAD BEEN A CLOSE-RUN THING, Balthazar knew. Perhaps he should have given up the business after that; but then, it was the only trade he knew. What would he do instead? Work as a farmhand? Try his luck at panning for gold? No. There was really no choice, he just had to keep on moving and hope that he could stay ahead of his pursuers.

Thinking about getting caught made him anxious again, and he shook the reins. The long-suffering old mare whinnied in annoyance, but she sped up her pace a fraction and the bright-ly-decorated wagon rattled on down the dusty road.

There was another town up ahead. A *new* town. A new town always refreshed his sense of hope; it was like a beautiful dawn full of rosy color. He forced himself to smile. You had to appear to be cheerful, to be positive, to be beaming with good health, or no-one would believe in you for an instant. And belief was what it was all about.

Entering the town, he turned the wagon into what seemed to be the main street.

The town was called Kirkstone. A saloon, a general trading store, a blacksmith, a stable and saddler, and a small chapel. Not a large town, which was all to the good. News would be slow in reaching such a place, and the townsfolk would be starved for entertainment.

They were already staring at him. Two old men sitting outside the saloon leaned forward, eyes squinting. A scattering of children began to trail him as the wagon creaked along. Several women coming out of a store stopped when they saw him and began to talk among themselves.

He drew to a halt in what passed for a town square—just a slightly wider area of dusty roadway in front of the chapel. The mare began to drink eagerly from a stone water trough.

Balthazar stood up as a crowd began to gather about the wagon. He grinned and waved his hat.

"La-ay-dee-ees and gentlemen!" he bellowed out in his rich baritone. "Thank you for this warm welcome to your lovely town." No welcome had actually been extended, but that wouldn't trouble him, no sir!

"I am Doctor Orville Balthazar, known throughout the land for curing the incurable, giving hope to the hopeless and consoling the inconsolable. You have heard of me, no doubt?" *I hope not,* he thought to himself.

Allowing no time for an answer, he went on quickly. "No? That can only be because the many thousands of my patients want to keep the benefits of my treatments to themselves. Who could blame them? Once my medicine has done its work they beg me never to leave. But do I agree? No! It is my mission—my sacred mission—to spread the benefits of my treatments as far and wide as I am able."

And so it went on. It was a lot harder, these days, without a shill in the audience. But Jackie Baker, his shill in previous times had... well, Balthazar had lost him four months ago. Jackie hadn't been able to run fast enough. Perhaps Balthazar should have stopped the wagon instead of urging the mare to a reluctant gallop? Perhaps. But no, that would have been the end of them both. They had stayed too long in that town, that had been the problem. He knew better now.

Even without a shill, his pitch would work. It always did these days. Thanks to the Miracle Cure.

"You sir!" he called out. "Yes, you there with the crutch. Why are you lame, sir?"

A grizzled old man looked up with a skeptical expression. "I was in the war, sonny. Fightin' the rebs, weren't I? Took a bullet in my leg, and had to wrestle the doc who wanted to take the whole thing off with his saw. Never liked docs since then. Don't like you."

The crowd cheered on the old man, who was clearly a well-known identity around the town, expecting to see Balthazar discomfited. "You tell 'im, Bill!" came a call from the back. But they didn't know Balthazar.

"I know exactly the type of doctor you mean," he bellowed back. "Cut off a man's leg or his arm rather than try to fix it. Well, that's not my style. Here, sir, let me give you a free draught of the Miracle Cure, normally five dollars a bottle."

Balthazar pulled out a green bottle with a bold, colorful label. "Come, sir, why not try it out? Free, gratis, no strings attached. Who could ask for a better deal? I guarantee that it will ease your pain and allow you to walk more naturally."

The war veteran was reluctant at first, but with the crowd urging him, he limped towards the wagon, leaning heavily on his wooden crutch. Balthazar pulled the cork from the bottle and poured a generous quantity into a glass, which he passed down to the man.

The old man sniffed at it suspiciously. "What's in it?" he asked.

"Natural herbs, spices, and a special ingredient known only to myself. That sir, is my trade secret." *And what a secret it is*, Balthazar thought, with a slight inward pang.

The old soldier looked at the greenish liquid as if debating whether it was poison or not. After a long pause (and the jeers of the crowd), he lifted it up and gulped down a generous swig. Nothing happened.

This was the problem with not having a shill, Balthazar knew only too well. A shill would have immediately thrown down the crutch, started dancing about, shouting with joy. This way took patience and a little time. But it would work. Oh yes, it would work.

He distracted the crowd by pitching on about the benefits of the cure for another good five minutes, and then picking on another subject. A middle-aged woman, her face drawn and sunken. "Madam, may I inquire what ails you? I can see that you are suffering."

With a half-sob, the woman said "Doctor says it's a tumor, a tumor here inside." She placed her hand flat on her abdomen. "It hurts, hurts real bad. Ain't got more than a few months to live, he says."

"Madam, my heart is pained for you. Let me offer you a draught of the Cure. It can do you no harm and will, I am sure, offer you comfort."

Her face lit up with a kind of half-hope that it truly pained Balthazar to see. Still, business was business. She came up to the wagon, took the glass from him and swallowed it down without hesitation.

There might have been enough time by now. Balthazar turned back to the old man. "Sir, how does your leg feel?"

The man tentatively put some weight on it. "Well..." he said. "I guess... Reckon it doesn't hurt as much as it did. Could be imagining it, but..." He handed the crutch to his neighbor in the crowd and tried a few steps. He still limped badly, but he was managing to stay upright without the crutch. *Perfect*, thought Balthazar.

"Ladies and gentlemen," he called out. "Like all good things, the Miracle Cure takes time. Your leg, sir, will feel better and better as the day goes on. Tomorrow you will be able to walk on it without a limp. The day after, and there will be almost no pain."

An encouraging buzz of comment arose from the crowd. He looked back to the woman with the tumor. Her face was relaxing, its deeply-etched lines softening. "Yes!" she said, almost with a smile. "Yes. It is working. Doesn't hurt quite so bad, anyhow." The crowd began to chatter noisily.

"Now then," Balthazar said. "You have seen what the Miracle Cure can do. I ask only a mere five dollars a bottle! A bargain at ten times the price! What is five dollars compared to the benefits of the Cure? Do you have pain? The Cure will ease it. Are you crippled or lame? The Cure will let you walk again. Are you blind? In time, the Cure will let you see. Deaf? In a day or so you will hear. Come, who will take the first bottle?"

Arms reached up eagerly, but then came a bellow from the back of the crowd.

"Stop! Stop, I say, in the name of God!"

Standing in front of the little wooden chapel was a man dressed in black with a white clerical collar. His face was red with anger. The padre, thought Balthazar with a pulse of annoyance. He'd had a little of this kind of trouble before.

The minister strode forward, pushing aside people in the crowd. He was a tall man in his fifties, well-built, no milksop priest like the ones with whom Balthazar had tangled in the past.

"Who are you, you charlatan, to promise what only Almighty God can deliver? Are you Christ himself, to whom it was given to raise up the dead and give sight to the blind? No. Begone with you, you and your trumpery medicine!" The townsfolk edged slightly away from the man and the power of his fury.

Balthazar forced himself to grin. "Well, now, padre, I'm sure it's not a sin to help people to feel better. If it was, wouldn't every doctor who sets a broken leg be committing a sin? Or every midwife who eases a woman when she's bearing a child? As for being a charlatan, why don't you ask old Bill here how his leg is feeling? Or ask this lady..."

"Meg Peterson," the woman chimed in. "And I really am feeling a little better, Reverend Andrews. The pain is easing, I'm sure of it."

But the minister wasn't going to be deflected. "The devil plays many tricks, Mrs. Peterson. Do not let yourself be taken in."

"Well now, Reverend," said the old soldier, striding across with barely a limp. "What I says is, what works, works. You been praying over my leg, and over Meg's belly, for many a long month, and I don't see as it did either of us any good. But now here we are, pretty near cured. I ain't been able to walk straight ever since the war, but look at me now. I give thanks to God like any Christian man. But I thanks Him for sending this here fella to give me his medicine."

The minister's face turned a deeper red, and his nostrils flared. He opened his mouth to speak again, but Bill's response had turned the mood of the crowd, and they began to jeer and call out. The minister tried to shout them down in vain. Finally he turned on his heel and stalked back into the chapel, slamming the door behind him.

"Now then, ladies and gentlemen," called out Balthazar. "You've heard the testimony of Mrs. Peterson and old Bill here. Testimony to the effectiveness of the Miracle Cure. Who will be the first to buy a bottle? You, sir? Here you are, a mere five dollars."

The crowd clustered around the wagon and he began collecting money and passing out the bottles. Within an hour, he was considerably richer, but was out of stock. He had to turn people away. If he'd still had an assistant, this was the point at which he would have had him filling bottles with colored pump water in the back of the wagon, no need to waste the special ingredient.

To the disappointed customers, he simply said, "Tomorrow,

my friends, I will have made up a new batch. Come back here tomorrow at noon." But Balthazar had no intention of being there to meet them. He planned to be well on the road by then. He'd learned his lesson.

That evening, after feeding and stabling the mare, he spent a little of the money he'd made on a meal at the local saloon. He didn't need to buy his own liquor, however. Grateful townsmen kept on coming up to him and telling him how the Cure had already done his wife, or his son, or his aged parent the world of good. One man even said that it had induced his cow to start giving milk again. They all wanted to stand him a drink. Normally Balthazar would find a way to politely refuse after the first drink or so, but tonight he was feeling weary and a little depressed. He accepted far too many whiskeys.

By the time he left the saloon to return to his bed in the wagon, the street was weaving and tilting beneath his feet. He fumbled with the keys for an age before he could unlock the door at the back. Finally, he was able to climb in. He closed and locked the door behind him, fell onto his narrow bed and sank into oblivion.

He woke with the light of morning streaming in through the cracks in the wooden paneling of the wagon. His head felt as if it were being crushed under a mill wheel. Someone was thumping on the door and each thump sent a bolt of pain through his head.

Feeling dizzy and nauseous, he went to the door. He had gone to bed fully dressed, he realized. He opened the door to a flood of painful light.

It was one of the townsfolk—the one who had given the Cure to his cow, if Balthazar recalled correctly. Tom something-or-other... Tom Denver, that was it.

"Say, Doc, someone's been doing you a mighty ill-turn overnight. Figured you ought to know about it as soon as could be. You'd better come see."

Balthazar climbed down out of the wagon, cursing the light, and cursing himself more. He'd meant to be well on the road before most townsfolk were up and about.

Tom pointed at the wheels of the wagon. Balthazar stared. Each wheel had been damaged: several pieces had been cut out of the wooden rim and pulled away from the steel tire, and some of the spokes removed. Bending down, he could see that the same had been done to the spare wheel slung underneath the wagon. It must have taken someone a good long time, and generated a fair amount of noise. Balthazar had heard nothing in his drunken stupor. He cursed loudly. Tom nodded soberly at his side.

Along with his anger, a tide of panic was rising within Balthazar. He had to get out of this town, and soon!

Tom was rubbing his bristly chin, still examining the damage. "Must have been kids, I guess. Dunno why they'd want to pick on you, though, Doc."

Baffled and angry, Balthazar was about to comment, but he stopped himself and looked across at the chapel. The minister was standing at the open door, looking out with folded arms, his face expressionless. Balthazar clenched his fists. It was pretty obvious who was responsible, but he could prove nothing. Who would believe that a holy man would do such a thing? Besides, an argument would just use up valuable time. Time he didn't have.

He turned back to Tom. "Is there someone in town who can fix this up?" he asked, trying to suppress the panicky catch in his voice. "A carriage-maker? A wheel-wright?"

"Sure," Tom said. "Jim Jonson does most of that kind of work around here. If it was just a spoke or two, most anyone with some tools could fix it up. But a whole new wheel, that takes a bit of knowing how. Jim's your man. I'll go and fetch him for you, you don't need to worry none."

Jim Jonson was a massive man with muscular, hairy arms and an impressive gut hanging out over his pants. He ambled along the street after Tom. He looked at the stricken wagon and shook his head. He agreed to make up a new set of wheels, and prompted by a handful of the cash Balthazar handed over, agreed to have them ready as quickly as possible. "Day, maybe two. That's the best I can promise," he said. "Guess you can leave the wagon right here until the wheels are ready to be fitted."

A couple of days! It *might* be all right. Maybe not. If only he hadn't sold so many bottles of the real stuff yesterday. What had he been thinking? Colored water would have kept most of the crowd happy once the first few cures had been evident.

He should have been—would have been—long gone down the road before they knew any different. Again, Balthazar cursed himself.

Now what was he to do? The townsfolk, the ones he had turned away yesterday, would be back wanting to buy more bottles. On top of that, those who had already bought bottles might be back wanting more. Everyone knew someone who had one affliction or another. That was what made the business so lucrative.

Unfortunately he couldn't fend them all off today with pump water and coloring. There would be enough time for them to find that out. He would have to make up another batch of the real stuff. If Jim Jonson was true to his word, it would be all right. And he wouldn't risk getting drunk again. It *would* be all right. It would.

Inside the body of the wagon, with the roof hatch open to give him more light, Balthazar sat at his work table. The saloon had sold him a couple of crates of empty bottles and he'd already spent an hour cleaning them up and pasting on his labels. Now it was time for the ingredients.

Water. Herbs. A pinch of chili powder. A dash of rubbing alcohol and last but not least... the secret ingredient.

With slightly trembling hands, he picked up a heavy box and unlocked it. He stared at the gray stone within. The stone which had fallen from the sky almost at his very feet. A stone which at first had been so hot that it had burned his hand and he'd been forced to drop it. Then moments later, it had begun to frost over. Though Balthazar was far from being a religious man, he knew that the stone must have been sent to him, that he was meant to have it. It was a sign. A miracle, if you like. So—at first—it had appeared.

He'd heard of Chinese herb doctors grinding up 'heavenly stones' to make medicine. If it worked for them, why not for Balthazar? The surface of the loaf-sized stone was surprisingly soft and powdery, like chalk or sandstone. Though he had removed a substantial amount of material from it over the last three years, there was still plenty there. With his pocket knife, he scraped off another teaspoonful of powder and added it to the mix, then locked the box again.

Half-an-hour before noon, he had several dozen bottles ready to go, and he climbed wearily out, carrying them in a crate.

The Reverend Andrews was there in the street, right in front of him, his face working with anger.

"You do the Devil's work!" The minister grabbed hold of the crate and tried to wrestle it out of Balthazar's hands. Balthazar pulled it back and turned his body to shoulder the minister hard. The man staggered back.

"Seems to me, Reverend," said Balthazar, "that some devil's been at work chopping up the wheels of my wagon. Hadn't been for that, I'd have been out of town by now."

"And deceiving the good people of some other town," Andrews said. "I know your type. You need to be stopped."

"Well, I'm stopped right enough. Stopped right here. Now, if you'll excuse me...?"

Furious, the minister turned away and marched towards the chapel once more. Balthazar gave a chuckle and went to the front of his crippled wagon. A small crowd of people was assembling, some with arms already outstretched holding out five-dollar bills. Balthazar climbed up with the crate and started selling.

Half-way through his supply of bottles, Balthazar's attention was distracted by someone running down the center of the dusty street. Balthazar's heart sank. It was old Bill, the veteran soldier. Running, Bill didn't even glance at the crowd or the wagon, he just ran right past and out of sight as he turned a corner. Heads in the crowd had followed him and a great deal of excited chattering began. After that, bottles sold even faster and soon Balthazar was out of stock again. He put the remaining people off with a vague promise of more in a day or so.

Later that day, Balthazar went to Jim Johnson's workshop, after having paid a passing boy a dollar to keep an eye on the wagon. Jim was hard at work shaping pieces for the wheel rims. So far he had assembled two of the new wheels.

The big man just shrugged when Balthazar asked about progress. "Tomorrow," was all he would say. Balthazar thought about old Bill running down the street and felt sick to his stomach. He had little choice; he would have to stay through another night.

He slept little, trying to keep alert enough to prevent any

further sabotage to the wagon. Each time he nodded off, he was woken by terrible nightmares.

At first light, Balthazar began to prepare for a swift departure. After paying his bill for stabling he tied the mare up at the hitching post nearest to his wagon so that no time would be wasted once the wagon had been fixed. After taking the necessary precautions he once again returned to Jonson's workshop. Unfortunately, the last of the four wheels was still being assembled and Balthazar had to stand there anxiously fidgeting while watching the slow progress. Finally Jonson looked up. "Right, let's get you on your way," the big man said.

As Jonson rolled the first wheel outside, however, they were stopped by a red-headed youth, who ran up gasping for breath. "Doc, doc!"

It's starting, Balthazar thought. *I've got to get out of here.*

"Doc," the lad repeated. "I've come from the saw mill. It's about Jack Dietrich." He stopped, gasped in some more air. "There's been a bad accident. Jack cut almost his whole arm off. There's blood just everywhere. But, but..."

"What?" Balthazar asked, though he was pretty sure he already knew what had happened.

"He's still walking about! They can't get him to lie down, or hold him still to bind him up! He took some of your Cure yesterday, for his bad back. Can you come and see to him?"

"Is he still bleeding?"

"Some, but not what you'd expect. He's like a crazy man, Doc, tells people it's just a scratch and he'll be right soon enough."

Jim Jonson was standing with his mouth agape. Balthazar knew there wasn't much time left. He couldn't be distracted. "Run back and tell them to get hold of Jack and force him to lie down. Tie him up to keep him still, tie him up strong with rope. Losing an arm, that's a bad shock, enough to send anyone a little crazy for a while. The Miracle Cure will see him through. I'll come along when my wagon's fixed."

The red-haired youth hesitated for a moment, but then turned on his heel and started running back up the track to the mill.

Jonson shook his head in puzzlement. "Powerful stuff, that Cure of yours," he said.

Balthazar had no time for polite conversation. "Yes. Let's get the wagon fixed, then I can drive up to the mill."

Jonson shrugged, and rolled the wheel down the street without further comment. He began to carefully fit the wheel on the propped-up wagon. Balthazar stood by, looking nervously about. After what seemed an age, Jonson finally had the wheel in place, and turned back to his workshop for the next.

In the distance, beyond Jonson's lumbering figure, Balthazar spotted someone running down the road. The red-haired kid from the saw-mill again? No. No, it was the old veteran Bill.

Balthazar felt a renewed surge of panic. He dodged behind the wagon, but Bill had seen him. He ran up to Balthazar, but couldn't stand still. Instead, he kept running in small circles, alternating between dashes back and forth. Nevertheless, his attention was fixed on Balthazar.

Short of breath, the old man tried to speak, failed, started again. He seemed to be forcing himself to slow down a little, but could still only manage short bursts of speech. "Have to run," he gasped. "That Cure... cured my leg... cured it so much... have to move it... all the time... can't stop running... How you... gonna stop it... Doc?"

Balthazar gulped and shook his head slightly. "I... I... I can't," he said.

"It *don't* stop... Do it? The Cure?" the old man forced out as he ran in a circle, raising dust.

Balthazar could only shake his head. At that, old Bill gave an inarticulate cry and ran off, fast, down the street, dodging horses and carts, then out of sight down a lane.

A group of women outside the chapel had overheard the incident with Bill, and now Balthazar could see them whispering, their heads together. Word would get out quickly. He had to get out of the town before it got any worse.

Jim Jonson had returned with another wheel. His expression was grim and suspicious. "Heard just now about little Emily Ransom," he said. His voice was loud, a bellow, Balthazar thought in dismay.

"Little kid, been deaf and blind since she had a brain fever two years ago," Jonson said. "Her mamma bought some of your Cure and gave it to her. Now the kid's screaming, they can't stop her."

"Screaming? Why is that?" Balthazar asked, trying to keep his face from showing what he really felt. If only Jonson would get on with fixing the wagon!

"Screaming that everything's so loud, so bright. Keeps holding her hands over her ears and keeps her eyes screwed tight."

More people had gathered near the wagon as Jonson talked. His voice had been so loud everyone in the street must have heard it. A crowd was forming.

"Just a temporary side effect of the Cure!" Balthazar announced with as much confidence as he could muster. "It will soon settle down again."

Angry mutters from the crowd. Balthazar desperately tried to regain the initiative. He jumped up to the step at the back of his wagon.

"Ladies and gentlemen," he yelled out. "Do not be disturbed! These are merely proofs of how well the Miracle Cure works! As you see, there is no doubt of the efficacy of the Cure!"

"Yes, it works," came a stern voice from the back of the crowd. It parted a little to reveal the Reverend Andrews, striding forward. "It works because it is the tool of the Devil, as I warned you. Tear this man down and we'll make an end of him!"

Hands began to reach up towards Balthazar, who shrank back.

He was saved by an awful distraction. Down the street from the east came the mail coach, driving at speed. And right in front of it, dashing out from a laneway, ran old Bill. In a moment, he was under the wheels of the coach. One, twice, the coach lurched as it ran over him before the driver managed to pull it to a halt.

For a moment the old soldier lay still on the road amidst a cloud of dust. Then he stirred, and in a horrible, lurching motion, swung back onto his feet. One arm was twisted at a funny angle, and the other swung loose like a sack of stones. Blood poured from his nostrils. But nevertheless, he stood. A woman on the boardwalk began to scream as Bill staggered forward several paces, then steadied. And then he began to run again, in a half-toppling, sickening motion.

More screams, and the crowd around the wagon scattered in horror as he approached.

Seizing his moment, Balthazar threw open the door of the

wagon, ducked in and grabbed up his cash tin and the box containing the 'heavenly stone'. Then out again.

All eyes were still on the shattered shell of the old veteran. In a high-pitched voice that sounded nothing like his own, the old man gasped out "It don't stop. It don't *stop!*"

It was true, Balthazar knew. That had always been the problem. The Miracle Cure worked. Worked too well. And it didn't stop.

Even while he was thinking this, though, he was down and running away from his wagon. Running towards the mail coach before anyone could gather their senses and stop him.

The coach driver was still in his seat, looking out in astonishment at the crowd now closing around old Bill.

"Here!" Balthazar said as he climbed up, shoving a handful of bills at the man. "Quick! You can have all of this. Throw out the mail, now! Then, for the love of God, drive on, as fast as you can!"

"Hey, mister, I can't do..."

"Damn you!" Balthazar picked up the man bodily and threw him off the coach. Still standing, he lifted the reins, shook them, and urged on the horses. He grabbed the whip and cracked it, and flicked it at the horses' backs. "Get going, dammit!"

Balthazar would never have succeeded in his escape had it not been for Tom Denver's cow. Up ahead, it was dashing from side to side in the street, trying to gore people. Its udder, Balthazar saw, was huge and swollen, and squirting jets of white milk. It plunged towards the crowd near old Bill, and they scattered again.

The mail coach was slowly, oh so slowly, gathering speed and rumbling forward. Reverend Andrews was yelling at the people in the street, trying to pull them together to block Balthazar's passage, but he was too late. The mail coach shot past them, going faster and faster. In a few moments, Balthazar was out of the town.

Another close escape, worse than the last town. Too damn close! And he'd lost his wagon, and the mare. What's more, he had just stolen a mail coach. That had to be a jailing offense, if not a hanging one. He would have to give it up. Change his name back to plain old Oscar Brown. Maybe try his luck on the goldfields after all, or find a job as a farm hand. Anything but this.

They would be following him. As soon as they regained their senses, there would be men on horseback setting out after him. The coach wasn't fast enough to keep ahead of them, and was too easy to spot from a distance. He would have to unhitch one of the horses and ride it bareback into the hills, hide out somewhere for a while.

He reached a four-way junction in the road. Here. He pulled the coach to a halt and jumped down, pulling out his knife to cut a horse free from its tackle. The one on the right looked the healthier and fitter of the two beasts. He began to cut through the straps.

He had only cut through one of the traces when a hand gripped his shoulder from behind, gripping hard, painfully hard. Balthazar shrieked with fright and dropped the knife.

"Doctor Balthazar?" said a soft, strangely unearthly voice. He turned. It was the woman to whom he'd given the free dose on the first day. She must have been inside the coach when he'd driven it off. What was her name? Mrs. Peterson. Meg Peterson.

Her hand squeezed tighter and Balthazar yelped.

"It's growing," she repeated. Her eyes stared at him without blinking. "It don't hurt any more. Don't hurt at all. But it's growing, see."

To his horror, as Balthazar glanced down, he saw her belly hugely swollen as though she was pregnant with some monstrous child. Beneath the woman's drab dress, now stretched taut almost to tearing point, he saw something squirm and pulse.

He stared at her, appalled and dismayed. Of all the awful things that the Miracle Cure had done, this was the most awful by far.

"It needs more," she said. "Give me more. More of the Cure."

"Madam, I... there is no more!"

"More!" she said, her eyes fierce and fixed. "You cured it, you see. Cured *it*. Cured it of *me!* Now it must have more. You must give me more!"

"I..." Her hand was like a steel vice, squeezing ever harder. Balthazar thought he could feel the bones in his shoulder begin to crack.

"A moment, madam, a moment. Just let me get..."

She released him, but her hand fell immediately on the collar of the nearest horse and gripped it tight. Her strength was immense.

Frantic, terrified, he scrambled up to the driver's seat and retrieved the box containing the 'heavenly stone'.

"Here!" he said, as he jumped down. "Here! Take it, take it! The stone..."

But she had already torn the box open and pulled out the stone. Like some starving dog thrown a bone, she began to gnaw on it, heedless of her teeth breaking as she bit down. With a rip, her dress tore open, and inside her gravid body, something alive moved and stirred and *grew*.

Balthazar didn't stay to watch what would happen next. He was running, running for the hills.

As he ran, his thoughts ran wild with him. Had this, he wondered, been the reason the stone had fallen from the sky? Had he been meant to dose one person after another just until the stone found someone with a condition it could really exploit? Had it been sent by the Devil, as Reverend Andrews would surely have said? In which case, *what was it* that was growing in Meg Peterson's womb? Growing, and about to be born?

Behind him, the woman gave a final, terrible shriek, and there was a loud, wet, ugly sound. Balthazar heard the horses squealing in terror and the clatter of the coach as they tried to flee. He glanced back and saw something red and angular struggling up from Meg Peterson's torn and fallen body. Were those leathery *wings?*

Balthazar shuddered and ran faster. Not, as it turned out, fast enough.

The Golden City

Jack Cobb, his breath steaming and his arms clasped under his armpits, stepped at last out of the shadow of the City and into the welcome morning light of the sun. He stood for a while in the middle of the dirt road, letting the sun's warmth find its way into his bones. Then someone behind him cursed, and he had to step aside out of the way of a man pulling a heavily laden cart.

When he had left the hut that morning, Jack had followed the custom of all of the Southwesters, and had shaken his fist in the direction of the City whose huge long shadow almost always fell over them. Life in the south-west was grim, and in winter, the layer of frost which settled on their thin tents and rough shanties made it just that much harder.

But now Jack was warm enough, and a long thin line of gold ran down the City's sunward edge. It was almost beautiful, he thought, despite how he hated it. Then Jack laughed at his own foolishness, and was on his way once more along the great road which circled the City and led to the market in the north.

As he strode on and left the south-west far behind him, he began to pass substantial wooden buildings, and even a few of stone. He saw more people pulling carts and leading cattle and a few horse-drawn wagons laden with goods for the market.

Those who had the wealth to choose lived in the north. Far enough away from the City that its shadow never fell over their dwelling. There, the City was seen, not as a black, lumbering silhouette blocking out the sun for most of the day, but as a vast, golden tower. Not that that stopped the Northerners from cursing at it, like all of the Squatters who were forced to live at its foot, instead of inside it.

Checking that the pack on his back was safe from being snatched in the crowds, Jack Cobb came at last to the marketplace. He found a suitable place where he could open out his parcel and place his wares before him, all in a row: handmade boots of the finest quality. *Well*, thought Jack, trying to be honest with himself, *perhaps not quite the finest*. His father had made the best boots ever seen in the market, but since his father's sickness had come on, Jack had been doing most of the work, and Jack's hands were too large to be delicate.

In time, well-dressed Northerners came by and asked the price of Jack's boots, and then the haggling began.

All around Jack, the market swarmed: rich men in purpled robes, their wives in white and scarlet; poor men in rags; cows, sheep, dogs and a multitude of laughing, scampering children; carts carrying timber and stone, drawn by tired, sweating horses, or by even more tired men; merchants selling wines, food, fine cloth and hand-worked wood and leather; the smell of dung and mud and spice; and the babble, a river of rushing sound. Above it all, like some golden mountain, stood the City.

It was well past noon before the last of Jack's boots were sold, and silver and copper coins jangled in his purse. He stood and stretched his large frame, complaining inwardly of the stiffness of his joints. A sudden waft of wind brought the smell of food to his nostrils, but he ignored it. To buy food here would be to waste a good portion of what he had earned. There would be time enough to eat once he was home.

What he needed to do before leaving the market was to buy more leather for the next batch of boots. He began to push his way through the afternoon crowds, helped by his height to see where he was going. Even so, he was pushed and jostled, and narrowly missed having his foot trodden on by a cow. But Jack's thoughts were elsewhere. Again and again he found his eyes wandering in the direction of the City.

Jack's father scorned all talk of the City, saying it was all pointless, idle chatter. But Jack couldn't help thinking about it. What did the city people do up there in the golden tower? Did they look down in the winter mornings at the miserable south-west lying in their shadow, and see the frost-laden tents?

A heavy jab to the ribs by a passing herdsman brought Jack back to earth. He was approaching the tanner's stall on the outskirts of the market. The smell of the freshly-cured skin was foul and overpowering.

The tanner was a small, sharp-faced man, his skin wrinkled and coloured like his stock. He glowered as Jack carefully examined various hides, looking for defects and trying to find the most supple leather. "These two," Jack said at last.

"Let's see the colour of your money, lad," the tanner said.

Jack brought out two silver pieces, but the man shook his head. "Not enough," he said. "For that, you can only have one hide. Four silver pieces for two."

"What!" cried Jack, his hand still out, offering the two coins. "Last time I was here you'd have given me change of this."

The tanner shrugged. "Things are bad, what with the drought last summer. Less cattle to slaughter. Leather's scarce right now."

"But..." Jack was confounded. "If I pay for two hides at that price, I won't have enough to buy our food. And if I buy only one hide there'll only be half as many boots to sell next market day..." He was overwhelmed by this unexpected alteration of his fortunes.

"That's your problem, lad," said the tanner. "You should have come here first and found out the price. Then you would have known to sell your boots for twice as much."

"But... Look, you must sell me the hides at the old price. I'll give you twice as much next time."

The tanner laughed. "Go walk into the City, lad!"

The insult stung Jack into a rage. He swung his fist and felled the tanner, sending him sprawling among his hides.

A sudden quiet fell, and then the crowd boiled around Jack, and people grabbed his arms and his clothes. He turned to hit at those holding him, but a hefty arm clamped down on his shoulder. A blow crashed into the back of Jack's head. The ground seemed to turn black and reach up to swallow him.

A long confused time passed. Jack heard arguing voices, and once, hands tugging at his boots. But he kicked out, and the hands tugged no more. Then came darkness again.

He awoke in pain. His head throbbed with every movement, and he winced at the light as he opened his eyes. He was lying on the ground amongst broken stones. Struggling to sit up, he saw that he was very close to the City, within the shell of a shattered stone building. The ruins were the remnants of the town that, it was said, had been here when the City had first been built long ago. Now the place was inhabited only by the poorest. The majority of the Northerners would never come this uncomfortably close to the great tower, unless it was to steal stone for the making of better houses further away. Or unless they wanted to dump a stupid Southwester somewhere to get him out of the way.

Jack rubbed the bump on the back of his head, and grimaced into the afternoon sun. Only now did he remember that the tanner had two brawny sons. On a sudden thought, he felt for his purse. Gone! Stolen, not a doubt of it, while he lay senseless.

Now were his problems fully begun. What a fool he had been! How could he return to his father with nothing to show for the boots? Worse still, would they ever be able to buy leather again in the market? Hitting the tanner had been the most foolish thing Jack had ever done. He put his head in his hands. He and his father might well starve if they couldn't gain enough money to buy hides again.

He stood up, feeling every bruise, and wondered if he should go back to the market and face the tanner, accuse him of stealing his purse. But that would only earn him another lump on the head, and he had no proof that the tanner or his sons had taken the money. It could have been anyone in the crowd. At least they had left him his boots and his tools, dangling in a leather bag at his side.

He began to walk aimlessly through the ruined streets. Every so often Jack saw a hostile, dirty face in one of the windows. Few wanted to live so close to the City, even though these collapsed walls would give better shelter from the wind than a tent or a wooden hut. The real disincentive was that this place was so close to the Fence, a bitter reminder of the way things were: an impassable barrier between the rich who had built the City and the poor who had been excluded from it.

The streets twisted and turned, but Jack, downcast, for a long while did not notice or care where he was going. When he became conscious of his surroundings again, he was within a street's width of the Fence.

The Fence was a very strange thing. It wasn't like a fence or wall anywhere else in the world. It didn't block out any light, nor did it hide the sight of the sculptured, empty gardens at the foot of the tower. All that could be seen of the Fence was a bright yellow, two-yard thick band on the ground, running off into the distance on either side, circling the City. It just looked like a pathway paved with yellow bricks. You could imagine that there was nothing much there, that all you need do was to stroll across to enter the grounds of the City.

But the Fence was there all right. Jack walked cautiously towards it. He felt quite a child again, dared by his mates to go closer and closer to that yellow line. One of his playfellows, he remembered, had broken an arm by getting just that little bit too close...

Jack bent and picked up a small chunk of stone from the scattered rubble, and tossed it lightly towards the yellow band. The chunk moved in a gentle curve until it reached the edge of the Fence. Then it seemed almost to disappear, and there was a flash of light as it struck the ground. The core of the stone lay glowing red, not more than an inch into the band of yellow.

Jack tried again. He took a fist-sized stone, bent his arm and his body back and threw it as high as he could towards the Fence. As it crossed the line, it was as though the stone had been knocked out of the air. The eye could barely follow its fall, and the flash it made as it hit was dazzling. It lay perhaps six inches into the band. That was how the Fence worked.

"It's too strong here, lad."

Jack gave a start, and turned quickly to see who had spoken. It was an old man, weight resting on one foot, head tilted to one side. His face was brown and wrinkled, like a sun-dried fruit. He was almost toothless, and his eyes were bloodshot and crusty.

"Too strong," the old man repeated. "Fifty times as strong as the Earth, just there."

There was an air of manic desperation in the way the raggedly-dressed old man looked about, first at Jack, and then at the cliff that was the City. He didn't seem senile, though his words verged on madness.

"What do you mean?" asked Jack, annoyed at having his foolishness observed and commented on.

The old man blinked twice, slowly. "I'll show you," he said. "Yes, I'll show you. Old Sam knows all about the Fence. Yes. Been studyin' the Fence ever since I was a lad like you. Always wanted to get across, like you." He beckoned to Jack to follow, and ambled off.

Jack frowned. On top of all of his other troubles, now he had this old fool to contend with. But... He looked across the Fence, and upwards, at the great City, where the golden people lived in luxury. Hadn't he always dreamed of going into the City? And, with no money in his pocket, there was no point in going home just yet. Sighing, he set off after the old man.

"They built the City in my grandfather's time, when he was just a boy, that's what he told me. Said they put it up overnight, that it was all done by giants, but I don't believe that. Maybe it was just one of his tales..."

All the time, old Sam was nodding to himself, glancing at Jack, and at the City. It was obvious that the old man seldom had anyone listen to him. They were walking parallel to the Fence, further into the region of shattered buildings. Once, they saw the skeleton of a man spread-eagled and broken a few steps within the yellow band. Sam stopped, and pointed with a laugh. "See him, lad?" he said. "He tried to carry twenty men on his shoulders, and found them too fat for him."

Jack frowned in puzzlement. He was already regretting following the old man. But Sam beckoned again, and after a moment, Jack followed.

Soon, they reached a building which retained a small portion of roof. This was obviously where Sam lived. The inside was a hovel. It was dim, but Jack could see a pile of straw covered with rags, and a few bare utensils filled with foul-smelling food. The place stank worse than a cattle yard.

Sam searched about for some time, and finally returned with a yard-long rod. He handed it to Jack. "You can carry this, lad," he said. Jack was surprised by the weight of the rod, which was cold to the touch. Metal. Iron, probably. Metal was very scarce at the foot of the City, and this rod could be sold for twenty coppers or more. For a moment, Jack toyed with the idea of stealing it from the old man to help make up his loss for the day. But it wasn't in Jack's nature to do such a thing.

Back towards the Fence they headed. Jack examined the rod now that they were in better light. It had been marked off into small, regular divisions. Old Sam was carrying a large wedge-shaped block of wood. Jack was mystified.

They quickly reached the place where Jack had been throwing stones. Sam winked at Jack, and cautiously approached the yellow band. Then he knelt down: a slow, painful exercise involving a lot of cursing. The old man pushed the wedge of wood ahead of him toward the Fence. It took quite a bit of effort for him to push it the last half-inch until its apex was exactly positioned over the edge of the yellow area. Then he backed away, and, cursing, got back to his feet.

"You do it, lad," he said to Jack.

Jack frowned in puzzlement. Old Sam stamped in frustration. "Fool of a boy," he said. "Rest the tip of the rod on that block there. Just the tip, mind you, or you'll break your arm."

Jack advanced with the rod, bracing it in his arms. It wasn't very heavy in itself, but Jack knew well the effect that the Fence had on things. The tip of the rod hovered near the block of wood; he let it move just a little further in, and then the Fence caught it and brought it down sharply on the wedge.

"Now let go," Sam commanded. The rod dropped to the ground, leaving one end still resting on the wooden block. Sam tapped the free end with his foot, again and again, nudging the rod a little further into the Fence. When the far end was a little less than an inch into the yellow, the near end slowly raised itself from the ground and the rod stood balanced on the block of wood.

"There! Do you see?" Sam said, grinning toothlessly. "See, that bit of rod over the Fence weighs just as much as the rest that isn't!" Then he squinted at the rod, and tilted his head to one side. "Your eyes will be better than mine, lad. How many marks are over the line?"

Jack peered at the rod. "Two," he said.

"And there's a hundred marks on the whole of the rod. So that makes it close enough to fifty times as strong as the good Earth. Am I right?"

Jack knew enough of figures to be able to take money and count out change. What Sam was saying seemed to make a sort of sense. "That's all very well," he said, "but what of it? What's the use of knowing that?"

Sam hopped up and down, impatient. "Damn and blast your stupid head! It's no wonder no one else in this blasted land ever thought to do any measuring!"

Jack frowned and turned away. He'd wasted enough time with the old coot. But Sam followed, abusing him and complaining of the stupidity of the people at the foot of the City. Eventually, he grabbed at Jack's arm and held on. Jack raised a threatening fist, though he was reluctant to strike such a feeble old man. Sam's eyes glistened.

"Come lad, it won't take long. Let me just show you another spot along the Fence. Do you have anything better to do this day?"

Jack bit back a sharp reply. The truth was that he would rather waste his time and go home only once his father was asleep. So, with a sigh, he shook his head and trailed after the old man. They retrieved the rod and the wedge – pulling the wedge out took Jack's full strength – and went on.

They reached the spot where the shattered skeleton lay, all tumbled about and broken with unnatural force. "Only twenty times here, like I told you," Sam said."Do you see that dark patch on the yellow?" Jack looked where Sam pointed, and saw that an irregular blotch of a pale brown colour lay in the midst of the yellow band. "Something goes wrong sometimes with part of the Fence," Sam said. "And when it does, the force is less by far."

Sam was tugging at Jack's sleeve again. Interested now, he followed. They reached an area where the remains of houses came right up to the Fence, and the pair were forced to pick their way through a maze of ruins and rubble-filled streets. Soon, though, they reached a road which ran down a slope towards the Fence, where it abruptly stopped. That was puzzling to Jack, too. Had the road once run right on, all the way to the City itself? On the other side of the Fence was what could be a continuation of the roadway, though it seemed to be made of a different, smoother material, not the rough cobbles of the road on this side.

Down the slope they went, and Sam hurried forward to the Fence with his block of wood. Jack could see that here there were several of the slightly darker blotches on the yellow band. Again they went through the ritual of balancing the rod. This time Jack had to be very careful in counting the marks on the part of the rod hanging over the yellow band.

"Twenty-two" he said at last.

Sam squinted up at the bulk of the City, calculating. Then he nodded and chuckled. "Less now than the last time I tried. It's getting weaker here. Nine times the force of the Earth! Only nine!"

The old man looked at Jack with an eager expression. "What do you think, lad?"

"What do I think about what?"

"You're a strong young lad. Could you carry nine men on your shoulders?"

Jack was speechless. His mouth opened, but he could say nothing. At last, he managed "Me? You think I would be mad enough to try to cross the Fence?"

Sam grinned and nodded, his eyes fixed on Jack's face.

"Then you're madder by far than you think I am!" Jack said in anger, and turned once more to leave the old man.

"Lad, lad!" came Sam's voice behind him. "Think of what you might find! They say the City People wear robes of silver cloth, and eat from plates of gold!"

Jack kept on walking, but gradually slowed,then stopped. It was true. All of the tales about the City told of the wealth of those who had built it and who now lived within. If he could steal just a single precious thing, his troubles would be over. But no, it was impossible.

Yet... there it was, the City. So magnificent and so close, and yet as far away, it seemed, as the Moon. To enter it and return with treasure... it had the very feel of a child's tale about it. Jack looked around. Sam still stood next to the yellow band of the Fence, his figure dark against the bright-lit backdrop of the tower. Jack Cobb set his shoulders and walked back to the old man.

"I can't carry nine men on my back," he said. "I might stand with that weight for a moment, but as soon as I took a step I'd break both of my legs."

Old Sam rubbed his hands, one against the other, and frowned. "But you're so young, so strong. I can hardly carry the weight of myself around. It's not far, just across the band..."

"No," said Jack. "It can't be done that way. Let me think for a while." He sat down on the cobbles. He gazed up the slope of the road, thinking hard.

There were perhaps two hours of daylight left. If anything was to be done, it would have to be done soon. Just then, as Jack watched, a four-wheeled cart came into view at the top of the slope and started down. It was loaded with lengths of wood and pulled by a small, thin man who was making hard going of it. Jack stood. Sam looked up from where he was staring at the weirdly-balanced iron rod.

"A cart!" said Jack, "that's what we need." He strode off towards the man labouring with the wagon.

"Here," said Jack, "I'll haul your load for you."

The man was very short and clearly not strong. "What for?" he asked, his eyes moving from side to side as though seeking a path of escape. "I've nothing to pay you with. I can do it. Go away!"

"I'll haul your load if you'll let me use your cart for a while."

The little man scowled. "Why should I?"

Jack laughed. "I could easily take the cart away from you. Instead I offer you a trade. It would seem foolish to refuse it." The man gave Jack an angry look, but was forced to agree.

It wasn't long before Jack returned, pulling the empty cart. He didn't approach Sam, but instead headed up the slope of the hill. At the crest, he paused and looked back. The slope wasn't steep, but it was long, and it would be enough to start the cart moving at a steady pace.

Jack drew a deep breath. He hadn't fully thought yet about what he was doing. But if he thought too much he might not have the courage to go through with it.

The cart wouldn't be easy to steer. Jack climbed on it, and lay on his belly, facing down the street, taking the shafts of the cart in his hands. He rested his chin on the wooden floor, trying to make sure that his weight was evenly spaced. Yes, it would have to do. He climbed off and pushed the cart forward until it began to roll. Then he jumped on board and settled himself again.

The cart moved slowly at first, with much creaking and groaning. It gathered speed, and Jack found that he could steer by shifting his weight from side to side. Every so often, the cart went over a loose stone, or into a pothole, and his chin jarred painfully. Faster and faster now, towards the City, towards the Fence.

Sam was there, waving his arms and yelling. Jack couldn't make out what he was saying. The bumping, jolting ride was numbing his senses. His stomach contracted. The Fence was very near. He should jump off, or steer the cart away from the approaching yellow band. He should...

The cart reached the Fence, rattling along as fast as Jack had ever moved. As the shafts hit the line, the cart began to tip forward, but that was only for an instant. Then the Earth seemed to fall on Jack's spine, and he tried to cry out, but could not. All the air inside him was squashed out. His chin smashed against the cart, and he couldn't see for the mountain of blackness that crushed him. He could hear a shattering noise as the cart came apart, then nothing.

After a time that seemed as long as Jack's life, he opened his eyes. For a moment all he could see was scarlet. He moved his arms and legs cautiously, found them painful but not broken, and sat up. His chin hurt. He touched it, wincing, and his hand came away bloody.

It took a moment for Jack's eyes to come back into focus. Across a yellow band, an old man was jumping up and down and yelling. Jack shook his head once, then twice, and it came clear. He had crossed the Fence!

He felt a surge of panic and tried to get up. But his legs betrayed him, and he sat back down again, trembling.

On the other side of the Fence, old Sam was crouching over, playing with his block and rod again. It was only then that Jack, dazed as he was, saw that where the wheels of the now-ruined cart had crossed the Fence, there were two ragged bands of pale brown on the yellow.

With a shout of joy, Sam looked up. Before Jack knew what was happening, the old man was edging his way across the Fence, his arms tight by his side, moving carefully along the path made by one of the cartwheels. And all the time, Sam was laughing and weeping and gasping and shouting:

"Lad, lad, my hero, my wonder, you've done it, my bonny boy. Ha ha! Ho ho!" And then Sam was beside Jack, pulling on him to stand. "Come on, lad, come on, we've got no time to lose, come on, come on."

Jack looked stupidly up at the old man for a moment. Then his bewilderment turned into action, and he stood up quickly.

"Yes, yes," he said to Sam. "We've got to run. The City People, they'll know we're here. We'll have to be quick." And he started to run, with old Sam hobbling as fast as he could behind him.

The gardens at the foot of the city were shaped into low grass-covered hills and shallow valleys. Small trees and artfully-arranged piles of rocks dotted the artificial landscape. To Jack, it was all strange, far more lavish than even the fanciest garden he'd seen, owned by the richest merchant living on the other side of the Fence.

He ran over grass and stone, weaving a little to follow the contours of the land, and all the time expecting to hear the sound of alarms and cries, or even to feel the pain of one of the magical weapons of the City People. But there was nothing.

After a time, as his breath started to come hard, he came to a sudden stop. He had almost run into the side of the City itself. He had always seen it from afar, and it was so huge that there was no scale to apply to it. The City. He was really here. He reached out and touched the smooth wall, ran his hands over it. It seemed to be made of a dark glass, so dark he couldn't see through it.

He looked back, to see Sam slowly working his way towards him over one of the low hills. Even over the distance that separated them, Jack could hear the old man wheezing and gasping. Jack waited for him, suffering agonies of impatience. When he finally caught up, Sam's nose was tinged with blue, and his breath came in great racking gasps.

"Stop... stop a moment.., lad, for the love of God. Oh God. Just a moment." And Sam sat down with his back against the wall of the City.

Terrified they were going to be caught, Jack looked about on either side. But it seemed they had not set off any alarms, and here so close against the wall, it was surely impossible for them to be seen from inside the City itself. They were safe enough for the moment.

After a few minutes, the natural colour began to come back to Sam's face, and his racking gasps of air slowed.

"Ah, lad, that wasn't too good. I'm too old, too old." Then he sat up and looked about them. "But lad, we're in. You broke the Fence, you wonder. This is the day I've dreamt of, lad, getting inside the City... I never thought you'd do it. I was sure you'd be killed stone dead."

"Then you should have stopped me," Jack said crisply. "But we're not inside the City, anyway. We're on the outside, still, and I don't see how we're going to get in." He had hardly thought beyond crossing the Fence.

"There has to be a door, lad. You go look for it while I catch my breath."

Jack nodded, and began to stride along the level pathway which ran beside the wall, perhaps circling the whole City. Surely there must be an opening in the wall somewhere?

It wasn't easy. In fact, Jack at last despaired and decided to head back to Sam. Perhaps the nearest door was in the opposite direction. He had almost reached the old man, who was still sitting against the wall, when one of the panels of dark glass slid silently aside and someone came out. Jack gave a cry of alarm and stopped in his tracks.

Not someone. Some *thing* had come out.

If it was a person, it was very short – a dwarf who barely came up to Jack's waist. And it was clad entirely in metal, like one of the knights in the old picture book his mother had shown him once. The dwarf came out, seemed to spin a half circle, and faced him. The glass panel closed again without a sound. Jack cursed himself a little for not dodging in when he had the chance. But then, the dwarf might have stopped him.

The dwarf had two enormous crystal eyes, spaced on each side of its head. The eyes swivelled up and down, examining Jack. He was ready to run at any moment. Surely he would be able to outrun this little person, with its short legs... Except that now Jack saw that it didn't have legs. It was moving, balanced, on a single fat *wheel*. Was this some kind of mechanism, then? Like the expensive, fancy clocks he had seen in the market, which popped out little tweeting birds every hour?

It turned its huge eyes downwards. From somewhere it drew a cloth, and before Jack could react, the thing was polishing the dust from his boots! It looked up again, and Jack fancied that the dwarf was examining his rough clothing with a degree of contempt.

But at least it didn't seem as though this thing was going to attack him, or sound some kind of alarm. Could it understand him if he spoke to it? Jack gestured frantically to Sam, who began to clamber to his feet, his mouth opening in astonishment when he saw the dwarf.

"We want to get into the City," Jack said to it slowly and loudly, as though talking to an idiot. "Inside, see?" He tapped the glass wall behind him. Out of the corner of his eye, he saw Sam hurrying up and could hear his wheezing breath.

"Let us in," Jack repeated to the metal thing.

The dwarf paused for a moment as though puzzled. Then it spun on its wheel and the huge glass panel slid aside again. It rolled in, its head turned so that it looked back at them as it went. Jack grabbed hold of Sam's arm and they quickly followed the dwarf.

Inside. *Inside the City!* Jack's heart was galloping inside his chest like a bolting horse.

They were in a short corridor, lined with the same dark glass as the outer walls. The dwarf sped ahead of them, and they hurried to follow it. Before long, they came to a great hallway, whose ceiling was covered in a fantastic pattern of crystal shapes. Its walls were lined with dozens of silver doors. There was no one in sight.

The dwarf looked up at them with its huge glass eyes, then apparently deciding that its work was done, a small glass panel slid aside in a wall and it dodged in. Before Jack could decide to follow, the panel slid back, and the dwarf was gone.

Jack and Sam stood looking about them. If they were going to find anything to steal, they would have to pass through one of these silver doorways, that was certain.

Jack fidgeted in anxiety. Now that they had performed the impossible feat of actually entering the Golden City, his fear had taken over his foolhardiness. At that moment all he wanted to do was get out of the City and run away to tell the tale. But then he glanced at Sam, who was looking around with his almost toothless mouth wide open, but showing no sign of fear.

Perhaps Sam was too old to be afraid? After all, the old man had little life left to lose. Then Jack cursed to himself. What was he thinking of, to let an old man show him up in bravery? He straightened his back, quietened his heart, and strode forward to the nearest set of silver doors.

He pushed at the doors, but they did not move. There were no handles, and the doors were perfectly smooth, meeting evenly together in the centre. Perhaps they were locked, only to be opened by a special signal? He looked about. There was a small square of crystal next to the doorway. He reached out, intending to see if it would turn, but as soon as his hand touched it, a light came on inside the crystal, and the doors opened. As simple as that.

Jack glanced quickly in through the open doors. No one was in sight, just another wall. "Sam," he called, and the old man looked around and nodded. To his surprise, he saw that Sam was now weeping.

The old man smiled and wiped away the tears with a ragged, dirty sleeve. "Well done, lad, well done. Now we have to be quick, or we'll be caught. We'll dash in and grab some of the golden plates, and we'll be off out again. Right?"

Jack nodded, and looked in through the silver doors. It seemed to be just a very small room. He stepped inside, with old Sam right behind him.

The room was hardly big enough for them to stretch out their arms, and there seemed to be no other exits. It was a dead end. Puzzled, Jack looked up, and saw that there was no ceiling to the room. It was like being at the bottom of an enormously deep well. He gave a grunt of surprise, and Sam looked up, too.

"It's a mystery, that's what it is, lad." Sam said. "Have a look down." Jack looked down, and his heart gave a leap. The floor of the room was the same yellow color as the Fence! They could have been killed, squashed flat, just stepping into the room. It must be a trap.

Even as he thought that, the silver doors shut with a click behind them. In sudden panic, Jack pounded on them, until Sam shook his shoulder. "Now, lad, keep calm. We're not dead yet. Let's have a think about this, and see what we can do." Trembling, Jack looked upwards. The shaft seemed to go on and on, with no end to be seen. In any case, the walls were smooth, and there was no way he could climb up even a few yards, even if he could see an opening above.

He looked down, and saw that old Sam was examining several long columns of tiny crystal squares set next to the inside of the doors. "Touch one!" Jack said. "Maybe they open the door, like the one outside."

Sam frowned. "Then why so many? There's a few hundred squares here, I reckon. Can you read, lad?" Jack shook his head, and Sam sighed. "No more can I, now that my eyes are bad. There's something written small on each of the squares. Never mind. Let's see what happens when..." And Sam reached out and touched one of the crystal squares.

Jack was expecting the silver doors to open at once. Instead, his stomach gave a lurch, and he was falling. He gave a cry, and flailed out with his arms, hitting old Sam, who was falling with him too.

At every moment, Jack was expecting to strike the ground with a shattering smash, and to die a moment later. But then his eyes, contradicting his senses, told him that something impossible was happening. They were falling *upwards*! Up the great well.

The walls whizzed by so fast he could hardly see them, and the yellow floor was disappearing rapidly below. Then, moments later, they seemed to slow, and eventually come to a halt. Another floor slid out from the walls under their feet, and with immense relief, Jack felt his feet on something solid once more. He gave a gasp, and sat down, feeling as though he was going to vomit. Old Sam was lying collapsed on the new floor, looking green and blue at the same time.

"Are we dead?" the old man said in a croaking whisper.

"No," said Jack, "more's the pity." Then he saw that there was a new set of silver doors in front of them, and that these doors were now opening silently. Not prepared to let the chance slip, Jack clambered to his feet, picked Sam up bodily and dragged him through.

Then Jack's legs gave way again, and he collapsed to the floor with old Sam sprawled loosely on top of him.

Jack looked around, expecting at any moment to be surrounded by a crowd of the City People, demanding to know what they were doing breaking into this place, but there was still no one to be seen.

They were in a wide corridor, lying on something soft: a thick, fawn-coloured carpet which stretched away on either side. Above, white light fell from panels in the ceiling, though Jack didn't think that it could be daylight. They couldn't be at the very top of the tower. They had "fallen" upwards a long way, but surely not that far.

Gold-coloured doors were set at wide intervals into the walls all along the corridor. Jack couldn't see the end of the corridor in either direction. There must be hundreds of such doors.

Sam sat up and groaned. "That's no way for a mortal man to travel, lad; that's for sure. Falling upwards! Them City People must be fools. What's wrong with a nice set of steps?"

But Jack was hardly listening. "Sam!" he said urgently, "Where are they?"

"Who, lad?"

"The City People! Why haven't we seen any of them?"

Old Sam shook himself, and stood up. "In their rooms, lad, have no doubt of it. They'll all be wining and dining and looking out of their windows at us poor folk, and laughing all the time. But it's lucky for us they don't much seem to like taking strolls outside their rooms. Come on, then; we'll have to have a look."

Together, Jack Cobb and old Sam walked down the corridor. Nervously, Jack glanced back to make sure they would be able to find the silver doors again, though he wasn't looking forward to going back down the well. He had thought of leaving his handkerchief to mark the spot, but now he saw there was a brightly burning sign hung on the ceiling outside the doors.

Old Sam came to one of the gold-coloured doors. Unlike the silver doors, there was only one, not a pair. But it too had a crystal square set next to it. Sam reached out and touched it. A light came on for a moment, but nothing happened. The door stayed shut. Frowning, Sam paced down the corridor to the next such door and tried again. Again, nothing happened. "It must be a kind of lock, that must be it," he said. "Anyone can use the falling-well, but only the owner can get inside his room."

"Perhaps we should just knock?" Jack suggested. But Sam just gave him a foul glance.

They were both becoming fidgety, nervous. Already, their exploit had taken too long. Jack had hoped, somehow, that they could just dash in, grab something valuable and then rush out again without being caught. He should have known it wouldn't be so easy.

Sam rubbed his grizzled chin with a rasping noise. "Can you

smash it lad, do you think? Not the door, mind you, but the crystal? It might be enough, if we're lucky."

Jack pondered, then looked down at his belt. His small cobbler's hammer was still in its pouch. He pulled the hammer out, sized up the crystal square, and delivered the hardest blow be could. It was on target, and the crystal shattered. Sparks flew, and there was a sudden smell of burning. The golden door quivered, seemed to hesitate, and then came half-way open. Jack stood with the hammer raised, expecting to hear cries of outrage from inside. But all was silent. Sam chortled, and squeezed through the gap. Somewhat reluctantly, Jack followed.

Inside was a palace. Or so it seemed at first to Jack, for whom luxury was a straw-filled mattress to sleep on.

A small hallway led into a complex of rooms. The first was clearly a bedroom, with a huge double-bed covered with a fantastically embroidered quilt. Strange devices whose purpose Jack could not imagine stood next to the bed. On the walls were what seemed to be glossy tapestries, showing scenes of cloud-capped mountains.

Another room contained a huge bath, plated with gold-specked tiles. Frowning, Sam fumbled with a lever on the wall. After a moment, steaming hot water came gushing from an outlet to fill the bath. Sam scratched himself underneath his rags, and turned away grinning.

One room had a desk and big grey panels of glass on its walls; there were another two bedrooms, each with its own white-tiled privy; and a room empty of furniture, whose walls were padded with soft material.

Yet another room had a huge table made of beautiful laminated wood. A small door was set into the wall with hundreds of tiny crystal squares next to it. Sam pushed randomly at a few of them, and in a matter of moments, the small door opened to reveal three plates of hot food, with what seemed to be pieces of real meat and fresh vegetables. Hungrily, they scooped up the food in their fingers and ate as they explored. Finally, they entered a large room filled with a dozen comfortable chairs and small tables. The carpet was white, and even thicker and softer than that in the corridor.

They had examined all of the rooms. There was no one here. The place was empty, though it looked and felt as though the owner had just stepped out for a moment, and would be back very soon. That was an uncomfortable feeling. They sat down on the soft furniture, still munching on handfuls of hot meat, and looked at each other. Almost anything they could carry from these rooms would be worth a fortune at the foot of the City. The embroidered bed-quilt alone could be sold for twenty pieces of silver in the market. And there were dozens of things here made from precious metal. Not gold, perhaps, but strong steel, almost as valuable.

Jack looked at old Sam, and wondered if he felt the same way Jack did. They could escape from the City now, and be rich, but that would leave behind a mystery that would nag at them forever. Why hadn't they seen any of the City People yet? Had they just been lucky? Sam shook his head. "I know what you're thinking lad. You don't want to go back without being able to say that you've seen just one of them Golden People."

Jack said fiercely: "Not just seen one. I'd like to kill one of them and carry back his head, just to prove I've been here. Imagine, living in places like this, while we..." Anger choked him.

Sam nodded. "It's no wonder they shut us out with the Fence, all those years ago. Otherwise, all of us Squatters would have rushed in and taken over this place. That we would."

Jack shook his head. "So will we try another door? Or the falling-well again?"

Sam gave a sad sort of smile, and said, "Well lad, I'd like to stay here for a while myself, have a bit more food, maybe a sleep. I'm terrible tired, and it must be night outside by now. Why don't you have a wander off, and come back a bit later?"

Jack frowned. "But what if I meet one of the City People? Or if the owner of this place comes back and finds you here?"

Sam shrugged. "In the first place, you're a big lad, and can take care of yourself. And in the second, well, there's not much of me to be missing if they haul me out and toss me out of the window. The truth of it is, lad, that I'm happy. Nothing I could buy outside the City would make me as happy as I am right now. We've shown them City People up, for sure, breaking into their City and whooping it up in one of their own rooms. It's paradise, lad, that's what it is. You go off, if you want."

Jack nodded slowly. He was reluctant to leave the old man,

but on the other hand, he wasn't happy about staying put, not knowing where the City People were, expecting at any moment to be surprised by one of them. He had to find out for himself.

So he left Sam enjoying himself, squeezed out of the broken door into the hallway and set off for the sign that marked the falling-well. He wasn't looking forward to using it, but there was no choice. He touched the crystal square, and the doors opened obediently. To his relief, there was still a floor there, and not an awful drop.

His legs trembling slightly, Jack stepped in. Before he did anything, he looked carefully at the long columns of tiny crystals on the inside of the doors. There was a faint green light behind one of them, which seemed to be the one that Sam had touched to bring them to this level. Counting carefully, Jack worked out that it was the thirtieth square from the bottom, on the left. He wanted to be able to get back here again.

There were hundreds more squares on the panel. Jack pondered for a second, and then, bracing himself, he touched the very top-most crystal on the right-hand column. In an instant, the floor slid back into the wall and he was falling upwards again. Though he had a flash of panic and his stomach lurched, this time it was a little better; he knew what to expect, and he could keep his fear under control.

As he fell upwards, his speed increased until the walls were just a flickering blur. Then at last, he slowed and came to a halt. The floor slid back under him, and the doors opened.

Jack gave a gasp of surprise. He was no longer inside the City, but out in the open. He stepped out. It was just after sunset and stars were beginning to twinkle above. It was quite cold, and the air seemed to be thinner, somehow. Jack stood waiting for his eyes to adjust to the gloom. He seemed to be at the edge of a huge area of farmland. What had happened? Had the falling-well transported him miles away from the City?

Then he turned around, and understood. He was on the very roof of the City, perhaps thirty yards from the edge.

Huge transparent walls ran along the edge of the building, keeping out the wind, and preventing anything from falling off. From here, Jack could see for what seemed to be hundreds of miles to the far western horizon, where the red-gold of sunset still hung. The whole roof of the City was covered with farmland, in raised tiers which at first he had thought were hills. Jack could see crops stretching away into the distance on all sides. And there was movement, lots of it. City People at last? Jack stepped back to the side of the falling-well, wanting to keep out of sight. He hefted his hammer and waited.

But, after a moment, he saw that he had been mistaken. Moving among the nearby crops, tending and weeding, was a steel dwarf, similar but not identical to the one which had let them into the City. Jack watched it in wonder. It was whizzing up and down between rows of what looked like cabbages, hoeing the soil with its arms. Jack stepped out from the shelter and went closer. The machine paid no attention to Jack at all, even when he came close enough to touch it. He looked around. There were dozens of such machines nearby moving among the crops. One of them was harvesting vegetables and piling them up in a hopper.

Jack began to understand. The City People would never soil their fine hands with such menial work as farming, of course. But they had to eat, and their food had to be grown somewhere. So their wonderful machines did all of the work for them, never stopping for lack of daylight, nor from tiredness.

Stimulated by curiosity, Jack followed one of the harvesting machines for a while, until its hopper was full. Then it turned and rolled towards an opening in the floor, and tipped the contents of the hopper into it. From the opening, Jack heard the sounds of busy machinery just below. His brow furrowed in thought, Jack went back to the falling-well. He would like to see what happened to the crops once they were harvested.

Inside the tiny room once more, he pressed the crystal square just below the one for the roof, and fell only for a fraction of a second as he dropped one level.

The doors opened onto a scene of intense mechanical activity. There were thousands of the mobile mechanisms moving around on a vast floor, and huge contraptions as big as houses were in operation. There seemed to be no inner walls here, just supporting pillars, and the activity stretched away as far as Jack could see. But still there were no City People, just machines.

Ignored by the steel dwarves, Jack moved into the area, amazed and filled with wonder. Food was being prepared automatically by the thousands of machines, cut up, cooked, seasoned, and then placed into a complicated sorting device that sped the food in different directions. Jack remembered the food Sam and he had obtained in the room far below, and realised that each of the City People's rooms must have a device which commanded those machines to select and deliver the right food from this vast cornucopia. Here then, thought Jack, was clear proof that there were thousands of City People in the City, though he had not seen them yet. *Someone* must be eating all of this food.

But then he moved on further, and saw that enormous quantities of cold and spoiled food were being emptied by the ton into a huge hopper of waste, and conveyed to a machine which churned it up and vomited forth a foul-smelling mash that seemed to be destined to be turned into fertiliser for the roof-farm.

Jack frowned in puzzlement, and paced slowly back to the falling-well. He went down again, stopping at levels at random, and walking out to see what he would find. Most of the top levels of the City seemed to be occupied by automatic machinery carrying out different kinds of manufacturing work. One level was nothing but clothes-making machinery, producing beautiful gowns, shirts and pants, gorgeously embroidered and coloured. And, to Jack's chagrin, superb and delicate boots and shoes tumbled from one machine. But in another area on the same floor, unworn clothes were being ripped to shreds and fed into a furnace.

As Jack moved further down the building, the living areas began. He wandered through the corridors, smashing at the crystal locks, sometimes gaining access to the rooms. Nowhere did he find another human being. Where were the City People? The busy machines were producing food and goods which were never used, but appeared happy in their ignorance, continuing to produce and destroy at the same time. What had happened to the people these things were intended for? Where had they gone? None of it made any sense.

Filled with confusion, and exhausted from his explorations, Jack stepped back into the falling well and carefully counted up to the thirtieth crystal from the bottom of the left-most column, and then touched it. He would go back and tell Sam that the Golden City was empty, and that he could, if he liked, stay here forever.

Jack found the broken door without difficulty, and squeezed through. He was in a hurry to tell Sam all he had seen. But as he entered the living room, he sensed something was wrong. There was a faint gasping sound. Jack ran in. Sam lay flat on a couch, his face quite blue. Scattered plates surrounded him. The old man was still alive, though just barely. He greeted Jack with a flicker of his eyes and tried to say something. "It's all right, Sam," Jack said in a panic. "Save your breath."

But Sam was determined to speak. His breath was a ragged wheeze, and it took him many attempts before he could get it out. "Enjoyed... myself... too much... good... happy... die happy..." Then he ceased the struggle, and was silent. After another few minutes, there came a sudden spasm and a terrible rattle from Sam's old throat, and it was over. Sam was dead.

Weeping, Jack stood up from the old man's body and turned away. Then his legs trembled, and he was forced to sit down on one of the plush chairs. He was completely exhausted from the combined effect of his emotions and the day's hard activity. Before he knew it, Jack was asleep.

He was awakened eventually by the sensation of nearby movement. His spine prickling with horror, Jack sat up, half-expecting to see old Sam's ghost standing over him. But poor Sam was still dead and motionless. The movement was that of one of the steel dwarves, busily moving around the room. There was an open hatchway in one of the walls, from where the thing had apparently come.

The machine was tidying up. It was picking up the discarded plates that lay about poor old Sam and placing them in its hopper. Some internal device was sucking up scattered pieces of food and dirt from the carpet, and as it passed a small table, it extended an arm to polish its surface.

Jack watched the machine working in pensive silence. The City People had never had to lift a finger to help themselves. Everything was done for them by their wonderful machines. No hard toil for them, no breaking their backs tilling the earth, no piercing their fingers with needles as they sewed garments to keep out the cold, no callouses forming on their hands as they made boots so they could earn enough to eat. Their lives must have been endless comfort and luxury. And now they were gone – wherever they might have gone to – yet their machines still kept on working, growing food, making clothes, all just as though the City People were still here, needing it all.

In fact, mused Jack, *so far as the machines were concerned, the City People hadn't needed to exist at all.*

Suddenly struck by the direction of his thoughts, Jack sat up straight. But the next instant, something happened which made him forget.

The dwarf had reached the body of old Sam, lying sprawled and blue on the couch. Touching the hand of the corpse, the machine hesitated for a second, reached out two powerful arms to pull Sam from the couch, and started to drag him towards the open hatchway.

Shocked, Jack leapt up and grappled with the machine, trying to break its grip on the body. But its mechanical arms were far stronger than Jack's. It paid no attention to his efforts. Seized by sudden anger, Jack pulled out his hammer and struck blow after blow at the machine, smashing its crystal eyes, and causing blue sparks to fizz and spit from the breaks. Jack kept on smashing until he broke the joint of one of the thing's arms. It let go of old Sam, spun in a circle, and retreated hurriedly towards the open hatchway. The hatch closed behind it so tightly that the hatch was almost invisible.

Jack gasped in relief and sat down. He could not have said why he had been so outraged by the machine's actions. But like all his people, he had a reverence for the dead. He also had in his mind the awful image of Sam's body ending up in that foul-smelling mishmash of wasted food on its way to be fertiliser for the roof-farm.

Then he frowned. Things were starting to become clear in his mind. Whenever one of the City People had died, the machines must have come and taken his or her body and then tidied up afterwards. There would be no sign, a few hours later, that the person had ever existed. So that would explain why Jack and Sam had not come across any skeletons of the City People in their explorations. But that didn't explain what had caused them to die out in the first place.

Jack stood up. It was time to be gone. Now that Sam was dead, he was starting to feel lonely and afraid, all alone in this vast building. But he wasn't going to leave Sam here to be turned into fertiliser. He hefted the old man's body up over his shoulder, and started off.

He was almost out of the broken door before he remembered

that the reason they had come into the City in the first place was treasure. He put the body down for a moment and went to the bedroom to get the embroidered quilt. He tied it like a thick sash over his shoulder and around his waist. Then he stuffed a few metal items into his belt and pouch. It was enough. At least he and his father would not starve now, and would be able to buy new hides even if he had to pay someone to deal with the tanner on their behalf.

Burdened by the quilt, it was hard to pick up old Sam as well. But he would manage.

Outside the door was another of the steel dwarves. This one was busily repairing the damaged crystal lock. Despite the heavy weight over his shoulder, Jack stood and watched it for a while. It was delicate and clever in its work, better than any human workman. And it needed no one to supervise it. *If thousands of these things had been created*, Jack thought suddenly, *why then, human life would be futile. What point would there be in a life where you needed to do nothing at all?*

And so, just like that, Jack Cobb understood why there were no City People left. Sobered and depressed, he turned away and walked smartly towards the falling-well.

Back in the crystal hallway on the lowest level, Jack made his way along the short corridor through which they had entered. For a moment, he wondered if he would need to wait for another steel dwarf to appear to let him out. But the dark glass panel simply slid aside as he approached with his burdens, and he was outside. It was still night-time, but the sky was becoming brighter as dawn approached.

Jack's arms and legs ached, and he felt utterly spent. Old Sam had been old and thin when he was alive, but now that he was dead he seemed to be growing heavier by the moment.

Shifting his burden to make it more comfortable, Jack slowly climbed the shallow hills which surrounded the base of the Golden City and made his way towards where he had broken through the Fence. It seemed a lot further away than he remembered, but he had no fear of missing the spot.

He came to it at last, marked by the shattered remains of the cart. He reached the yellow band and stood looking at the two faint lanes of pale brown that lay across it where the cart's wheels had passed. He put the old man's body down and looked back at the City, pondering.

Now that Jack had broken through, any curious person might come along and walk safely across the Fence here. In time, the news would get about that luxury and wealth lay in the City for the taking. Nothing could stop everyone who heard of it from moving into the City. And once there, their lives futile, they might also die out within a generation or two, leaving no one at all left in the world.

"Sam," said Jack sadly, "I'd like to bury you properly, but I think you'd be happier doing something else." He lifted the old man's body and tossed it onto the yellow band to one side of the ragged lines of brown. The body fell with an awful wet, crunching sound, and Jack was forced to look away, feeling sick. Had he done the right thing? He thought so. Old Sam would be happy to be left within the Fence he had studied so long, and no carrion could come near him where he now lay.

Then Jack picked up the pieces of the smashed cart and one by one tossed them onto the Fence so as to mostly cover the lanes of pale brown. Only when that was done did he pick up the quilt again and carefully pick his way over the shattered wood until he was across the Fence and back in his own land.

He looked back to examine his handiwork. It was perfect. The shattered boards and wheels of the cart, the crushed body of poor old Sam. To anyone who came along, it was clear what had happened. Some fool had tried to drive a cart across the Fence and been killed doing it. No one would try to cross, knowing they would suffer the same fate.

The sun was rising. Jack Cobb looked up at the Golden City for one last time, sighed, and then turned and headed home.

After a while, he began to whistle.

On the Cold Hill Side

ANDY STEVENS WAS IN THE LEAD, his bright red snowmobile moving smoothly over the hard-packed snow, when he suddenly gave a shout and waved back at Lee, who had been following several yards behind in his own lime-green vehicle.

They had been driving cautiously. Though the snow was deep, there were often hidden hazards so near to a town. Andy's snowmobile had been overturned a few days ago when it had hit the roof of a buried lorry. It had been a bugger to get the vehicle and its trailer upright again.

Now Andy pulled to a halt, and in response, Lee throttled back his own machine, stopped, and turned off the engine. Every drop of fuel was precious.

Pulling off his ice-coated face-mask and goggles, Andy ran a hand over his fur-lined hood to clear it of accumulated ice and then pointed ahead. "Smoke!" he said. "Can't you see it?"

Disbelieving, Lee took off his own goggles. Sure enough, a thin plume of grey smoke was ascending from somewhere in the abandoned city.

He shook his head. "Can't be people, surely. Maybe a lightning strike, or something, set fire to one of the old houses?"

Andy's warm breath turned to white mist as he spoke. "I guess... But it's hardly been thunderstorm weather, has it? Can you even get lightning in these conditions?"

They both gazed forward, unspeaking. "Say what you like," Andy said after a while, "it looks for all the world like smoke from a chimney to me."

It hardly seemed possible. Though it was high summer right now, the air temperature was minus 25 degrees Celsius. In winter, the temperature up here was estimated to fall below minus 60 and stay there for months at a time. The whole of the North had been abandoned years ago. If the smoke they saw was from a man-made fire, then it was the first sign of human life they had seen in nearly ten days of traveling north.

"Well," said Lee at last. "No point in guessing. Let's go and have a look."

They remounted their snowmobiles and started off again.

They were on the outskirts of Edinburgh, once the proud capital of Scotland. But Scotland didn't exist any more. And neither did a lot of England, though the areas around London were still hanging on. It was just too damn cold up here, ever since the disastrous attempt at geoengineering eight years ago. It had stopped global warming all right. With a vengeance. The end for this city, when it had come, had been very swift, with forced evacuations and the Army rounding people up into transports at gunpoint.

From the slight hill they were on, they could see that much of the old city was now submerged in deep layers of snow. In some places the outlines of streets were barely visible, marked out only by the sparse taller buildings whose roofs peeked out from the snow. But in other areas the snow did not look so deep. It was from one of these that the smoke rose.

The pair drove forward, even more slowly now. Urban areas made for hazardous traveling.

As Lee and Andy rode they tried to keep the smoke trail in sight and head in that direction. It was hard work. They kept losing it behind buildings, and Edinburgh's crooked streets kept pushing them away from the direct route. In most of the streets, deep drifts had been piled up by a strong prevailing wind. In many places snow reached to the roofline of the houses on one side of a street, but was almost clear on the other. That meant they were often riding along the contours of a steeply angled slope.

But they kept on getting closer, until finally, as they turned onto a long, straight avenue, Andy shouted and pointed out the smoke rising up ahead.

Many of the houses here had roofs which had collapsed under the weight of years of heavy snow, snow that built up year after year, never melting. But the house that Andy was pointing out had a steep roof only lightly covered with snow. An unmistakable thin grey plume of smoke drifted upwards from its chimney. Someone must still be living there.

They slowed their machines to a halt outside the house. It was a tall, three-level Georgian affair, connected to its neighbors on either side in a long terrace. Its windows were largely blocked off with something white up against them on the inside. The front door must once have been green, but the paint had nearly all flaked off. A drift of snow reached up to be almost level with the bottom of the door.

"Well," said Andy, taking off his goggles and ski mask again. "What do we do now, go up and knock and ask if they ordered a pizza?"

Lee hesitated, feeling a sudden strange but surprisingly deep reluctance. "We don't have to stop at all. We don't want them asking awkward questions about what we're doing up here."

"We don't have to answer," said Andy reasonably. "Maybe they know something which would be useful. Besides, why have we been trying to reach this place for the last hour or so if we're not going to find out who's here?"

Before Lee could answer, however, the decision was taken away from them. The door opened. Standing at the door, fur-coated, stood a young woman. Her right hand came up. In it she was holding a double-barreled shotgun. She proceeded to aim it expertly at them.

"Who are you?" she said in a voice with a strong Scots accent. "What do you want?"

Andy recovered quickly and responded before Lee could overcome his shock. "We've been sent by the Government," he said smoothly. "Part of an expeditionary team, looking for survivors like yourself. We can take you back down south with us." Lee stifled an exclamation. Andy had always been the one with the slick answers.

Incredibly, before the young woman could answer, they heard a baby begin to cry, near at hand. An astonishing, unexpected sound, it rose and fell in the still, cold air. The woman turned her head a little and made soothing sounds, and only then did Lee realize that she was carrying a baby in a papoose on her back, its little head topped with a knitted beanie.

As though there had been no interruption, she turned back to look sceptically at them. "I'm not going south," she said firmly. "D'you have any food with you? Fresh food?"

Lee shook his head regretfully. "Just rations, mostly dehydrated stuff. It's taken us nearly three weeks to get here, and we had to haul all of our own fuel," he said, indicating the trailers.

The woman gazed at them in silence for a long while. Her fierce stare was disconcerting. Behind her, the baby started to grizzle, but she paid it no attention.

She seemed to come to a decision. "Go on with you, then," she said, gesturing down the street with the shotgun.

"Wait," said Andy. "Surely we could talk for a while? You mustn't see many people up here. Don't you need any help? Things for the baby? We could fetch you things with our snowmobiles."

Lee wasn't really sure why Andy was persisting. Well, he did have a suspicion. Andy had always been one for the girls, and this strange young woman was quite pretty in her own way, though she showed not the least sign of friendliness.

She was certainly intriguing. How on earth had she managed to survive up here by herself? The baby didn't seem very old, but wasn't tiny. It must have been born months ago, in the depths of the terrifyingly cold winter.

Well, he reflected, she can't have been entirely by herself, or where had the baby come from? Maybe she *wasn't* alone, perhaps there were others living in the house? But somehow, he didn't know how, he knew that she was indeed alone. She hadn't made the smallest motion to look behind her or to call out to anyone else. Just raised the gun, which she still aimed unwaveringly in their direction.

"I could shoot you both now," she said after a long while. "Take your motors for myself." She paused again, and Lee started to really worry that she might actually do it. Then she dropped the barrel a little and the tension eased a fraction. "But you're right. I haven't had anyone to talk to since... well, for a long time now."

There was another long pause, during which the baby began to cry lustily.

"Ah, hell," she said wearily, and lowered the shotgun fully to her side. "You can come in for a wee while. But I need to feed the wean first, so you'll stay outside until I've put him to bed."

She closed the door firmly in their faces. They could hear a heavy bolt being slid into place.

"You'd think she doesn't trust us," said Andy, genuinely if only slightly offended.

Lee laughed then, an explosion of steam from his open mouth. "Andy, if I was a young woman with a kid, I wouldn't trust you within a mile of me. And what was all that business about 'I'm from the government, I'm here to help you'?"

Andy smiled. "Seemed like it was worth a try."

"Can you believe she's been living up here through the winters? No water. Sewerage system frozen. No electricity. They had to evacuate. No way food supplies were going to get through in future. What's she been living on?"

Andy shrugged. "Maybe she'll tell us."

"Would you really take her and the baby south with us once we've found the stuff? What if she told somebody?"

He shrugged. "Don't know. But it doesn't come up. You heard her, she wants to stay here."

Lee shook his head in exasperation, and looked back at the door, thinking about the woman. And the shotgun. It just seemed wrong. A woman with a baby on her back and a lethal weapon in her hands. He stamped his cold feet and slapped his gloved hands together.

After a long while, the green door opened again. The shotgun was back in her hands. "All right, then, come in. But you'd better not wake the wean, or I'll skin you alive. And no sudden moves, or I'll have to shoot you, and that *will* wake him up." No smile accompanied this flat statement.

She stepped aside from the door, and gestured for them to go in first. "Take the first door to the left," she said. "That's where we're living. I call it my Igloo Room."

It was a big house. They entered a passage with doors to left and right. Up ahead they could see a staircase. Strangely, it had no bannisters. They paused, and Lee, who had entered behind Andy, could feel the gun being jammed against his back. "To the left," she said brusquely. Meekly, they obeyed.

They entered a dark room. After the brightness of the snow outside, it took a long while for their eyes to recover and start making sense of what they saw. At first, Lee thought that the walls were painted white, but as his eyes adjusted he saw instead that something white was stacked up against all of the walls, big white blocks of some kind.

In a gap left clear of the blocks, there was a large fireplace, and in it, burning merrily, was the fire which must be generating the smoke they had seen. The room was very warm compared to the chill outside, and they were soon sweating in their fur jackets and pants. Andy quickly unzipped his jacket and took it off. Lee copied him.

In front of the fire, on a thick rug, was a bright orange sleeping bag. A couple of big leather armchairs, an ottoman and a small table were the only other pieces of furniture in the room. Oh, and the baby's crib next to the windows, or where the windows should be.

The room was dark because the high windows also had big white blocks stacked against them, almost but not quite covering all of the glass. Lee realized now that the blocks were big pieces of polystyrene packaging, the kind of thing that household electrical goods were shipped in. Insulation, he suddenly realized. 'Igloo Room' was a good name for it.

There was a rich, sharp smell in the room. As he wrinkled his nose and looked around, Lee saw that it was generated by the contents of a nappy pail near the door.

The woman had followed them into the room. She had taken off her jacket in the corridor, and now she shook out her honey-brown hair. "This is it, then," she said. "This is where I live mostly. I can only keep one room warm, d'you see? Though sometimes I light the Aga in the kitchen for a spell."

Andy nodded and looked around admiringly. "How long have you been here, then? Surely you don't spend the winters up here?"

She made a derisive snort. "I've lived here all of my life. This was my father's house, and my grandfather's. Not that they would be happy with what I've done to the old place, but you have to survive, don't you see? You have to be prepared to do anything to survive." She stared at them for a long moment. "Sit down, then, if you like."

The two men sat in the armchairs. She sat perched on the ottoman. Another long silence ensued. "I'm Janet McDiarmid.

What do you two want up here? Don't tell me any more lies. You're no more from the government than I am."

Andy, his face lit mostly by the flickering orange light from the fire, looked slightly abashed. "OK, I'm sorry for that. I'm Andy Stevens, and this is my friend Lee Baxter. I guess you'd say we're on a hunting expedition. Have you seen anyone else traveling north?" It was a fair assumption, Lee thought, that anyone who saw the smoke from her chimney would come here to investigate. She must have to keep that fire burning night and day in order to survive.

Janet looked skeptical. "You're no hunting any kind of beast. They're all mostly gone to the south, though in the summer I've seen deer. I shot a stag two years ago. Fresh meat is very hard to come by, you understand?"

Andy shrugged. "No. We're looking for something else. Something we think will be very valuable, that we can sell." He stopped suddenly as she pointed the barrel of the shotgun directly at him.

"My, my, you're the smooth one, aren't you?" she said. "You'd better tell me straight now, or we'll be having an awful short conversation."

Andy's confidence was gone as he stared into the barrel of the gun. "I... we... we've been commissioned to find something left behind in the rush. Computer drives and the data that's on them. Designs for equipment, processes. Test results. Even after the crisis that data is still valuable to competitors."

Her gaze didn't waver. "I see. It doesn't sound very ethical, to me. I'm sure it's not legal, taking gear that doesn't belong to you. But that's not my concern." The gun barrel lowered yet again. "D'you want a wee bite to eat, now? That dehydrated stuff doesn't sound much good for two grown men. Mind you, all I have is tinned. Oh, and frozen, of course." She gave a soft, cold laugh, and stood up.

On the table were stacked about a dozen cans and two small saucepans. She rested the gun on the table within easy reach, and opened two cans, pouring them into the larger saucepan without turning her back on the two men. *My God, she's cautious*, Lee thought. Still, she had let them into the house.

She picked up the gun again in one hand and with the other carried the saucepan to the fire, where she set it atop a metal tripod. She put another couple of pieces of wood on the fire. They looked like they had been the legs of a chair.

"Your baby's father," asked Andy suddenly. "What happened to him? Is he still here?"

She gave a bitter laugh. "He's gone." She paused, seemingly thinking back. After a moment, she went on. "He came up north like you did, maybe a year and a half ago. But he didn't have a machine. He had a sled, and dogs." At Andy's sound of surprise, she looked at him with that unnerving gaze. "Aye, dogs. Real huskies. He'd been raising and training them for an expedition to commemorate some famous explorer's polar trip. But then the cold came down, and the north of Britain might as well have been the pole, so he set off anyway, from London. That's what he told me, anyway."

She turned back to the fire. "But he's gone now," she said, adding very softly something Lee had trouble catching: "I *hate* him." A pretty understandable emotion, Lee thought, if the man had left her here to cope by herself.

Lee thought of something which made his stomach turn. "So he wasn't here when your baby was born?"

She looked at him with a grim expression. "No one was here. I managed it myself. Here in this house, before that fire. It was hard, very hard. I thought that I was going to die. But I managed it, and my child was healthy. I was lucky. A lot could have gone wrong. But it didn't."

"But why did you stay here?" asked Andy. "When the evacuation was on, I mean? Why didn't you go south?"

She stirred the contents of the saucepan. "I told you. This has been my family's house for generations, and I'm a Scotswoman through and through. I wasn't going to abandon Scotland, even if every other man, woman and child did. Go and live as a refugee in England? No."

She lifted the saucepan from the stove, and poured its contents into three large mugs and handed them out, one hand on the shotgun. Lee sipped at his mug. Hot soup. Canned soup, but better food than they had had while traveling.

She went on. "So I hid. It wasn't hard. There were quite a few others like me in the city at first. But most didn't survive the first winter. Those that did didn't survive the second. But I did."

"But how did you survive? How do you cope in the winter?"

She smiled. "I might show you tomorrow, if you'll fetch me some stuff. Like you said you would."

"All right," said Andy slowly. "And can we sleep..."

She cut him off before he could finish. "No," she said firmly, lifting the shotgun again. "Finish your soup, and then get out of the house. You'll be having a tent, I'm thinking?"

Andy gave a sigh and shrugged. "Yes. OK. We'll see you in the morning, then." He looked across at Lee, and they both stood up and went out the front door. It was swiftly closed and bolted behind them.

Darkness came late here in the summer months, but by the time they had unpacked and assembled the tent in the middle of the snow-covered street, the stars were coming out. They shuffled into their sleeping bags.

"I think she fancies me," said Andy.

Lee laughed out loud. "I don't think so. That's one tough lady."

"Just playing hard to get." And with a self-satisfied smile, Andy rolled over and went to sleep.

Lee lay unsleeping for a while, thinking. Janet McDiarmid didn't seem quite normal, quite sane. But then living alone up here, giving birth all alone, surviving the terrible conditions; that was enough to dent anyone's sanity. He sighed, and eventually dropped off to sleep.

In the morning, they got up, stiff from sleeping on the firm snow, and made a simple breakfast.

"Andy," Lee said, "why don't we just go on into the city and look for the computer drives? We're just wasting our time with Janet."

But Andy shook his head. "If we get in good with her, we'll be able to stay longer. Give us a better chance of finding everything we're after. She can tell us where to find food, maybe fuel too. Besides, we only just got here yesterday. An extra day can't harm."

Reluctantly, Lee went back to eating his breakfast in silence. As they ate, they watched the green door, but there was no sign of movement. Eventually, Andy shrugged and went over to knock. He waited a long time with no result, but as he retreated to the tent, the door opened. Lee suspected that she had been waiting for Andy to be far enough away for her safety.

Janet stood there, the shotgun as always in her hand. But at least now it wasn't raised and pointing at them, instead hanging loosely by her side. The baby was again in its papoose on her back, apparently asleep.

"You can come in for a bit," she said. "You've seen my Igloo Room. Now I'll show you my tunnel."

"Tunnel?" said Andy.

"You'll see."

Lee and Andy went in, Janet following.

"To the right, this time," said Janet.

Obediently, they turned into the room at the right of the corridor. It was empty, bare of any furniture, except for a small wooden sled on skis and a massive wooden wardrobe on the wall opposite the door.

"I kept the wardrobe for the doors," she said cryptically. "To keep the cold out, do you see?" Andy looked at Lee with a raised eyebrow. *Mad*, thought Lee, *off her rocker*.

Then she opened the heavy wardrobe doors. A big hole had been cut out of the wooden back. And behind that, a hole smashed through the brickwork, right into the house next door.

"Go through," she said, and gestured with the gun. Andy laughed, and climbed through. Lee followed.

They were in another completely bare room. In fact, it was a shell. Most of the floorboards had been pulled up, leaving only a narrow platform on which they could walk forward. Everywhere Lee looked, he could see that every scrap of wood had been torn out. Where the ceiling would have been, he could look through up to the floor above. Floorboards, floor joists, door frames, furniture. It was all gone, except for a few remaining boards down here to walk on.

Janet urged them forward, into another corridor, then another room. With another hole smashed into its far wall.

Suddenly understanding, Lee turned to Janet. "How far?" he said.

Janet gave a grim smile. "Twelve houses so far. I knock through the walls with a sledgehammer. It takes a long time, but then I have lots of time. Next year I'll start going in the other direction."

"And you strip them of wood!" Lee laughed. "But why not just break down their front doors?"

She looked at him scornfully, disappointed in him. "Because in winter it's *death* to go outside. The houses retain just enough heat to be safe, and I can travel down my tunnel out of the wind and blizzards. I must have wood, d'you see, for the fire?"

"Very clever," said Andy.

She was contemptuous. "It's not clever. It's just what I've had to do to survive, me and my son," she said fiercely. "And I intend to survive, at least until he's grown. So far as I know, he's the last Scotsman ever to be born in Scotland."

Andy shuffled his feet uncertainly. Lee was amused. Andy's habitual charm was having zero effect on this woman.

"Now, You'd fetch me some stuff, you were saying?"

Andy nodded. "Sure. What do you want, and where do we find it?"

"Cheese," she said. "Frozen, of course, deep frozen, but it thaws out well enough. I'm running short. I need the calcium for my baby's milk. I can fetch some myself, but only as much as I can pull by hand on my sled. If you can haul me all you can find..." She stopped, seemingly unable to frame any kind of expression of gratitude.

"OK," said Andy. "Anything else?" Lee almost laughed. Here they were in Arctic conditions, in the middle of an empty city, and Andy was behaving like a hen-pecked husband sent off with a grocery list.

"Tinned meat. See if you can find any. There's not much left, I'll be thinking. Protein is hard to come by now."

"Where do we find this stuff? Is there a supermarket?"

Janet McDiarmid shook her head. "The supermarkets were all emptied the first year. I told you there were other people here then. But I found something that no-one else did. A supermarket supply truck, broken down. Slid off the road, I think, just before the evacuation. I visit it as often as I can manage during the summer, build up my supplies for the winter."

She gave them brisk directions. It wouldn't be far on the snowmobiles, but it would be a long slow trek on foot, Lee thought. Again, he marveled at her determination.

They emptied Andy's trailer of the containers of fuel and other stores they had brought with them, and set off.

It wasn't easy to find. Only Janet's precise directions enabled them to locate an upper corner of the truck's container poking out of the all-enveloping snow. They had to scoop away a thick drift of snow with their hands to gain access to the contents.

"This is taking too long," Lee said after ten minutes of this. "We should be off hunting up the data. We don't owe her anything."

Andy shrugged. "It will pay off, you see. Have a bit of patience."

Finally a gap into the back of the truck was clear of snow. Flashing a torch inside, they could see that it was more than half empty now.

They found the plastic-wrapped blocks of cheese, each block frozen as hard as rock, and piled up several cartons of it on the trailer. Lee could only find one carton of corned beef to add to their load. He added a couple of cartons of tinned soup and vegetables, noting that most cans had bulged and some had split open as their contents froze. Still, they had stayed deep frozen, and presumably the contents were still good.

When they arrived back, Janet opened the door to them. As before, she stepped aside to let them carry the first cartons into the house while, as always, she kept the shotgun loosely by her side. *My God, when is she going to start to trust us?* Lee thought.

"Up the staircase," Janet ordered. "Two flights, then right out the back to the garden. It all needs to stay frozen until I want it, you understand?"

The back of the house was dark, and only as they reached the second floor did they see that it was because snow was piled up against the windows on that side. On the top floor, though, bright light streamed from an open window, and through that they stepped out onto the snow.

Lee could see that the terraced houses here formed a huge rectangular block, all of their backs facing inwards. The interior of the block had now all but filled up with snow. Several cartons of food were stacked neatly in rows on the snow nearest to Janet's house.

She directed them to put the cartons with the others, then waited in the garden as they traipsed back and forth to the trailer. It was hard work, climbing the stairs with the weight of the food. And dangerous, too, with no bannisters.

"Look," Andy said to her, panting, after the third trip. "Can't you put the gun down for a bit? We don't mean you any harm. We've been helpful. Can't you be a bit more friendly?"

She gave him a cold smile, but turned and put the gun down to lean against the back wall of the house. It was still easily within her reach.

They brought the last of the cartons through. "Thank you," she said grudgingly. "That will be a big help come winter. Just one more thing before you're done. It's best if I bury some of the food, to make sure it stays hard frozen. Can you dig me a wee trench in the snow, about three or four cartons long? I've got a couple of shovels here. Won't take you long."

Lee was getting more and more annoyed about the waste of time, and was about to make a sharp reply when Andy cheerfully said "Sure!" Lee gave him a sour smile. Andy thought she was warming to him, but Lee strongly doubted it.

Janet watched, arms folded, as they dug the trench together. It wasn't difficult, though the snow had packed quite firmly. They reached a carton's depth, and Lee looked up at her enquiringly. "A wee bit deeper," she said, "to make sure I can cover it all." So they continued.

Suddenly, Lee's shovel struck something buried in the snow. He bent down and pulled it out. It was a short bone, just an animal bone. He tossed it aside. On the next stroke, though, he came across something much larger, an elongated shape. He scraped the snow from it. Whatever it was, it was covered in brown fur. He scooped it out with his shovel. It was a complete animal's head, frozen solid.

Then, as he lifted it out of the trench to put it to one side, he realized what it was, and a sudden electric shiver ran through him. It was a dog's head. A husky dog. He held it in his hands, staring at it, his mind whirling.

Andy looked across at it with a frown and turned to ask Janet a question. He found himself facing down the barrel of her gun. She was only a pace away.

"That'll be deep enough, I'm thinking," she said, and pulled the trigger. There was a horrible sound, and suddenly the white snow was splattered with shockingly bright red blood.

Lee found that he was screaming. He jumped reflexively from

the shallow trench but stopped moving on the instant as the gun centered steadily on him.

"Steady, now," she said.

Lee wobbled on his feet, and then sank to his knees, stifling his mouth with his gloved hands. He couldn't bring himself to look at Andy's body lying in the trench. From the house, he could hear the sound of the baby crying.

"I never lied to you, you know," said Janet. "Not once. And I gave you the chance, at the start, to go on your way. It would have been a big loss to me, yet I offered it. But your smooth friend thought he could get the advantage of me, wasn't that the way of it?"

Lee nodded mutely, and she went on. "Survival. That's all that this is about. There's nothing personal in it, I want you to know that. But I must survive to raise my son. And protein—meat—is hard to find. I have to take it where I can get it."

He stammered out: "Your baby's father..."

Her gun centered on his face.

"The bastard raped me," she said flatly. "But I had my revenge. I *ate* him."

She paused for a moment, and then went on, in a matter of fact tone, "And all his dogs. You have to avoid their livers, did you know that?"

There was a long silence. He was shaking; hard, uncontrollable tremors were jerking through his body.

"I should kill you too," Janet said. "Feed me for another few months, you would."

"No, no, please..." Lee found that tears were trickling down his face, and beginning to freeze. He was all too aware that she was assessing him dispassionately, considering him entirely as an object, valuable only for his flesh.

Another long silence.

Finally she said: "All right. You're not as bad as your friend, I'm thinking," and lowered the barrel. "Besides, I only need one of your motors. Get up, get out."

As he stumbled to his feet, she said "I reckon you'll be telling them down south about what I've done."

A thrill of renewed fear ran through him and he stood stock still. "No, no, I promise I won't..."

The shotgun steadied on him again. "Don't lie to me, Lee. A lie will be the death of you. I've had enough of lies. Of course you'll tell. But I reckon they'll not be bothered coming up here after me. They have enough problems as it is keeping people alive down there, isn't that right? Now get out before I change my mind."

He stumbled toward the house, forcing himself not to look at the red splash on the snow where Andy lay. Through the window, expecting at any moment to hear the blast of the shotgun. Down the stairs and out, onto the snowmobile, fumbling for the starter, and then away and out of the frozen city.

He drove ahead, alone, long into the night, never looking back.

This Too, Too Solid Flesh

I PULLED MY GABARDINE COAT CLOSER AROUND ME against the thin drizzle of rain which was now falling as I stood in the graveyard, watching the men working. My leg was aching abominably – the result of an injury I had sustained fighting the Boers in the recent South Africa war. I shivered a little. I hadn't thought to bring an umbrella. It had been a fine day only a few hours ago, but now, not long after sunset, the weather had turned against us.

"We're losing the light," said Jacobs, my assistant. "They'd better hurry up." He was rather older than me, grey-haired and bearded. I had first been appointed to my post just over a year ago, and I knew that he had been angry to be passed over for the position, but, to his credit, he seemed never to have held it against me, and we had developed an excellent working relationship. Now, his face was grim, as it surely should be, given what we were doing here in the graveyard.

He was right about the light. But we had needed to wait until the graveyard was closed to the public, not wanting to attract any unwelcome attention. In any case, the workmen were now bringing the coffin up from the grave. Nearby, the horse harnessed to the black van snorted and whickered softly, disturbed by these proceedings.

I picked up one of the paraffin lanterns, struck a match and adjusted the wick. The light was dim at first, but began to strengthen. I took it over to where the coffin was now resting on the trestle legs we had brought for the purpose, a little loose earth falling from it. I gave a sign to the chief gravedigger. He produced a chisel and began to work it under the lid. The wood was still firm, and the gloss of the varnish still shone here and there. It had been in the ground for less than a year.

Wood shrieked as the lid was prised off. I lifted the lantern and Jacobs and I leaned over cautiously, expecting an unpleasant stench. But there was none.

"Damn!" I said, realising what we had found. Jacobs cursed too, rather more colourfully.

"Another one. Just like the first!" He shook his head in bafflement.

The body, such as it was, was wrapped in a yellowing shroud. But what had caught our attention immediately were the four large stones in the coffin, neatly boxed in at the corners so as not to move around.

The gravedigger peeled aside the shroud. Underneath it was a white skeleton, the bones seeming to gleam a little even in the dim lantern light. No smell. No remnants of mouldering flesh, as there should have been after so short a time. No stains on the cloth or inside the coffin. Nothing, in fact, to indicate that there had ever been a whole body. Just the skeleton. And, of course, the stones.

Jacobs looked across at me quizzically. "What do we do now, Coroner?" he asked.

I was thinking hard. This development cast a whole new light on my earlier investigation.

I glanced over the neighbouring fields towards the nearby manor. Lights were shining in windows here and there in the big house. "I'm going to call on the District Commissioner. If he's free tonight, I'd better talk to him. Take the coffin back to the morgue just as we planned. But, Andrew, keep quiet about this, mind. And tell the men here the same. Give them an extra shilling apiece. We don't want the newspapers causing a fuss again. Not until we understand this."

⊰⊙⊱

Sir Charles Fellman was seated in a plush leather armchair when his butler showed me into the library that evening. I had been here a few times before, but I was always impressed by the beauty and luxury of this room. An antique mahogany desk stood to one side. Two stuffed deer heads, complete with magnificent antlers, were mounted above the doors. And then, of course, there were the books. Shelf upon shelf of books, all beautifully bound in leather, rising up to the ceiling on every side. I wondered idly if Sir Charles ever had time to read more than a fraction of them, and if not, what was the point of such a collection. But then, Sir Charles' wealth did not derive from his modest salary as District Commissioner of Police, but had been inherited. This manor had been passed down in his family for many generations.

Sir Charles stood up to shake my hand. "Good evening, David. Are you well? How are things in the Coroner's office?" He was a tall, strongly-built man in his middle fifties, with dark brown hair and thick eyebrows, his contrasting reddish beard neatly trimmed and cut in the current fashion.

I inclined my head slightly in deference. "Evening, Commissioner. I'm pretty well, thank you."

Sir Charles moved to a small drinks cabinet. "Brandy? It's very good, well-aged. Yes? Have you finished that book I lent you? Stirring stuff, that Kipling, eh?"

I wasn't there to socialise. "Not yet, sir. I'm here on business, I'm afraid. As you are probably aware, we have had a couple of disturbing cases over the last few months."

He proceeded to pour the drinks. "I heard about that case a few months ago, of course, very upsetting what you found on the exhumation. Case of poisoning, yes?"

I sat down in one of the leather armchairs and took the brandy gratefully. "Not quite, sir. That was what was alleged, certainly. That was why we exhumed the young man's body."

"But there was no body in the coffin, was that it? Forgive me, I've been very busy lately." He eased himself back into his armchair, stroking its soft leather pensively.

"Of course. No, it wasn't that the coffin was empty. We found a skeleton, and several heavy weights – cobblestones, actually, fastened down so that they would not move. That was the point. It had only been a few months since the burial, but inside the shroud was just a clean skeleton. No flesh. We think that the weights had been placed there before burial to give the impression of the weight of a normal body to the pall-bearers."

"So it wasn't possible for you to do an autopsy?"

I shook my head. "The undertaker was questioned, of course, and claimed there had been a break-in at his premises the night before the funeral. We had no reason to dispute that."

Sir Charles pursed his lips, looking thoughtful. "Some student prank or other, then. I wouldn't concern yourself too much about it."

"That's what we thought at the time. But that was before the second exhumation we carried out today."

Sir Charles put down his brandy glass abruptly and frowned. "Second...? I didn't hear about that. Good God, man, I can't remember the last time we had *any* exhumations in this district. In my grandfather's time, I think. Now you're telling me we've had two in six months? You should have informed me."

"I did write you a letter a few days ago, but perhaps you haven't seen it yet. The second exhumation came about solely because of the first. You might recall that the young man's parents had disputed my finding that he had died of a self-inflicted over-dose of laudanum. They alleged that a young woman called Christine, who was romantically involved with their son, had in fact poisoned him. They are well-connected and created quite a fuss, so we felt obliged to try the exhumation. After that, though, with no body and no obvious motive, we couldn't hold the girl, who strongly denied the accusation. But then..."

The Commissioner was still frowning, and he fiddled irritably with the stem of his glass. "Then?"

"I received a letter making further allegations against the young woman. Wild claims, really, suggesting that Christine's own sister had also been a victim of her schemes. The sister died about nine months ago, five months before the young man. In normal circumstances I would have ignored this poison-pen missive. In fact, just between you and I, Sir Charles, I suspect that the letter was written by the young man's mother, who it appears had taken against this Christine from the start. But given the on-going mystery about the first case, I felt obliged to seek an exhumation of the girl's sister."

Sir Charles was clearly annoyed. "Really, David, I think that was going too far on such flimsy evidence. I'm sure I wouldn't have agreed if I had known. I was against even the first exhu-mation, if you recall."

"Yes. But the point is what we found when we opened the second coffin today."

He was silent now, his nostrils a little dilated in anger. I went on, feeling nervous. Sir Charles' temper was legendary, and I could see it building now.

"It was the same thing," I said. "Skeleton, weights, no sign there had ever been any flesh or organs in the coffin."

"But... nine months, you say, since the sister died. Perhaps you are mistaken about the rate of decay. The ground is damp hereabouts."

"That wouldn't explain the stones placed in the coffin, sir."

"Ah, no, no. I suppose the local police station has questioned the undertaker again? Old Carruthers, isn't it? Time the old duffer retired, seems to me."

This was where it was going to become difficult. "No sir, we haven't spoken to him yet. I need to gather some more evidence. I propose to close the cemetery to the public early tomorrow morning and carry out more exhumations."

"More! Oh dear, no. That is going too far, David. The public outcry! The newspapers would blow it up into a severe embarrassment, a disaster. No, no, completely out of the question." He stood up, began to pace around the room. "Complete disrespect for the dead. No."

I was firm. "I believe that we must. We need to know the extent of this... this interference with the bodies."

"Nonsense. It's clearly something to do with this young woman. Christine, did you say? Yes. Perhaps she really *is* a poisoner, and has found some way of disposing of the evidence. That must be it. No, I'm certainly not going to give my permission for further exhumations. It simply will not do."

I took a deep breath. "I'm only here as a courtesy, sir. I'm sorry to have to remind you that I have wide discretion as Coroner to conduct my own investigations when I see fit. My powers ultimately derive from the Crown, not from the Police Department."

He was silent for a long time, one hand stroking his red beard, thinking. Then he shook his head, an unreadable expression on his face. "I see," he said coldly. "Very well, then, you've informed me. You had better leave now and get on with the ugly business. I have my own work to do."

∞∞

Late on the following day, I was in my office when Andrew Jacobs came in to the room. He looked tired to death. He had spent the day, at my order, out at the cemetery. I had been too busy to spend all of my time out there, and I knew that I could trust Jacobs.

"Sit down, Andrew," I said, "you don't look well. What did you find?"

He rubbed his hand across his face wearily and sipped at the glass of water I poured for him.

"Well, we dug up the five graves that you and I decided on this morning. Three were perfectly normal, and we put them back. The two others... it was the same thing. Skeleton only. Stones. We brought the coffins back to the morgue."

We had picked five relatively recent interments carefully. None of them, so far as we could tell, had any connection with the young woman Christine.

"Which ones? Have you got that list we made up?"

He passed it over, a little grubby with smears of dirt. I looked it over carefully. It included both of the earlier exhumations and those that had been done today. Was there a pattern discernible? I thought that there was, even with so small a sample, but it wasn't helping much with the mystery.

Of the normal burials, two were of people over seventy years old, and one of a young man run over by a carriage. All of the burials which had been interfered with seemed to have been of younger people, none of whom had died violently. Consumption, of course, is nowadays the major killer of young people outside of wars.

I gazed out of the window for a while, thinking. Then I got to my feet.

"Come on, then," I said. "I want to examine the coffins closely. We might find some clues. Is the police sergeant still here? What's his name? MacTavish? Good. Let's take him down too."

The morgue is equipped with the newest electric lighting, so much brighter than gas, and a great benefit to our work these days. With its aid, the three of us moved slowly from coffin to coffin, carefully examining every part of the contents; the shrouds, the skeletons, even the stones which had been used to weigh down the coffins.

Jacobs drew my attention to the wooden brackets which had been used to hold the stones in place. "These seem almost to have been part of the coffin construction, Coroner. Same type of wood, anyway."

I looked across at the policeman. "MacTavish, I think you'd better go and talk to the undertaker. Clearly what has been going on must involve him. That business of the break-in was just a ruse."

Sergeant MacTavish nodded. "I'll take one of the lads from the station with me. Mr Carruthers will have some questions to answer, all right."

Jacobs and I went on with our examination. There wasn't much to go on, but we located a couple of hairs trapped in a corner of the woodwork of one of the coffins. I pulled them out with a pair of tweezers and looked at them thoughtfully for a long time, not quite believing where my thoughts were leading me.

◑◑

Two days later, I went to see Sir Charles for the second time that week. I chose to see him in the evening, when I knew he would be home. I didn't want to carry on this conversation at his office.

Sir Charles was again in his library as the butler saw me in and quietly closed the door behind us. I was limping a little as I walked in; my damaged leg seemed to ache more when I was under stress, as I certainly was that night.

Once more I looked around at the splendid room: the expensive furniture, the deer heads, the books reaching to the ceiling on every side, and my skin prickled a little. All that wealth, all that tradition. It was intimidating, as I suppose it was intended to be.

Sir Charles rose from his leather armchair and looked me hard in the eyes. "You've done it, then? Dug up more graves? Do you have an answer?"

I shook my head. "Part of an answer. There's a lot I still don't know. I am hoping for your help in finding out the rest."

"You have suspicions, then. No proof. You had better tell me what you do know. Why don't you sit down?" He waved towards the other armchair.

I repressed my immediate visceral reaction. "No sir, I would rather stand, if you don't mind."

"Very well. I shall sit, however." And he did so. "Tell me."

"On Tuesday we found two more coffins like the earlier ones.

No sign of any flesh. On that basis, I ordered a few more targeted exhumations yesterday. We've now found a total of six such cases, including the first two. All of them relatively young people, none of them having suffered violent deaths. Does that suggest anything to you?"

Sir Charles looked grim. "No. Should it do so?"

"I believe it should. We also found some evidence in the coffins themselves. Some human hairs which didn't match the hair type, so far as we can tell, of the people interred. In total, in all of the coffins interfered with, we found a total of seven hairs. Two white ones, which we suspect may have come from old Carruthers, the undertaker. Three dark brown hairs and two shorter ones with a reddish tint."

"Hairs. It sounds rather flimsy as evidence to me." Sir Charles settled back in his chair and folded his arms.

"Yes, you are right, of course. Matching hair samples is notoriously unreliable, but still, the results were suggestive. They pointed me in a particular direction, which I have been busy researching over the last few days. What I have discovered is very interesting."

"Hmmm. What does Carruthers have to say about the matter?"

"The police went to question him again on Tuesday night, but he wasn't there. Not at his premises or in the attached residence. According to his staff, he had left town late on the previous evening, the night just before we started the new exhumations. He had left a brief note, saying that there had been a sudden unexpected death in the family, somewhere in Scotland. No details."

Sir Charles gave a slight smile. "Well, then, you can interview him when he comes back."

I paced to and fro for a moment, silent, trying to decide how to frame my words.

"I doubt that he will be back. I don't believe the story in the note. So far as we can discover, Carruthers had no relatives or even friends in Scotland. No, I think he fled because he was tipped off."

"A leak, then, in your department. Or the local police..."

"I have reason to doubt that, but I'll return to the matter later. I was telling you that I have been conducting some research. Financial research, rather out of the way for my position. I found out, for example, that the local graveyard is situated on land which used to be part of the Fellman estate. The title, it seems, is still in your family's name. Essentially, you own the graveyard, which is just leased for the community's use."

"That is no secret," Sir Charles said coldly, sitting up straight again and leaning forward, "but I cannot see what right you have to investigate my affairs."

I could see his anger, but I went on. "Furthermore, it seems that your family owns quite a large number of businesses. Through a couple of trust companies, for example, it seems that you own the local funeral director business, as well as some other such firms in neighbouring towns. Carruthers, it appears, is your employee."

He stood up, his face grim. "Where are you going with this nonsense? What are you saying?"

So now we had reached the heart of the matter. I felt a moment's uncertainty but pushed on. "I believe, Sir Charles, that Carruthers fled because *you* tipped him off."

"Me? Are you serious?" He paced about angrily, then moved over to his desk.

"You, Sir Charles, are the only person to whom I told my plans for Tuesday's multiple exhumations. It was a surprise even to my own staff. That fact, together with those dark brown and red hairs in the coffins, suggested to me that you might be personally involved."

His face was red with anger. "You're rambling, man. Making wild accusations! You're clearly incompetent. I shall certainly demand that your position be reviewed."

I went on, ignoring him, "The strange thing is," I said, "I am not even sure that a crime has been committed, unless it is simple theft."

"Theft? Theft of what, for God's sake?"

Here it came. "Theft of their skins, Sir Charles."

He shook his head, but he said nothing.

"What I imagine," I said, "is that you consider that what is in the graveyard or in a funeral parlour to be your own property, to be put to your own use. I am quite uncertain whether a charge of theft would stick. Are the dead their own property? Do they belong to themselves? It would be a nice judicial point."

He leant on the desk, arms outstretched, resting on his fists. "And your evidence for this ludicrous, this extraordinary, accusation is simply that the old undertaker had to make an unexpected trip north? That, plus some nonsense about my family finances? Really, David, this is beneath you."

I straightened my shoulders. "I do have one more piece of evidence. A strong piece of evidence. You gave it to me yourself. Do you recall that book you lent me of Rudyard Kipling's stories? A book that you had recently had bound in leather?"

His face changed, became like stone, both grey and cold. "Yes. I'd like it back, thank you."

"It will be returned to your estate. But I took the liberty of having a small piece of the leather examined microscopically and some chemical tests done."

Sir Charles was silent, but he slid open the desk drawer and pulled out something from inside it. A revolver, which he now aimed steadily in my direction.

I swallowed against the sudden dryness of my throat. Had I miscalculated? Nevertheless, I was compelled to go on.

"I can see that you know what we found," I said. "It wasn't calf leather or pig-skin. It appears to be tanned human skin. What I want to know, Sir Charles, is *why*?"

He laughed bitterly and looked defiantly at me. "Tradition, that's why. Centuries of tradition."

"*Tradition?*" I was bewildered, thrown off my stride. This was the last thing I had expected.

Sir Charles smiled, still aiming the gun unerringly in my direction. "Do you want to know my family history? I can assure you that I am proud of it. Do you know where the name Fellman comes from? It comes from the trade of my ancestor, Tobias. A fell-monger, a dealer in hides and skins. A smelly, unpleasant trade, it was considered in those days. Not much money in it."

He looked around at the accumulated wealth and luxury in the room, smiled and continued. "But Tobias also had a side-business, a lucrative one. He was secretly supplying cadavers and cleaned skeletons to the medical schools, digging them up from the local churchyards, or, I suspect, even knocking a few homeless souls on the head to supplement his supply. Sometimes he even had more bodies than he could sell. It seems that he was a parsimonious man, not wanting to waste anything, and he developed a special process. What he discovered is that human skin, properly treated, makes for the finest of leathers. Unique. Tobias discovered the best process to treat it. And he found that there was a market for it. A select market, which is prepared to pay highly. It still exists. As you can see, over the centuries it has made us rich and influential."

I was shocked, and took a step back. I had been convinced that Sir Charles alone of his family had succumbed to some recent psychological mania. I looked up at the ranks of books again. *All* of these books...? Was it possible? I shuddered.

His gun was still steady in his hand. "Alas, I can't let you tell anyone about my family's interesting history. It was foolish of you, David, to come here alone." He reached over and pressed a button on the wall. Summoning the butler, I thought, and realised with a sickening feeling that some at least of his staff must be aware of his secrets.

"Besides," he demanded, with another flare of anger, "who have we harmed with this? What use is a person's skin to them once they are dead? Why let it rot in the ground, wasted, when it can be turned into objects of beauty and comfort? That was what Tobias thought, and I think it also."

I swallowed, hardly crediting that Sir Charles was trying to justify himself. "You talked yourself," I said, "just the other night, about 'respecting the dead.'"

"You think my treatment was disrespectful? Not at all. That's why I returned the skeletons to the coffins instead of leaving them empty. In another fifty years, what will be the difference? All that will remain will be the bones, the coffins fallen apart, the stones lying unnoticed at the bottom of the grave."

The door behind me opened, I could feel the draft without looking around. Sir Charles looked towards it, no doubt expecting his butler. He wouldn't want to shoot me here. Too much mess on the expensive carpet.

"You were right," I said. "It *would* have been foolish of me to come here alone. That's why I didn't do it. Jacobs?"

"Coroner," Jacobs said from the open doorway. Sir Charles had turned white.

I didn't dare look away from Sir Charles' eyes. "Did you hear all of that, Andrew?" I asked, "And Sergeant MacTavish?"

"Mr. Jacobs was here the whole time, but I only heard the end of it," came MacTavish's voice. "I've been down in the cellars. There's a whole room hidden behind the wine cellar. It's a rather unpleasant sight. Vats of chemicals. Drying skins stretched out. And we found old Mr Carruthers in there, dead."

Sir Charles lifted the gun and looked at me with hatred. Would he shoot? Had I lost my gamble? I had had so little real evidence. The bluff had been necessary to get at the truth.

After a moment, he spoke, quiet and calm. "Hanging," he said, "stretches the skin abominably. Can't have that."

I jumped involuntarily as the gun went off, a shockingly loud sound in the room, muffled not at all by the ranks of leather-bound volumes. It was not myself but Sir Charles who fell dead, slumped over his desk, the gun smoking in his lifeless hand.

Demonslayer

LET ANY WHO CAN, HEAR MY TALE. Singlehandedly have I slain the demon Gorgoroth, which had laid waste to the place called Gehenna and terrorised and murdered travellers in that region for more than a thousand years.

Could I but return to my town of birth, all honours are due me. But I cannot return. I am trapped and bound by my own valour. Hear me, then, and pity me.

My tale begins in my youth, when, with my fellows, I would play at arms. fighting great battles with swords of wood and helms of cloth. We laid seige to many citadels, my comrades and I, though they were in truth no greater than a midden-heap. But in this way, at least, we learned the glory and joy of valour, and many of us vowed to be warriors when we grew to manhood. I boasted to my friends, vowing to be the greatest swordsman of all time, and in truth I believe that I have been faithful to this childish hope.

Often, when I was a child, I used to listen to tales told by the town elder, and it was from this aged one that I first heard tell of the terror of Gorgoroth, the demon who tore men apart with bare hands and ate their hearts raw. There is a road which leads through our town, leading in the east to the sea and to the ports. Westwards it winds into the mountains, to pass through the place called Gehenna and then on down to a city where many of the guilds have their home. For this reason there is often traffic on this long road, and often one lonely merchant has to make the perilous journey unaccompanied by any of his fellows. Many of these single travellers enter the pass called Gehenna and are never seen again. Even when travelling among many, men are oft snatched away from the van of the company before their fellows can help them. On these rarer occasions, men tell of seeing the demon itself: a great hairy beast shaped almost like a man, but twice the size, carrying off its luckless victim to its cave high in the hills.

This tale struck terror and fascination into our young hearts, but I. wishing to appear valiant, boasted that one day I would slay the demon and bring home his head for all to see. Half only of this boast have I fulfilled.

As the years passed, I became a man, and went off to the King's service, there to learn the skills of warriors and to fight in the wars against the southern hordes. Many enemies I killed then, and many acclaimed me as the greatest warrior they had seen. After seven years, my service was done, and I made my way homeward to bring tidings to my family and friends. When I reached my home, I recalled my childhood boast, and enquired whether or no the demon still ravaged in the mountains. The town elder, now more wrinkled and aged than ever, told me of it:

"Aye, the demon still lives, as it has these many years. It is immortal. Demons and dragons never die, nor can they yet be slain. The tales of dragonslayers are all empty wind, lad, do not heed them. "

"Nay," I said, "this can not be true: for no foe can stand against the touch of cold hard steel," and I showed him the great sword Sanglamore, carved with many runes, which hung at my side. "I have vowed to slay this demon, and I shall."

The aged one shook his head. "Others, many others have tried this thing. The legends tell of their setting out, but none ever return when they go against Gorgoroth. I remember the last who left this town to do this thing: Edouard Twoknifes, it was, a lionheart of a man. A score of years ago he left, and no mortal has seen him since. Do not go, lad, there is only death and no glory in Gehenna."

I mocked the old man then. and called him a fool, and kicked at him so that he fell and stumbled into the dust of the street. This I should not have done.

With pride and courage in my heart I began my quest in the bright morning, with my sword at my side and my helm of gleaming brass tied to my saddle, as I rode forth on the long journey towards the mountains. I was dressed in the finest of black livery, and my horse was a pure white stallion. There were crowds of women crying and children cheering, and great banners flying and the sound of trumpets. I was magnificent.

The next day I reached the foothills of the mountains. It was very clear, that day: everything I saw, every sound that I heard was sharp and fine. I paused my horse for a moment, looking up at the hills, and I loosened my sword in its sheath. I had taken that sword from a wizard of the Southrons, in return for my promise of his life. He had told me how he forged it, with great magic in the dark depths of the night, and he swore that it would slay any foe that it touched. To test that boast, I slew that wizard with his sword, and left. Wizards are not to be trusted.

Above the hills. an eagle flew, and the wind blew cold around me.

I urged my horse forward, and we passed over the small stone bridge that spans one of the streams that seem to encircle the mountains: a great river splits in the north into a myriad of small waters which pass on either side of the mountains. to rejoin in the south. As my horse and I went over the bridge, I felt a strange thrill, as of anticipation in my heart.

I had no plan of how I should seek out the demon Gorgoroth: if it did not show itself as I passed along the narrow road through the mountains, I would have to dismount and seek it in the high hills and rocky cliffs. I had food and water with me: I would seek it down though it ran from me for a score of days.

Yet as the fates would have it, I did not have to seek out Gorgoroth. the demon found me.

My horse was making slow progress where the road climbed steeply through a narrow pass: rocks overhung the road on either side. There came a sudden cry, as of a beast in pain, and a brown fury fell on the neck of my horse. My steed reared with the hellish thing now at its throat, and I was thrown to the ground, and near stunned.

When I looked up, the demon was tearing great gobbets of flesh from the neck of my horse: the animal was dead but still jerking. I was on my feet in a moment. and made to draw my sword. The demon, seeing my movement. leapt at me, and before I had time to move, plunged at me with one of its paws. I felt a cold, tearing pain in my left shoulder, and I dropped to the ground, my sword still in its sheath. I was back on my feet in an instant, but by then the monster was running up the hills, leaping from rock to rock like a mountain goat.

I can not describe what the demon resembled. if indeed it was like any other thing in the world this side of the grave. It was covered in brown fur, and had sharp, sharp claws, that is all that I can say. I could see no face.

I looked about me: the damage to my mission was very great. My faithful horse slaughtered and myself wounded, and as it seemed some of my provisions stolen. But I still carried my rune-sword, and I still had my courage. I would track the demon to his very lair, if need be. But first I must bind up my shoulder: this I did with strips of material torn from my livery. I then took some food and water, all the while keeping alert for the return of the demon, and then rested for a while. Then I set off up the slope after Gorgoroth.

The wound in my shoulder was painful, but it had stopped bleeding, and I did not fear that it would harm my ability. I had suffered greater wounds than this during the wars. I climbed the slope grimly and slowly. Rocks were all about: any one of them could have concealed the demon. I was alert and prepared this time.

But the demon was cunning, and hid from me. I could find no trace of its lair. I wandered the hills for hours. seeking, but caught no glimpse of it. The night drew on, and the shadows became long. Then I lodged myself in a narrow cleft between two rocks, my back to the stone, my sword in hand. I was confident that were I approached, I would wake easily in time to hew the demon in two. I slept, but dreams troubled me.

In the cold morning, I began to search again, and this time luck was on my side. Before the sun had yet risen over the mountain top, with the grey sky still heralding its light, I came on a shallow pool of water in a depression high in the slopes of the mountain. There were rough footprints about the murky water, and I knew then that this must be where the monster came to quench its thirst. I smiled gently to myself, knowing now that I must triumph, and hid behind a rock overlooking the pool to wait.

At last, it came. Shuffling along and making rough bestial sounds, it came down the faint trail to drink. A little way from the pool, it stopped and sniffed at the air, as if it could sense danger. I crouched hard against the cold stone and prayed that it would not catch my scent. But it stopped sniffing and came down to the water, bending and sucking up with loud, crude noises as it drank.

At that moment I leapt, Sanglamore my great rune-blade in hand, giving a battle cry. The demon looked up, started, and in that instant I saw that it had an almost human face, with bright eyes staring from its hellspawned head. It gave an incoherent shout, and tried to raise its claws against me, but my sword was swinging down, and it smote the monster's head from its neck as I fell on it. I was wounded by one of the demon's claws as it struck at me even in its death agony, and blood was spurting over me, but the demon was slain. It would waylay no more lonely travellers on the mountain road in Gehenna.

I stood up from the body of the demon, triumphant. I was covered in gore, and I was wounded savagely in my leg, but I raised my sword in glory, and placed it back in its sheath after wiping away the blood. All I need do was return to my town with the head of the monster to gain a hero's welcome, my childhood boast satisfied.

I came slowly down the slope, favouring my leg, to where my dead horse lay, his throat torn out by the demon's claws. I did what I could for my faithful steed, hoping that wolves would not find him too soon. I took what gear was left there, and began the slow walk back towards the town.

At last I came to the hills overlooking the stone bridge I had crossed days before. My leg wound was still paining me, yet I managed to stumble and run down the slope to that bridge, such was my joy and triumph.

But as I began to cross the bridge, a thing of mystery happened. As I half-ran, half-hobbled across. I was struck such a blow on my face that I fell down in a swoon. How long I lay insensible there, I can not tell. When I recovered my senses, my nose was bloodied, and my head still gave me pain. I stood and looked about to see what had struck me. There was nothing in sight, only the bridge and the muttering stream beneath.

I walked forward over the bridge cautiously. Suddenly I came to a halt. My outstretched hand had touched an invisible obstacle blocking the way back across the bridge. I rapped at it with my fist: it was as though someone had placed there before me a wall of the most exquisite crystal, so fine and clear as to evade the sight. A mystery indeed. I determined to knock at it with the pommel of my sword, to see if I could smash the crystal. And then an even stranger thing occurred.

The hilt of my sword passed through the wall as if it were the thinnest air. stopped only when my encircling fist reached the barrier. I knew then that there was great magic at work here. I tried the blade: it too swept through the wall as it would through a cloud; but my hand took a sharp knock when it reached the limit of this barrier, and it was all I could do to retain my grasp of the sword. There was no doubt: here was an artifice of powerful sorcery, created by some treacherous wizard. Perhaps the demon had been the familiar of this wizard, and by slaying it I had incurred his wrath.

I decided to test this thing. I went back over the bridge, and came down by the side of the brook. Wading across the cold, chilling water, I found the barrier lay there also,, centred in the middle of the water. It seemed to pass into the earth itself.

I had no choice. Before I could return and claim the glory due to me I would have to seek out this wizard and slay him as I had slain his demon. I rose out of the water and began the trek back into the mountains. In truth I was very weary, for my wounds pained me and my food was now gone, much of it having been stolen by the demon. But still I pressed on.

I spent a night and a day wandering the mountains in which I was enclosed by this diabolical wall of wizardry, and my weariness and hunger were great burdens. But I could find no sign of the sorcerer who must be enclosing me thus. What I found was the lair of Gorgoroth. There were many human bones there, gnawed by the demon's teeth. And also there was yet a portion of the provisions that the monster had stolen from me. I filled my belly gladly and my strength began to return. The lair was high on the mountain top, a dark cave with a view of the valley and the pass: travellers approaching would be visible from afar. I decided that this filthy hole was better than the open wind-swept mountain-side, and slept there that night.

The next morning, much refreshed, I espied a small figure on the trail: a traveller. I realised suddenly that all I need do to obtain assistance was to stop this man and ask him to tell my town to send me food and provisions and the help of a friendly wizard to free me from my crystal trap. I ran down the slopes in haste, limping hardly at all.

The man was a merchant: a skinny little fellow on a small pony, much bejewelled. A foolish man, if he did not fear brigands or the demon. I ran my hardest to catch him where the trail led out of the pass and began to descend towards the plains.

Suddenly, he saw me, and sat up in his saddle with a start. I hailed him as best I could, but I was out of breath in my haste and my voice came out only as a croak. Before I could form fair words, the skinny merchant gave a high shriek and dug his heels into his pony's flanks: the beast jumped and fled past me. I waved vainly as he rode away.

I realised then that I was not the image of nobility and valour that I had been when I rode forth on my mission: my livery was torn and stained with the demon's blood and my own: my face was similarly spattered and my hair and beard were awry and matted with filth. I was enough to frighten any skittish merchant. There was again no choice left open to me but to do as I had thought before: track down that damnable wizard who had so imprisoned me.

It took me five days to find the wizard's cave. By that time my food had run out again and I was bone-weary and greatly burdened with the weight of my misfortune. Byrol son of Bantor had never fallen so low in all of his battles before.

The cave was half-hidden by a huge boulder that stood in front of it, keeping out the sun. It was very dark within, and it took my eyes much time to adjust to the murk. The wizard was there, seated in a rough chair. He had been sitting there for a very long time, I would vow: only his bones remained, still sat upright. A death's head grin was all that greeted my challenge. Around the cave were scraps of things which long ago might have been herbs and medicines. There were dusty books which fell apart at my touch, and glass bottles filled now with nothing more than ashes. But on the table before the wizard's corpse was pinned a yellowed message. It was difficult to read. and parts were missing. But it went thus:

"Greetings, mighty warrior, to the abode of long-dead Carpathius, and hear of his death-spell. Thou art great in warrior's skills, and have suffered much to reach here. else thou would not have come. Know then my spell; he who slays the demon of Gehenna shall not leave that place... a barrier of most potent force shall keep him trapped: a force which shall only bind those who are known as heroes. Long ago I learned that heroes were more to be feared than demons or dragons: for the people allow heroes, even praise them, yet heroes slay more innocents than demons ever shall ... ... thee well, mighty warrior..."

I fumed. I raged. I tossed the dead bones of the wizard from his crumbling chair and threw them one by one down the mountain-side. Yet it was all to no avail. I was trapped in these mountains, and there seemed no way that I should ever again be free.

The days since then have been full of despair. My hunger is never satisfied. I have killed rabbits. since that day, and eaten them raw for lack of a fire. I hide against the cold at night in the demon's lair and watch the stars. Last week I ate what was left of my horse: there seem to be no wolves. The meat was bad: it made me sick.

My hair is getting long, I have no way to trim it. My livery is torn and in rags. I lost my helm of brass some days ago. Each morning I go to the pool where I slew the demon and see the face of a stranger: a wild man with horror in his eyes.

My hunger is intense. I chased a mountain goat this morning, up and down over the rocks, but it got away. My hunger is almost beyond endurance.

About an hour ago I spied a lone merchant coming along the trail. I will wait for him on a rock above the pass.

I hope he's fat.

No Direction Home

DUNCAN MASTERS HAD A MIGRAINE ON THE FLIGHT. The worst ever, with flashing zig-zags all across his right eye, and a raging pain in his head. One of the benefits of flying business class, though, was that it was easy to get prompt attention. A flight steward brought him a couple of pills. He swallowed them down and eventually the pain began to recede and his vision clear. He was able to drift off into what turned out to be a surprisingly deep sleep, though in normal circumstances he was rarely able to sleep on international flights.

He woke to find that the steward was tapping him on the shoulder and indicating that he needed to put on his seat belt. Duncan felt the sinking feeling that indicated the aircraft was now on descent. Blinking, still very drowsy and confused, he sat up and complied. He must have been really out of it. Perhaps it was some after-effect of his migraine? Or the pills he had taken? He shook his head, but that did nothing except give him a momentary stab of pain in his left temple.

The aircraft touched down safely, and a moment later the pilot made an announcement. But Duncan couldn't understand what she was saying. He frowned. The pilot must be speaking in some foreign language, and he'd missed the English version somehow. Perhaps he had dropped off again into a micro-sleep? He shrugged. It didn't matter.

After the plane had taxied to the gate, the usual bustle followed as everyone gathered their belongings and trooped off the plane. Duncan checked that he had his passport and the customs and entry forms, which thankfully he had filled in earlier on the flight. He wasn't sure that he'd be able to concentrate on them now.

Then he was in the long queue waiting to pass through border control procedures. Duncan idly looked around. There was something odd, which at first he couldn't put his finger on. Then it came to him. He couldn't see any signs in English. None at all. That was puzzling.

He was, of course, in a foreign country. In...in...where had he been heading? Impatient with himself, he forced himself to think. Europe. He was going to Europe, on business. He seemed to spend his life travelling to meetings or conferences. Where was it today? Italy, wasn't that where the conference was being held? But as he looked at the signs, trying to make sense of them, he was certain that none of were in Italian. He knew at least a smattering of that language, but the signs here weren't even written in a script he could understand. He could see shapes which must be letters on the signs, and knew that they must spell out something, but the shapes didn't connect in his mind with any sounds, let alone any meaning.

Then it came to him. Of course! For some reason, while he had been deeply asleep, the plane must have been forced to divert to another airport. Perhaps there had been an engine problem, or there had been an ash-cloud from some newly erupted volcano. Anyway, the plane had been forced to turn aside and land at an unplanned destination. Somewhere with its own language and its own way of writing. He felt reassured. There might be an annoying wait for another flight to Italy, but that was all. The airline would look after him, maybe put him up in a hotel if they had to wait for a long while.

He reached the immigration counter and handed over his passport and other papers. The middle-aged lady behind the counter looked them over, checked his face against the photograph in the passport, examined the forms. She pointed to one of the forms and asked him a question, which he didn't understand. She must be speaking in the language of this country, wherever it was. Duncan had a moment of panic, but decided simply to nod and hope. He smiled. A smile always defuses suspicion, doesn't it? In any case, it seemed to satisfy the official. She nodded in return and stamped the form and the passport, and Duncan went on. He felt very uncomfortable, though. He didn't even know where he was. That was an odd feeling.

What now? Well, he'd have to sort things out with the airline and see how long it would take to get another flight. He looked about, and finally recognized the logo of the airline over a service counter. As he went towards it, however, he started to become uneasy. He could recognize the symbol and the colors of the logo—it was impossible that he was mistaken about that. But the words underneath, and the sign on the counter in front of the attendant were written in the same incomprehensible script that he now saw everywhere.

There was another puzzle as he joined the queue. It was so short—there were only two people in front of him. But why weren't there dozens of passengers from the diverted plane queuing here to find out what the airline was going to do about re-booking them onto connecting flights? Perhaps...maybe...no, he *must* have missed an important announcement while he had been asleep. The pilot would have explained why they were being diverted and must surely have directed the passengers to go to a particular location once they disembarked. He had missed the instructions, that was all. A pity they hadn't been repeated. Still, the airline staff here would soon set him right.

He reached the counter. The customer service representative, a plump middle-aged woman, smiled and greeted him. He didn't understand the words, but her intent was obvious.

He launched into his account of how the plane had been diverted (although surely they knew that well enough by now?), and showed her his boarding pass. The woman frowned and asked him a question. But not in English.

"I don't understand," Duncan said. "Can't you speak English?"

The woman's frown deepened, and she said something else which Duncan didn't fathom.

Now, normally Duncan was a placid sort of person, able to cope easily with minor irritations, unlike some people he knew, who would start yelling and making demands if their pizza arrived a minute late or missing a topping. But this was all very annoying, and he was feeling more and more anxious. He started to become more animated.

"Why *don't* you speak English?" he demanded. "How can you work for an American airline and not speak English, for God's sake? Isn't there anyone here who can talk to me?"

The woman flushed at his angry tone, and she shook her head slightly before turning to a man standing not far away, obviously her supervisor. He approached and spoke to Duncan. But it was still in that maddening foreign language.

"Damn it, this is ridiculous!" Duncan said in a loud voice,

thumping his fist down on the counter. "Get a translator, then. Someone—anyone—who can understand plain English."

The man's eyes narrowed and he said something in a placating tone. He handed the boarding pass back to Duncan and shook his head.

Now Duncan was *really* angry. "For Christ's sake, I need to get to Italy. Italy! Italia! Rome! Roma! Capische?" He realized belatedly that he had begun to shout, but he couldn't stop himself. "Your damn airline brought me to the wrong place. It's your responsibility to fix it, to get me where I'm going. I swear I'm going to sue the airline and sue you personally if I don't get some help soon. Find someone who can understand me!" And he mimicked a mouth opening and closing with his hand.

The supervisor made calming motions with his hands and then pressed a button on the woman's console. Using simple signs, he indicated to Duncan that he should sit down on a bank of chairs opposite the counter.

Grumbling, Duncan did as he was bid. He tried to regain his composure. His doctor had been warning him recently about his blood pressure. All of this nonsense wouldn't be helping that, not one little bit.

There was something seriously wrong here. All of these signs in a script he couldn't read. All of these people speaking some incomprehensible gobbledygook. It was all wrong, wrong, wrong. He felt so alien, so out of place. There was a kind of continuous prickle of wrongness all over his skin. He shivered, tried to breathe slowly and steadily.

A minute later, though, and his blood pressure must have shot up alarmingly again. Two burly security guards came up to the counter, and the supervisor pointed at Duncan. The men turned towards him, and one drew out a taser.

Without a moment's hesitation, Duncan leapt to his feet, and abandoning his carry-on bag, ran for his life.

The guards shouted and raced after him, but panic drove him to run faster still.

A trolley piled high with luggage trundled in front of Duncan, but he dodged behind it, and shoved at the orange-uniformed man pushing the trolley so that he stumbled and fell over with a cry.

Hidden by the piled luggage, and briefly out of sight of the pursuing guards, Duncan dodged around a corner. There were shops everywhere here, selling handbags and jewelry, duty-free alcohol, cameras and so on. He hurried through a camera shop and then into a bookstore. He moved quickly behind a rack of magazines, then picked one up and held it in front of his face. After a moment, he risked a peek over the top of the magazine and saw the two guards run by, not looking in his direction.

Duncan waited for some time, letting his breathing and heart rate settle back to a normal pace. After all, what had he done wrong? Nothing, really, except lose his temper. That had been a mistake.

What should he do now? It was clear that he wasn't going to get any sense out of the airline staff here at the airport. He spent a little time enjoying thinking about the furious letter that he would write to the airline once he got back home from here. Wherever *here* was. He glanced at the magazine he was holding in front of him. Though he was pretending to read it, it was incomprehensible, as were all of the others in the rack he was standing behind. Not one of them was readable, all were in that bizarre foreign language.

About five minutes later, still hiding behind the magazine, he glimpsed the baffled guards heading back towards the airline counter. He abandoned his thoughts of going back there for his carry-on bag. There was nothing in it which he couldn't easily replace. He needed to get out of the terminal, get into the city. There was sure to be an American consulate there. He'd find that, and they would help him.

Avoiding going anywhere near the airline counter, he found his way to the baggage collection area, following a series of standard universal icons which were impossible to mistake. He grabbed his suitcase, by now the only item still circulating on the loop, and headed for the exit, also indicated by a familiar icon. He waited patiently in the queue for a taxi.

The driver popped the trunk and threw Duncan's bag in. Then he climbed back into the driver's seat and said something, a question. Duncan didn't understand a word, but it was obvious he was being asked where he wanted to go. For a moment he was baffled. How could he direct the driver without knowing his language?

But it was daylight, and in the distance, Duncan could see the skyscrapers of a modern city. He simply pointed. "There!" he said, and the driver shrugged and started off.

It was quite a long ride, and on the way Duncan was looking out at every building. Not a single sign bore any words he understood, not even on the billboards for familiar brands like Coca-Cola, though he recognized the logo easily enough. This is was a *strange* country. Again, that shiver and unease, that feeling of being out of place, an utter alien.

The taxi reached what was clearly the central business district of the foreign city. Foreign, but judging by the dress and coloring of the majority of the people on the street, it was a Western society, or one heavily influenced by it. Yet what such society used a written script which he couldn't pronounce, let alone read? Duncan racked his brains, but couldn't think of any such place.

The driver was asking him another question. Judging by his annoyed expression, he must have been asking for some time. "Oh, here, here," Duncan said, and pointed to the nearby sidewalk. He would get out and walk, ask everyone he met if they could direct him to the American consulate. It might take a while, but he would get there.

First, though, he had to pay the driver, who now had his hand out and was looking suspiciously at Duncan. "How much?" Duncan asked. He'd be damned if he would give the man a tip. The driver tapped the display on his meter. Duncan looked at the brightly-lit red LEDs. He couldn't understand what they were showing. That gave him pause. Surely *everywhere* used standard Arabic numerals, which looked like...which looked like...he frowned. His head hurt. A common LED display like that shouldn't be showing numbers he couldn't understand. It didn't make any sense.

The driver was becoming impatient, and angry. He shouted at Duncan. Desperate, Duncan pulled out his wallet. He didn't want to risk any problem with his credit cards, so he pulled out a bunch of notes and started handing them to the man. American banknotes. US dollars were acceptable almost everywhere, weren't they? At any rate, there was no problem. The driver's angry expression vanished, and he took three notes—two Jacksons and one Grant—before refusing the rest. Did that include a tip? Who could tell?

Then, as Duncan started to put the money back into his wallet, he stopped. He looked hard at the notes. Really hard. He recognized the engravings of the Presidents. He had two Benjamin Franklins, three Ulysses S. Grants, two Lincolns and a handful of Washingtons. But *every single word* on the notes was incomprehensible. The figures in the corners were surely numbers. *What* numbers, though? Duncan found that he didn't know.

The taxi driver was becoming impatient again, and Duncan stumbled out. The driver popped the boot and brusquely handed Duncan his case, spat what sounded like a curse, and then drove off with a squeal of tires.

Duncan stood on the sidewalk, glancing down at the money and then back up at his surroundings.

With a sinking, sickening feeling, he pulled out a couple of his credit cards. The logos were familiar, and he knew the cards were his own—he recognized that scratch across the corner of his Amex card. But the words... he couldn't read any of the words, nor recognize the digits.

There was something wrong, all right. But for the first time Duncan realized that what was wrong was *him*.

He stopped the first person who came by, who shrugged him off with an oath. Then the next, and the next. "Help me," he pleaded.

No one understood.

We, the Dead

I LAY ON THE BED, AND I FELT MY LIFE COMING TO AN END.

It was night, the darkest hours after midnight. That time when the human spirit is at its weakest, when every dread is magnified and every hope revealed as futile.

As I lay alone in that darkness, all of the regrets of my life seemed to be dropping down upon me: all of the things that I wished I hadn't done, and all of the things that I hadn't done which I wished I had. They fell upon me, mounted up and began to crush me; their heavy weight gathered in the center of my chest.

I'd always worked too hard; that was at the heart of it. Absorbed by the mental discipline of my profession as a civil engineer, relishing the creative challenges, I had spent long hours in the office away from my wife and young children. Too many hours. There had been arguments, bitter arguments. In the end, Sophia had taken my two sons away, and rarely let me see them. The boys were in their teens now, and although I tried to keep in touch, they never called me by choice.

So now I was alone, with a pile of stone settling on my chest, and I was dying.

The weight grew heavier still. Then came a moment when my life seemed to suddenly recede; a slow ebb at first, and then a rapid retreat, like that racing withdrawal of the sea from a beach which ominously foretells the coming tsunami.

But there came no returning wave, and I knew that I was dead.

Time passed, a time without measure.

I was dead. And yet, and yet... I was dead but not yet gone. A long, long time went by as I puzzled over this paradox.

At last, hour by hour, the darkness of the night began to ease, and light slowly grew. Beyond my window, a grey, grey dawn arrived, revealing a cold mist lying over the city buildings. Condensation ran down the window and obscured every detail. Every sound seemed distant, far away: someone arguing, a dog yapping, a truck reversing with its beep-beep warning signal.

Inside the room, too, everything seemed to be filmed with grey. I surveyed it all with little emotion, as though I were floating high above it. The small, anonymous room of a man whose interests had been elsewhere. A well-equipped desk, the better to go on working while not at the office. A bare kitchen, the kitchen of a man who lived alone on take-out food. A wardrobe. A chest of drawers and on it a faded photograph with the smiling faces of a once-happy family. A bed.

A body lay on the bed. It was mine. With that realization, my viewpoint seemed to fall from its high vantage above the room and collapse back into the body.

Reposing there in cold silence, I finally came to understand that although I was dead, I was still trapped inside this useless slab of flesh. Panic fluttered up then. I felt a terrifying sense of claustrophobia and I gasped in despair.

The chest of the body rose, and air entered its lungs. The panic receded a step. It still worked, then, this mechanism of meat.

I lay contemplating this fact. As I lay, my memories of an earlier life, even my memory of what it meant to be alive, seemed to be fading. This gross, physical object felt so distant, so unconnected with my spirit. I felt no ownership of it, and I seemed to have forgotten even the names of its various components.

Would it obey my will? Could I animate it in some way? I tried willing an upper limb to lift. On my first and second attempts, the limb remained motionless. But on the third attempt, concentrating hard, the length of flesh and bone did indeed rise, and I felt an absurd sense of triumph. Try the other limbs, then. One by one, with an intense effort of will, I was able to make all four extremities respond to my command.

What now?

What was the point of all this effort? Now that I was dead, why not just remain at peace here on the bed? I wondered how long it would take my body to begin to putrefy. It would start in a few days, I imagined. Or perhaps given the coolness of the season, it might take as long as a week. Would my body have to dissolve completely away to set my spirit free? That could take much longer. An interminable time to wait. And besides, something outside seemed to be calling me, something far away. I felt an overwhelming urge to go to it.

However hard and futile it might seem, I had to make an effort. I had to find a quicker way to free myself from this cage of meat.

Propping the body up and making it stand was a very difficult exercise. I had to summon my professional expertise and treat it as an engineering problem of weight, tension and stress. That knowledge, that life, all seemed so remote now. Still, I managed it at last.

The body was upright. How unstable the whole thing was! It swayed back and forth as I tried to control the shifting balance. It took intense concentration, but I began to learn how to manage it at last. It stood, a little unsteadily, but not about to topple.

Directly in front of me was a full-length mirror set into the sliding door of the wardrobe. It took me long minutes to recognize that the image I saw there was a reflection of my own body.

Slumped shoulders. Slack stomach, revealing an incipient paunch. Dark hair, receding. Eyes vacant and bloodshot. Gray, sagging face. An ugly, ugly thing, from which I recoiled. I was trapped inside this loathsome thing, cloaking my true spirit.

I had to turn away from the mirror in disgust, and in so doing I took my first steps since I had died. Lumbering, lurching steps, but I managed to keep the body upright. Impelled by the urge to escape, I propelled it towards the window and looked out.

There was still some fog over the more distant buildings in the old city centre, but here I could see clearly down to the street. All of the colors were muted, barely more than shades of grey. Cars and trucks moved slowly in the heavy morning traffic, bleating their anger.

Behind me, I heard the bedside alarm click on and begin playing a radio station. It was badly tuned and full of static, but I heard snatches of a news report: "....hospital authorities welcome a recent improvement..." I could barely comprehend the words, and I ignored it.

On the opposite side of the street, a woman came out of a doorway and staggered awkwardly along the sidewalk. She was naked, breasts flopping as she swung from side to side, black hair on her head and at the junction of her legs. Naked, her flesh a blue-grey in the cold morning air.

I looked on dully, without much interest, as cars stopped and passers-by reacted to the woman and halted her progress. Someone brought out a blanket from a car boot and wrapped it around her. She showed no recognition of this and continued to try to walk down the street until prevented by the crowd now surrounding her. She made ugly, incoherent sounds and struggled. But she was overpowered and soon I heard the distant sound of an ambulance siren.

She's dead, I thought. Like me. Why are you bothering her?

It was then that I felt the urge again, stronger than before. I had to leave this building, had to travel to... to where? At that moment, I wasn't sure. All I knew then was that I had to get away, find someone or something to get me out of this physical trap. The naked woman had been trying to go there, too. That only made sense.

I looked down with a shudder at my horrible flesh. All it had on was the white singlet and boxer shorts in which I had slept. I knew that I needed to cover the body, so that people in the street wouldn't seek to stop me the way they had stopped the naked woman. If she had been clothed, I thought, people would not have bothered her.

In the wardrobe was a long black coat made of some thick woolen material. Discovering how to command the body's upper limbs ("arms"?) so that they would push through the coat's sleeves was an exhausting, frustrating exercise, but I managed it at last. It hung loose at the front, and it was beyond my skill to fasten its buttons or the belt. But once I had placed my forelimbs into the coat's pockets, I found that I could pull it together to hide my flesh.

Every move was a struggle of will managing to triumph over recalcitrant flesh. Opening the apartment door took an age, but I persisted.

A corridor outside. I directed the body along it towards the elevator. A young woman was standing there waiting, stepping in as the doors opened. I had known her once, hadn't I? My neighbor. She had a label – a "name"? – which I must once have known, what was it? I couldn't bring it to mind and simply followed her into the elevator.

As the doors closed behind me, the woman looked up at me. Its – *her* – mouth started in one shape, but rapidly changed to another, and she cowered back into a corner of the elevator with a sharp sound.

I knew that I should make some noises back at the woman. But that involved very difficult control of the vocal apparatus of the body I was trapped inside. Trying to do that while also managing the business of balancing the body on its lower limbs was nearly impossible. All I could manage was a grunting sound. The woman cringed further back into the corner, and I turned my body away.

It was only three stories down. The elevator doors opened, and I directed my body out. Glass doors slid apart in front of me and I was out into the street.

Across the roadway, I caught a glimpse of a headline outside a news agency: "Road Deaths Drop". I could recognize the words, but it meant little to my clouded mind.

Moving the body was like a continuous toppling fall, each step a hairsbreadth away from disaster. But at least I was making progress, pulled along by the urge I had felt in the apartment. Somewhere ahead, towards the centre of the city, something was drawing me onwards. I walked on. None of the people in the street tried to stop me, and I congratulated myself on putting on the black coat.

After a while, I began to be aware of unpleasant sensations arising from the lower extremities of the body. I looked down, and immediately lost control of its balance. I fell forward and managed to bring up its upper limbs only just in time to prevent the head cracking into the hard sidewalk surface.

I pushed the body over so that the face was upwards, and looked along its length. The lower appendages ("feet"?) were bare of any covering. From somewhere far distant in my mind I recalled that when I had been alive, I would have protected these appendages with some form of covering. It didn't matter.

My own desperate and burning desire was to be rid of this clumsy thing. Its state of repair was of no concern to me.

As I went through the complicated exercise of returning my body to an upright position, an elderly woman glared at me, and called out: "You damn drunk! Get off the street!". It meant nothing to me.

Finally, with the body back up again, teetering precariously on stiff lower limbs, I set off again towards the source of the urge.

All color was washing out of the world, like a photograph left too long in the sun, leaving only pastel shades of blue and grey. Above, I saw that a faint mist was still shrouding the higher towers of the city. The sun was a vast watery patch of light.

I reached an intersection and turned into a wider thorough-fare. It was then that I first recognized that I was not alone.

Now that I paid attention, I could hear the wailing of sirens from many different directions. Here in this street, traffic had come to a halt. People were standing in the roadway, yelling up at the driver of a large white truck. He was sitting in the cab, his hands no longer on the wheel, his eyes empty, staring forward, his face drooping. Another one of the dead.

On the footpath, a tall woman dressed only in a thin night-shift walked ahead of me, stiff-legged, long dark hair trailing in tangles down her back. People were stopping to stare at her. A man in a grey suit said something to me, pointing down at my body's bare feet. I hugged the black coat tighter, and went on, not wanting to be stopped.

Others. There were others now. As I walked on, I began to see more and more of the dead. Many were scantily clothed, those, I assumed, who had died in their sleep like me. Others more fully dressed, but their faces immobile, their gaze fixed. There must be more of the dead behind me, I thought, but I dare not risk toppling the body by looking back.

Some of the dead seemed to be wandering at random, but many were moving in the same direction as myself, along the street towards the river and the old city centre beyond.

I could hear screams now, here and there. And more sirens. Then I heard a distinctive chopping sound. Above, in the still-misty sky, I saw the spinning blades of a helicopter.

The non-dead (the "living"?) were beginning to panic now, scattering from the sidewalk into the roadway to avoid us. In the near distance I heard a gunshot, then another. I couldn't understand these events. Were these people *afraid* of us? All they had to do was to leave us alone and let us go on, to whatever it was that was drawing us.

Just as I approached a narrow lane-way on my right, a trash-can toppled forward out of it, its contents whirling across my path: drink-cans, bottles, moldy sandwiches, food wrappings. I looked into the lane-way. A large man had fallen there, knocking over the trashcan. He was dressed in red-striped pajamas and was struggling to get up, his limbs stiff and awkward.

Grasping a drain-pipe with one of my body's upper appendages ("hands"?), I stretched out the other to the man so that he could pull his body up. He stood, pieces of trash falling from his pajamas. A bulky man, beer-gut prominent, his hair orange-red. His face was slack and expressionless, unshaven and freckled. But in his eyes I caught a glimpse of gratitude. It was enough. We went on together.

The helicopter flew lower, the beats of its rotors loud now. Above its sound, I could hear someone yelling through a megaphone. It was all meaningless. None of it could be applicable to the dead. The red-headed man and myself, and dozens of others, continued to walk on, drawn irresistibly on towards the river, and the bridge.

The streets were now beginning to empty of the living, as they ran from us. Cars, hopelessly stuck in the traffic jam, were being abandoned. I saw a white sedan with a woman inside trying to open the driver-side door. Her face was blank, her eyes distant, as she scrabbled clumsily and apparently without method at the door. I glanced at RedHead, and he stepped into the street. Apparently without effort, he wrenched at the car door and it came open with a shriek of metal. The woman, dressed in a dark pant-suit, climbed jerkily out and came to join us on the sidewalk. Together, we walked on.

I had no sense of time passing. It could have taken us ten minutes or ten years to reach Centenary Plaza, with the modern City Hall at the far end.

Ranks of policemen in riot gear were hurrying into place to form a line across the plaza. *Do they think we are here to protest?* I wondered in a remote part of my mind. *To complain about the most recent rate hike?* If I could have remembered how to laugh, I would have done it then.

I heard a megaphone bellow again. Some kind of demand that we disperse. But that was impossible. We were being drawn on, compelled to advance and cross the river that lay beyond the park behind City Hall.

There were perhaps a hundred of the dead now, with more joining the crowd with every moment. We walked on towards the line of police.

Canisters trailing smoke came arching towards us, bouncing among our bodies' lower limbs, then exploding in great clouds with a dull thud. My vision became impaired and my body began to have difficulty in bringing in enough air to keep it operating. But I found that with an effort of will I could over-come these problems. PantSuit, RedHead and I kept on moving forward together. On either side of us, all of the other dead did the same.

Through the clouds of mist, I could see the police standing shoulder to shoulder, wearing helmets and gas-masks. We, the dead, moved closer and closer, slowing to a stop before the ranks of police. We stood there in silence.

The police were nervous, shuffling in indecision, some of them tentatively raising their heavy batons and shields.

Immediately in front of me was an old lady in a flannel night-gown patterned with small violet flowers. She, like so many of us, must have died in her sleep. I couldn't see her face, but I could hear her body gasping for breath as she struggled to cope with the tear gas. Still, she was managing to keep it upright. She took a step forward.

The young policeman confronting the old woman stared down at her as though in disbelief. He raised his baton suddenly, as though to strike her, then suddenly dropped it down to his side again. She took another step, almost stepping onto his boots. A moment later, and he had turned to run, discarding baton and shield. To my right, I could see another gap open up as another police officer did the same.

A bulky policeman wearing sergeant's insignia tore off his gas mask and yelled after the defectors, to no avail. He turned back to face the crowd of dead, his face red with anger, his eyes weeping from the remaining effects of the tear-gas.

Then I saw him die.

He stiffened, and all of the color ran out of his face, from forehead to chin, like the water draining from a bath, leaving his face as white as paper. His eyes unfocused, and his arms dropped to his side like lead weights. His knees buckled, and he fell forward with a limp thud onto the paving.

It triggered a wave of panic, and the police line broke. The dead stepped forward.

As I passed the sergeant, I touched the arm of RedHead at my side. Locking our upper limbs together for balance, we used our feet to roll the man over onto his back. Red fluid ("blood"?) oozed from his nose, and his eyes stared vacantly upwards. I saw that it was too soon for him to join us, and so we left him and went on. The crowd passed on either side of the City Hall and on towards the park.

There were hundreds of us now. Above, helicopters swung back and forth in thundering impotence.

The city park ahead of us was a modest affair the size of a single city block, but planted with many trees and featuring a small ornamental lake. I could see a few of the police rallying and two of them began to stretch out coils of barbed wire in front of the greenery in an attempt to halt our progress. That done, they ran.

Night-Gown Lady ahead of me encountered the wire first and began to pull it taut between two of the trees. I could see the barbs slashing into the flesh of her body. She began to struggle, but she was quickly entangled in the coils, and could make no further progress. Blood began to ooze from the cuts in her arms as she flailed at the wire.

Moving to one side of her, I felt the wire begin to cut into my own body, and rip the flesh of my arms and chest. But I kept pushing forward insistently. The urge to go on was now stronger than ever.

I was not alone. We, the dead, pushed hard against the wire. There were only a few strands, quickly laid, and as we pushed forward remorselessly, it was pulled through the trees and here and there stretched and snapped, was trampled down and broken.

I still faced an intact length of wire, but I was able to back away for a moment and free myself by letting my arms slide out of my heavy coat, which had been caught in the barbs. The coat then made a bridge and I was able to step on it and over the wire, though several long barbs came through and penetrated the soles of my body's naked feet. Fluid began to leak out of them.

RedHead and PantSuit followed my footsteps. I could do nothing for NightGown, though. She was hopelessly entangled, though she kept trying to move forward despite the wire. In time I might have been able to help, but the urge to go on, on, drew us away.

The lake was shallow, and in a ragged line we crossed it, splashing.

On the other side of the park we reached the river bank. Well to our right was the bridge leading to the historical centre of the city, with its many cultural buildings and churches including the magnificent St Mark's Cathedral. As soon as I saw the cathedral I knew that it was my destination, the source of the urge which drove me onwards.

As we left the park, our numbers were spread wide, but as we neared the bridge we were forced to funnel together. RedHead, PantSuit and myself had been towards the left of the crowd, and now we found ourselves well back from the front as it moved onto the bridge.

The bridge was blocked.

Somehow it had been cleared of vehicles, and half-way along it was a barrier, made up of short stretches of metal fence embedded into concrete footings. In front of it, more barbed wire. Behind it, soldiers, and two armored cars. Low-flying helicopters roved up and down over the river surface.

Someone was yelling through yet another megaphone, but what he had to say was difficult to make out over the noise of the helicopter blades whenever one drew near.

"Go back," came the voice. "...victims of suspected biological warfare... will be treated... cannot allow you... suffering from ICS... Induced..."

The swelling crowd of dead ignored the incoherent shouting and pushed forward onto the bridge. There was the sudden snap of a rifle, and I saw a body fall at the leading edge. Another snap, another body down. More yelling through the megaphone.

I put a hand on RedHead at my right. I tried to control the speaking apparatus of my body to communicate with him, but it was too difficult. Only clumsy sounds came out. Still, I pulled at him, and pointed to one side of the bridge. I turned to Pant-Suit and did the same.

I knew this bridge. That distant part of me which had been an engineer had once been part of its design and construction, decades before.

Pushing through the crowd of slack, vacant faces, we moved off the roadway and down the slope of the riverbank to the cycle path, and then under the bridge. The urge pulled at me, demanding, implacable. I *had* to get my body across the river. Only then, I knew, could I be free of it at last.

In the deep shade beneath the bridge, against the concrete support, there was a metal ladder locked in a retracted position several yards above the ground, too high for any one of us to reach. I pointed, and RedHead turned to PantSuit. Without a word, he made a cradle with his hands, and the tall body of the woman stepped into it. He boosted her up with effortless strength. She reached up her arms and I saw the fabric of her jacket begin to tear as she stretched. Finally, she caught hold of the lowest rung of the ladder and began to swing her body up.

Above us on the bridge, I could hear more bellowing, distorted now even when the helicopters weren't near. "...will be treated... your condition... induced Cotard Syndrome... please halt... forced to..." And again the snap of rifle fire.

RedHead had found a metal bar on the ground It might have been part of a discarded screwdriver, or a piece of the bridge structure which had fallen away. He tossed it up to PantSuit, straddling a metal beam above, her once-neat business clothing now covered with dirt and grease. She caught the bar and began to use it to work on the rusty old padlock attached to the ladder.

With an awful clang, the lower length of the ladder dropped down. I led the way up, RedHead following me. At the top, we were able to step onto a narrow walkway used for bridge inspections, rarely used these days and poorly maintained. It was filthy with soot and grease. PantSuit clambered up from the beam to join us.

We began to cross. PantSuit went first, with RedHead following. I came behind.

To one side, I could hear the approach of one of the helicopters, and on the surface of the river I saw the characteristic radial pattern of the downwash from its blades. From above, more incoherent shouting from the officer with the megaphone, and again a few snaps of rifle fire.

I wondered how many of the dead there were now in the city, all of them entombed within their bodies. I had seen hundreds myself, but perhaps by now there were thousands, and more each moment dying where they stood like the police sergeant. Was my wife, were my sons, among them? Once, that would have mattered terribly to me, and even in my dulled state I felt a pang of sorrow at the thought. But there was no way for me to know their fate.

With every step beneath the bridge, I felt the awful drag of my own imprisoning body. How I yearned to be free of it!

The suspended walkway swung and shuddered beneath the weight of our bodies. Rust fell in showers from the attachment points above. Below, through the open metal grid of the walkway, I could see the brown surface of the river gliding by.

Halfway across, I heard the shriek of metal. PantSuit was several paces ahead, still moving, but RedHead had stopped. To his left, one of the suspension rods came loose from its attachment above, and then swung down like a pendulum. A moment later, there was another shriek, and the next rod in line also gave way and the walkway began to twist and tilt. RedHead had been thrown off balance and was tottering and sliding to the left.

I willed my body to grasp the rod to its right and grip it with all the strength it could manage. Then I lunged forward to reach for RedHead, but could grip only the cloth of his pajama top as he toppled away. His body was big and weighty, and even though my grasp swung him around so that I could see his face, I felt the cloth begin to tear. His face was as slack and expressionless as ever, as I knew my own would be. But even in his eyes I saw no fear, only a calm acceptance. A moment later, the pajama top ripped free in my hand, and he plunged without a sound into the opaque waters below. After the splash, there was no further sign of him.

I stood gazing at the water for a long time. I finally looked up to see PantSuit standing quietly beyond the broken section of walkway, waiting for me. She stretched out her body's arm, but it was too far off to reach. One side of the walkway was still attached above, but my engineer's brain recognized that the remaining attachment points must have been severely stressed and were likely to break under my body's weight. Still, there was no alternative. The urge to go on was as strong as ever.

Still holding on to the suspension rod to my right, I reached my body's left arm out to grasp the next rod forward on that side, my feet placed on the now tilted edge of the walkway. More rust fell and groans of tortured metal came from above, but in this way, rod by rod, I was able to maneuver my body across the damaged section until I could reach an arm out to hold on to PantSuit's limb. Even as I swung myself across, another suspension rod behind me gave way and we both lurched a little sideways. But then we were past the weakness, and moved on across the river.

At the other side, we were able to drop safely to the ground from the walkway, though this caused some distracting signals from my body's feet. This wasn't disabling, however, and I walked cautiously up the river bank, with PantSuit following.

I retained enough sense to keep us out of sight. I lay my body down and peered through a gap in the railings. We were now behind the soldiers on the bridge. Beyond the barrier part-way across I could see massed the silent ranks of the dead. The officer with the megaphone was still trying to shout commands, though his voice was hoarse.

"Return to your homes. You *are not dead!*" came the voice, almost pleading. "Medical treatment..."

His words were futile, and meaningless. We knew our own state better than he did.

I looked across the river to the part of the city from which we had come. I could see crowds of still figures standing on the far river bank. Here and there some were attempting to make their bodies swim – but the current was strong, and the motions of swimming are complex to control. Heads in the water sank out of sight even as I watched. None managed to reach even half-way across the river.

Now PantSuit and I faced a problem. We had crossed the river; but now we needed to move further into the old part of the city. I needed to reach the Cathedral, which was several blocks away. But there seemed to be soldiers everywhere in the streets, and above us, the helicopters still ranged back and forth. Although their focus was on the other side of the river and the massed ranks of the dead attempting to swarm across the bridge, it was only a matter of time before someone spotted PantSuit and me.

I looked down and along the river bank. Not far from the bridge, to our left, there was a grilled opening spilling water down a concrete gutter into the river. Around the opening, wild swirls of graffiti indicated that teenagers had been active there. I indicated the opening to PantSuit, and together we slipped down the grassy slope to the bicycle track that ran on the river's edge. It took only a minute to reach the opening – though it was a minute during which at any second we could have been spotted by the panicked military.

The grill was old, and broken in several places. Deliberately broken, or more likely cut, I thought. I distantly recalled the council's battle to keep young people from exploring the city's underground waterways.

In any case, it was not difficult to squirm our bodies between the remaining bars and for us to enter the storm-water drain. It was too small for us to stand, but we could make progress on all four limbs. There was a steady stream of water at the bottom of the drain, and here and there smaller side-drains jetted water over our heads, but it was not enough to prevent us moving forward.

As we moved away from the opening, the light grew dimmer and dimmer, and then we were in almost complete darkness. After a long while, there was a faint light from above, and I could see there was a vertical shaft with embedded rungs, leading up to a grill. I looked at PantSuit, following me, and shook my head. The urge was pulling us on, and we had not yet gone far enough. So, we moved on forwards, back into the darkness. With every inch gained, I cursed the miserable and now damaged shell of flesh which surrounded me.

We passed a second vertical shaft but went on, splashing, into the darkness again.

The third time we reached a vertical shaft, it felt right. I stood and began to climb my body up the rungs. At the top, a metal hatch, perforated with several openings which let in a dim light. I lifted the hatch, and it fell with a clang to the sidewalk. I looked out.

At first, the streets here seemed empty of both soldiers and civilians. But then I spotted a few staggering figures approaching. More of the dead, who like PantSuit and myself, had managed to evade the military. Or else those who had fallen dead here on this side of the river? No way to tell.

I climbed from the shaft and then turned and looked towards the Cathedral, now no more than a hundred yards away. And I saw fire.

A rough barricade had been piled across the street. Furniture, barrels, trash, lumber, whatever had been to hand. I could see people beyond it, still throwing items onto the heap. And someone had just set fire to it. Even as I watched the flame gained strength and began to spread.

PantSuit had emerged from the shaft and was now again at my side, her clothes and hair dripping with filthy water. Without a word, we began to move our bodies forward towards the fiery barricade. Slowly, clumsily at first, faster, then we were both loping at speed. I leapt at the barricade just as the flames covered it. Up, climbing, reaching for handholds – the leg of a chair, the edge of a burning desk. Up, and I was at the peak.

Behind me, a hand flailed at my body's lower limb, and I saw that PantSuit had become trapped, a rough length of wood piercing her jacket and preventing her from climbing. Flames were all about us now, but I forced my body to seize the piece of wood. A nail embedded in the wood pierced through its palm, making more blood leak. But I grasped it firmly and threw my weight back. It ripped loose from her clothing, and PantSuit was free. She scrambled through the fire and I followed.

Up and over, and into the street. I heard screams, and before us, people scattered in terror.

Smoke and steam came from our clothing. More distracting sensations came from my imprisoning body. I ignored them. They were unimportant. I was almost at the source of the urge which had driven me.

One person did not run as we emerged from the flames. A young Catholic priest. He was holding up a crucifix and declaiming something in Latin. We paid him no attention.

PantSuit reached out an arm and rested her body's hand on my shoulder. Her face was black with soot, her hair singed on one side. She looked into my eyes and there was a sensation of farewell. Then she turned and ran past the gesticulating priest and on into the city. Whatever the source of her own urge, it was not the same as mine.

I looked away from her, just in time to see a grey-haired older priest storm up behind the younger one, grab something from him, and throw it over me. Water. Only with its cold shock did I realize that my hair must have been on fire.

"You bloody fool," said the older man to the younger. "Don't you see that these are just ordinary people? People deserving our help? You! And you! And you!" he said, pointing at the cowering bystanders. "Get buckets of water. Put out this damned fire before anyone else is burnt." Under his fierce gaze, men and women ran.

I stood before him, my arms slack, faint wisps of smoke still coming from my clothing and my burnt hands and feet.

The priest's face was crinkled in an expression I interpreted as concern.

"My son," he said. "You need urgent medical help. But the city's resources, as I understand, are already desperately stretched in this emergency. Come with me and we will administer what first aid we can." He took hold of my body's upper arm, away from its burnt hand, and began to lead me towards the Cathedral.

As he went, he turned to the younger priest and to the shame-faced men and women in the street. "Pull down the barricades. Let the others come through."

The young priest objected. "But there are hundreds, Father. Hundreds of zombies!"

The senior priest was angry. "Not zombies, Richard. *People!* And they need our help. Let them come. Now, round up all of the medical supplies you can. Organize the community. I want to talk to this man first. I need to understand what has been going on."

Inside the cavernous Cathedral, he led me forward towards the altar and then sat me down on a pew. I looked up, to the crucifix with the martyred Christ bleeding upon it, and I felt a flash of fellow-feeling and hope. *His* spirit had at last been freed from the earthly clay.

The priest stood up to go, perhaps to fetch first-aid materials. But I turned my body's head back and forth to signify a negative. Then I began to try to master my body's speaking apparatus. When I was alive, it had been simple. Now it took intense concentration to command the breath, the tongue and the vocal cords. Clumsy, ugly sounds were all that came out at first, but at last I began to make the sounds intelligible.

"Father," I said, "help..."

The old man sat down beside me. I could hear shuffling behind me. More people were coming into the Cathedral.

"Dead," I managed. "Died... morning. But... stuck. Inside. Need... get out."

The priest looked deeply into my eyes and then nodded slowly. "I see that is what you believe," he said. "Are you a Catholic, my son?"

Faintly I remembered the distant days attending Sunday Mass with my mother. "Once. Long ago," I got out.

"It is not the business of the Church to separate body from soul," the white-haired priest said. "That remains in the hands of God. Let me tend to your wounds, at least."

"No. Body. Not important," I said.

The old man looked at me, considering. Half to himself, he said: "The authorities are blaming what has been happening today on some kind of terrorist attack. A virus, or a poison, affecting people's minds. It has been happening all over the country today. Hundreds, perhaps thousands of people, all believing that they are dead. Feeling driven to seek out places of spiritual guidance. Churches, mosques, synagogues, temples."

He looked back, and I turned my body's head to follow his gaze. Many others as dead as myself were now coming into the church, shepherded by the younger priest and his helpers. Dozens of them now, and more coming. Vacant, slack faces, all staring forward towards the altar.

"I'm not sure what the atheists are doing," the priest continued with a half-laugh. "Perhaps they are marching on the University."

He turned back to me. "Personally, I don't believe this business about the terrorists. I think this is something far deeper. Something strange has been going on for the last month. There have been far fewer deaths than usual. For example, I attend a hospice for the dying as part of my pastoral duties. No one has died there for three weeks. And the newspapers have been reporting a sudden drop in road fatalities. Murders are down, too."

His words rolled over me, but I could muster little interest. I could tell that my body's physical state was growing weaker. "Help," I repeated.

He nodded, and then beckoned to the junior priest, whispering a few words to him.

"I am going to try something," he said. "My superiors in the Church might not approve, but still... I am going to administer the Last Sacrament to you."

As the younger priest hurried up with a silver cup and tray of consecrated wafers, the old man said: "It is not for us to understand God's will. But perhaps this is the beginning of the end of all things. I do wonder whether the last few weeks, and what has happened today, are not part of His plan to remind us of what we so readily forget. To remind us that we are all mortal, that all of us must die."

He kissed and then donned the purple sole which the younger priest handed to him. "Perhaps you, my son," he continued, "would have died last week from a heart attack. Perhaps that young woman who accompanied you here today was meant to die yesterday in a motorway accident. And so on for all of those here."

He looked around at the pews filled with silent, suffering faces. "Perhaps this is His way of telling us never to forget those who die. What better way to do that to hold back some fore-or-dained deaths and then raise those people to walk through the streets so that we cannot ignore them?" He sighed. "I don't know. Our understanding of these matters is so feeble. Perhaps we are not meant to know."

My vision was narrowing. I saw the priest as though he was at the end of a darkening tunnel.

He knelt before me and began to speak the words of the Eucharist, giving me the wine to sip and raising one of the wafers to my body's mouth. I felt it placed on my tongue and heard his closing words.

As he spoke the last word I saw a bright light growing at the end of the dark tunnel of my vision. As I saw it, my memories seemed to return with a rush and within the light I saw my life laid out like a great tapestry filled with infinite detail. My parents, my school days, my work, my wife, my sons, my loves and regrets; all were present at once.

Then at last the useless shell of my body pitched forward and fell slack to the ground. My spirit broke free and soared, soared, towards the light.

Flashes of Inspiration

very short fiction inspired by prompts

The Bastion

SHE HAD ARRANGED TO MEET HIM BACK AT THE CASTLE. Robert had laughed when she suggested it, thinking it one of her whims. It was where they had first met, over 25 years ago now.

Marian Schloss had been a first-year university student, working as a tour guide during the holidays to help pay for her second-year fees. Leading tour groups around the ancient castle, describing the historical points of interest, mostly to bored coach-loads of Americans, eager to be done with this, probably the tenth castle they had seen that day, and keen to get back to the hotel and the smorgasbord dinner awaiting them.

But there had been a few independent visitors from time to time, as well. Robert Ritter had been one of these. It had been drizzling, she remembered, and there had been hardly any visitors that day. For the 2 pm tour, there had only been Robert, and a nearly-deaf old lady. So Marian had spent most of the tour talking directly to Robert. He was a professional writer, he said,

171

three novels published. He was here to get some background for his next novel, his first venture into historical fiction.

He had been charming, and all through the tour made sly innuendos based on their historic surroundings, and his reference to the castle as 'she'. Talked about storming her defences, mounting an assault, invading the breach, widening the gap, and of course, dropping her drawbridge and forcing through the gate. She ought to have found this kind of talk crude and demeaning, but somehow he had made it witty and arousing. She had been so naive.

At the end of the tour he had invited her to dinner. Two months later, they were married and soon thereafter she found that she was pregnant. She dropped out of her university course. Her parents had furiously objected to the marriage. Robert Ritter was thirteen years her senior, and had been divorced from his first wife.

Too late, Marian realized that she didn't know much about Ritter. He was a published writer, that was true enough, but his books – mediocre crime stories poorly aping Raymond Chandler in an inappropriate British setting – hadn't ever sold well. The historical novel never eventuated. The couple's income was pathetic, and in the long gaps between publishers' advances, Ritter had to rely on the dole to get them by.

Soon enough, too, she realized that she should have asked more questions about why he had been divorced. That was when she had to start buying more make-up to hide the frequent bruises on her face.

She had thought back ironically then on those innuendos during that first tour of the castle, and realized how weak her defences had been. She hadn't represented the castle as it had once stood five hundred years before, strong, independent and impregnable – oh, the irony of *that* word! No, she had represented the castle as it was in today's world, its walls broken, its drawbridge long gone, wide open to the first assault.

So they had had their children, a boy and then a girl, and somehow struggled on. With his income so erratic, she had taken a series of menial jobs, and managed somehow to keep from him the fact that she scraped aside a tiny sum each week to put into into a savings account he didn't know about.

As the children grew, she had started to fight back, a little, mostly to defend them. There had been a memorable incident where she had knocked him unconscious with a thrown jar of jam. A small, temporary victory, a battle won in the midst of a longer war that she was inevitably losing. And she had paid in pain for that victory. He was too strong, too well armored, had all the weapons.

She should have left him sooner, before the children had grown up, but it would have meant admitting her defeat to her still-disapproving parents, and she couldn't bring herself to do that. Stupid. She should have swallowed her pride. Sought help, looked for reinforcements from her parents or from the law. Instead, she had stayed with Ritter, her life a continual siege, with her defences continually failing.

But when her daughter left home to study abroad, she had somehow found a reserve of strength and walked out on him.

She had half-expected him to come after her, hunt her down and make a frontal attack, perhaps to kill her as so many violent men do to their ex-wives. When he finally discovered where she was living and what her number was, there had been the expected storm of verbal abuse, but also, near the end of his rant, a stifled sob.

Of course, he was a lot older than her, and not long after she filed for divorce, he suffered a mild stroke. He recovered well enough, but it had left him with a slight limp, she had heard. And he'd used the stroke as an excuse to give up writing, though heaven knew he hadn't sold more than an odd short story in several years.

The divorce proceedings were taking far longer than she expected, and now he wanted to talk to her about them, about the settlement.

As it happened, the old castle was about half-way between the two towns where they now lived their separate lives. Hardly any tourists went there now – with the change in the exchange rate the Americans seemed to prefer Ireland these days – and the gift shop and the tour guides were long gone. She suggested it to him as a quiet place where they could talk. He agreed readily. Doubtless he thought it a half-romantic gesture, perhaps aimed at their eventual reconciliation. She knew better.

He met her on the grassy courtyard. "Marian, my dear!" he

exclaimed. "You are looking so well!" The same oily charm. How could she ever have been taken in by it?

He didn't look so well, his hair now nearly white, and carrying a thick cane, which clearly was needed and not one of his affectations. "Robert," she said neutrally. "Why don't we go up on the battlements? I always loved the view over the headland."

He bowed his head, and she led the way up the rough steps. The view from the castle wall was as spectacular as she recalled, with the steep slope beneath the wall falling to the sea surging over the rocks. In another few hundred years, she supposed, the castle wall would be undermined and fall into the sea. And there on the battlements they talked.

It was very much as she had predicted to herself. He wanted far more than she wanted to give, far more than was fair. He had found some lawyer, some drinking mate, no doubt, prepared to give Robert some cheap but potentially valid advice.

His charm had gone now, it was back to the bullying, the threatening. "You've got money," he said. "You paid for that cottage with it. Money you hid from me. Money you *stole* from me while we were nearly starving. Half of it is mine, Chandler says, says I'll win if we take it to court."

Though she had been expecting something like this, she was rightly outraged at his shamelessness. Her rage added strength to her fortifications against him, helped with her plan.

"I didn't steal it," she said angrily. "I managed to save it from what I earned by my own hard work while you were lollying about pretending to be England's next great novelist. If I'd told you about it you would have drunk it all away, you *bastard*." The last word was a weapon.

Here it came again, the incoherent rage. And now came the moment she had been sure would occur. He lifted his heavy cane like a sword, like some ancient crusader about to slay the Saracen.

Marian stood calmly. Bitter experience had taught her his every move.

As his cane swept down, she ducked neatly aside and he stumbled forward against the broken crenellations, here only knee-high. He dropped the cane and flailed his arms to try to regain his balance. The cane tumbled down towards the sea. He cried out in terror, unable to stop himself still toppling forward.

She had meant to push him if the need arose. Dreamt of doing it. That had been the plan. But when the moment came, with an impulse she couldn't explain but would later be grateful for, instead she grabbed hold of the back of his jacket and halted his fall, though he was still leaning well out above the drop. She leaned back and braced herself against his weight. She could hold him like this, but not for long, she thought.

"Help me! Help me, you bitch! Pull me back!"

"Why should I, Robert? Give me one good reason. I'm thinking, Robert, of all those times you hit me. All the times you threatened to kill me."

"Please Marian! For God's sake!"

"My arm's getting tired, Robert. Shall I let you go?"

"No, please. Anything, anything. I won't take you to court, I swear. I'm... I... I'm sorry. Sorry." He seemed to sag a little, his knees about to give way.

"*I don't forgive you.*"

He gave a gasp of horror, thinking that was the end. But instead she hauled him back. He collapsed to his knees then, shaking uncontrollably and beginning to sob with reaction.

She looked down at him with contempt, and then without another word she walked away from him with strength in her every step, her head held high.

The long war was over and she had won at last.

The Teeth of the Sea

photo by *Georgie Pauwels* on *Flickr*

I'VE ALWAYS KNOWN ABOUT THE SEA. Hated it. Feared it. Understood what it is really like. But you don't, do you? How innocent and stupid you are.

When I was a child, I already understood. My brothers and sisters would run laughing into the waves on a sunny day at the beach. Not me. They would call and call for me to join them, but I never would. I would never go down the sandy shore towards the sea, but would turn my back on it; creep into the farthest corner; hide behind my mother's body, or any nearby tree. Anything to hide myself away from its lusting eyes. The sea wanted me, but it could not have me.

Once, exasperated, my father picked me up and dropped me into the shallowest, warmest water at the edge of the sea. Screaming I ran out of the water, screaming I ran up the beach, screaming I ran so fast my father had trouble catching me despite his longer legs. He caught me only when I collapsed, blue in the face. He had to hit me, hard, so that I would take a breath. Then I vomited all over him. It was an experiment he never repeated.

Why do I hate the sea? I hear you asking why? Isn't it obvious? The sea is a monster, and it eats people in great watery gulps.

Oh, it can pretend, put on a charming, beguiling face, like any psychopath.

Come in, it says, *come in just a little way. I'm warm and welcoming, and I'm full of beautiful coral and pretty little fishes.*

Don't listen! Don't you understand, don't you know, what it's *really* like? When it is roused to anger, when the wind howls and the sky is grey and huge foam-flecked waves come crashing on the shore like the closing mouths of a great, many-headed beast? That's what the sea is really like.

Deep in its depths, nameless horrible creatures dwell, fishes out of your worst nightmare, with impossible teeth and huge freaky eyes.

Down there, too, lie the bones of drowned men and the drifting hulls of their long-lost ships, hulls a-gape with the holes that the sea has torn in them before sucking them down.

Back when I was young, all I knew was that the sea was something I hated. But my understanding has grown over the years. Now I know that the sea is alive, awake, and *evil*.

As I grew older, I learned and understood more and more. Now I understand that I have been *chosen*. God wants me to understand the evils of the waters. Didn't He use water to destroy mankind in the time of Noah? Didn't he part the dreadful waters to allow the passage of Moses and the Israelites, and then let them rush back, destroying, over Pharoah and his men?

God wants me to watch. I cannot stay away from the sea's edge. No one else will listen to me when I rave of the evils of the ocean. They've locked me up many a time to stop me talking. I endure such treatment. I know that I have been appointed to warn the world and to keep a watch over the sea. No one else understands it the way I do.

I don't go too near! Oh no! But I creep close enough to watch. I travel on, from place to place, always on the coast. Watching.

Watching its moods, its shifting faces, its deceitful calms, its honest rages, and I take note. Every so often I write down what I have seen, and send letters. To the newspapers. To the government. I warn them to barricade the beaches, to stop children playing in the shallows, to stop adults from testing the sea's patience. I warn them to stop sending out ships, ships which may travel safely for a little while, but which ultimately are doomed when the sea decides that it is hungry, which is often.

From time to time in my travels, I visit a library, and read all I can about the sea. The ancients knew all about its manifold evils, evils we have somehow forgotten. The god Poseidon, smashing ships with his huge trident; the beguiling Sirens, luring men to their doom; sea monsters like the Kraken; the many-headed serpentine Scylla; and the monstrous whirlpool Charybdis. All faces of the insatiable, greedy sea.

Reading of such tales, of the heroes of old, I have been making myself a weapon. A piece of steel found by the road. I have been shaping it and sharpening it carefully with stones picked up along the way. Like Perseus fighting the sea-monster Cetus to save the maiden Andromeda, I shall be armed and ready.

Hardly anyone now knows of the old tales and their warnings. Everyone is blind to the danger. Everyone but myself.

Today I came upon this place. Walking, as I always am, walking and watching. And waiting. Today I found what I had been looking for.

Here, at this place, twin rows of black teeth stretch out from beneath the water. Who could look at those teeth and not understand the nature of the beast which has thrust out its gaping maw towards me, trying to snatch me up?

Well, I have had enough of watching, of always being a wanderer whose voice is never heard. Now I understand why I was chosen, and what it is my divine task to perform. There is only one way to end this. Did Perseus draw back from saving Andromeda? Did Hercules hesitate to destroy the monster Scylla? No.

Inspired by those heroes, I shall leap into the very jaws of the beast and thrust my blade into its abysmal throat.

Understand, the death throes of the sea will be awful. There will be tsunamis everwhere, floods and earthquakes, storms and lightnings. It will seem like the end of the world. Oh yes. Prepare yourselves!

I take my sword in hand. It is time to begin.

Motive

image by Victoria Pickering *on* Flickr

DETECTIVE GRABOWITZ FINISHED HIS CUP OF COFFEE with a sigh, looked at his partner and indicated the interrogation room with a nod of his head.

"We try him again?"

"Might as well," said Jefferson. "See if we can make any more sense of it."

They entered the room, closed and locked the door and sat down with the suspect. Grabowitz turned on the recorder and did the required introduction spiel with the date, time and name of suspect.

The suspect was a short, angular African-American man in

his late twenties. His hands were clasped tightly together, and he was still staring at the table they were resting on. He hadn't even looked up when the detectives came into the room.

"OK, then, Mr Baker. I want to go back over when you first believed you were related to..." Grabowitz hesitated. He wanted to be formal, but it seemed ludicrous with that name. Never mind. "...to Mr Megabuck Bhang?"

The suspect glanced up with a resentful look. "I don't *believe*, I *know*," he said. "He's my identical twin. You can tell that just by looking at me."

"All right, Mr Baker," said Grabowitz. "Just go on. You were telling us about the posters."

"The posters. Yes, they're all over town, damn it."

Indeed they were. Megabuck Bhang was one of the most popular recording artists in the world, and there was a big nationwide concert tour on, playing in Philly this week. The posters showed his dark, handsome face with a knowing, self-confident smile, and MEGABUCK in huge letters underneath it.

"Seeing the posters," went on Baker. "That's what made up my mind to do something about it, to make him pay for what he's done to me. I found out that he was my twin years ago."

Jefferson cut in. "How did you find out?"

"I already told you about that."

"Tell us again."

"Well, I knew I was adopted. Mom told me when I was a kid, wanted me to know. And then when Megabuck hit the scene, released his first album, you know, the one with his face on the cover, people kept telling me how much I looked like him. It was true. The more I looked at it, the more I knew."

"Identical twins, separated at birth," said Jefferson laconically.

"That's it, that's it. That's what I started to tell people when they asked if I was related. Lots of people ask, all the time. It got worse the more famous Megabuck got. But it's not fair. Not fair. He was getting all that money – he made up that name, you know..."

"You surprise me," murmured Grabowitz.

"He made up the name because he knew one day he would be

rich. And then they made that film, and his records took off, and he was. Rich. Rich. And I'm so..."

Grabowitz consulted his records. Baker had been brought up in a middle class home. His adopted parents had saved and were able to send him to college. He had had a reasonable job as an insurance assessor, but had been laid off during the financial crisis. The bank had foreclosed on his home, now worth only a fraction of the outstanding mortgage, and his wife had left him. Sad but very common story.

"And you tried to contact Mr Bhang?" asked Jefferson.

"Yes, yes. Sent him photos of myself. Told him I was his brother, his twin. Needed his help."

"But you received no reply?"

"No," said Baker with a half-sob. "It would have been his minders. Damn them. They wouldn't have passed on my letter, would have thought that I was just some crank."

Grabowitz took over again. "So when you started seeing the posters last month, you said that you came up with a plan. What was that?"

Baker shook his head and his hands, despite still being tightly clenched, trembled on the table. "I don't want to tell you. I'm tired."

"Mr Baker, you must talk to us. You've waived your right to have a lawyer present. Tell us about your plan."

Baker gave another sob, paused a long, long moment, and then finally began. "It was when I was trying to figure out how to prove that I was his twin, his identical twin. I thought about DNA tests, you know. I mean, I thought, if I can get some of his DNA and show that it is identical to mine... But I couldn't work out how I could do that. Then I got angry, really angry. And I thought of my plan."

Stony-faced, Grabowitz said "Go on."

"I... I found out the hotel he's staying at. And I thought, I thought..."

Grabowitz and Jefferson were silent.

"If I could get him accused of a crime... he's done time in jail, you know, before he was famous, beat up his girlfriend. His DNA is on record."

Grabowitz glanced across at Jefferson, who nodded and flashed him a glance of the report he had brought in.

"So, if I didn't leave any fingerprints... but left my DNA... he would get the blame. Jury would convict him based on the DNA evidence, bound to. I've never been arrested, never done any crime... well, until now... so my name wouldn't be connected, no one would know. And even if someone saw me, you see..." Baker was excited now, and glanced up. "Even if they saw me, they would think it was him. Because we're identical twins!"

"But someone did see you, Mr Baker," said Jefferson grimly. "Saw you leaving the back entrance to the hotel, with the maid's blood on you. And we tracked you down through that witness' description."

"But you couldn't, you couldn't..."

Grabowitz leaned across to Jefferson. "Want to try him with the mirror again?"

Jefferson shook his head. "Nah. Time to get the psych guys in."

They both stared across at Baker.

There was only a slight accidental resemblance to the posters of Megabuck Bhang. And Baker was at least a foot shorter.

The Waters under the Firmament

photo by Giuseppe Milo on Flickr

"WILL THE BARRIERS HOLD?" Amaya's mother asked, her face full of anxiety.

"Of course they will," her father replied with a touch of impatience. "We developed force-field technology more than twenty years ago, and the barriers have been in place for fifteen. We're improving the technology every year. Really, 'Mina, there's nothing to be worried about."

Amaya looked across at her father, sitting relaxed in his armchair, and was comforted. Her mother's anxiety had been affecting her, too. But her father Armand, tall and grey-headed now, was an engineer. Amaya wasn't entirely sure what an engineer did, but her father was always calm and certain, a solid rock amidst any storm. That was enough.

Hasmina, Amaya's mother, still fretted, looking out of the

window again and beginning once more to count through her rosary. Amaya hopped up beside her and looked out, too.

From here, it was easy to see the glittering, transparent barrier holding back the sea from the city a few kilometres distant. The level of the water was as high today as Amaya had ever seen it, almost level with the top of a four-storey office building close by. A framework supporting a huge lift-shaft ran up the side of the barrier to the floating docks at its top, where there were tall cranes which unloaded the cargo from container ships. That was the beauty of the force-field barrier, Amaya had been told by her father: it could be easily adjusted to stay just above whatever water level the sea now reached.

"But what if the power were to fail?" Hasmina asked.

Amaya's father put down the tablet he had been reading. "I've explained that," he said, by now obviously annoyed. "The systems are triple-redundant. All the power comes from a geothermal source, which can't fail until the Earth grows cold. Every coastal city has similar systems in place, and they are always being tested. Really, 'Mina, you don't have anything at all to worry about. Get a grip on yourself."

Hasmina was silent, but her fingers moved ceaselessly through the rosary and Amaya could see her mother's lips move slight-ly as she mentally recited the "Hail Mary" again and again. Hasmina's faith was a continual irritation to Amaya's father, who was an unbeliever, and the source of many an argument in Amaya's home.

Now Armand simply frowned. "Amaya, go out and play for a while. It's a beautiful day out there, and you're annoying your mother." That clearly wasn't true, and even a ten-year-old like Amaya could see that her father just wanted her out of the way so that he could have a full-on row with her mother. But it was best not to argue with him.

As she reached the door of their apartment, her father stopped her. "Don't forget your Nanny," he said, picking up the elec-tronic pendant from the table and handing it to her. "And don't go too far. If it starts to rain, come back straight away. They are forecasting a storm this afternoon."

With a sigh, Amaya put the pendant around her neck. It was quite heavy, and annoying to wear, but its tiny brain and sensors were always on the lookout for danger, and could sound a loud alarm and electronically call for help without her needing to do a thing. At any moment, her parents could check on her whereabouts and see video of her surroundings. Since the introduction of the Nannies some years ago, children had become much freer to roam without their parents worrying. That didn't mean, however, that children were particularly keen to carry them.

"I'll just take my skateboard down to the Plaza," she said. Amaya had few playmates, and had learned to entertain herself as best she could.

"All right," her father said. "Be back for dinner. Two hours max, OK?"

She nodded and ran off down the stairs and then onto the street, hopping on to her skateboard and speeding it along. It was a hot, humid day. The sun was shining and there wasn't a cloud in sight. Maybe the storm would arrive later, but there was no sign of it at present.

A pathway meandered through a nearby park, and Amaya scooted down it, dodging the occasional pedestrian and cyclist, feeling happier now that she was away from her parents' continual arguments. She sped by a small lake, frightening into flight a group of ducks and making a swan honk at her, which only made Amaya laugh. Through the park and down another few streets and finally into the City Plaza. It was heaven for skateboarders there.

Amaya spent a long time whizzing across the open spaces, speeding up ramps and leaping over gaps, once rather too close to a seat where two old people were sitting relaxing in the sun. They yelled after her in annoyance, but Amaya wasn't concerned. There were lots more old people than children these days, and young people like her were treated with a good deal of forebearance.

The afternoon went by. Amaya was hot and sweaty. She was just beginning to get tired and think of going home when she noticed heavy drops of rain hitting the paving and looked up to see a dark, threatening cloud approaching. The wind started to blow strongly.

Rather than going home immediately as she'd been instructed, though, Amaya ducked beneath a colourful canvas awning at the edge of the Plaza. The barrier holding back the sea was only about a half kilometre from here, down a wide sloping boulevard, and she wanted to watch the waves at the top. She could see their foamy peaks splashing against the barrier. Some water was now even starting to slop over, and even as she watched the force-barrier was raised higher. The floating dock was being anchored into place and the cranes were being moved into their rest positions. No more unloading today!

The wind whipped up even harder, blowing gritty dust into Amaya's eyes. Perhaps she should start for home after all. But the rain was now falling more and more heavily. She could always tell her father that she'd been caught by surprise and had to shelter until the rain was past. He could see through her Nanny where she was and what she was doing, anyway.

The storm now really arrived, and the wind began to howl, scattering paper and leaves across the plaza. The sea was lashing against the barrier, waves towering. The barrier was raised yet higher to try to control it, higher than Amaya had ever seen it, and she wondered how much power it was using. Her mother would be terrified, but Amaya thought that she could trust her father. The force-field technology would keep them safe against the rising sea, as it had done all of her life.

That was when the man-hole cover nearby jetted into the air atop a fountain of water. Cracks opened up between the paving stones, and first one, then another, then dozens and dozens of spouts of water shot high into the air, filling the plaza with an impromptu water display. Amaya looked on amazed, her mouth dropping open. Where was all this water suddenly coming from?

It was remarkably pretty. Amaya ran out into it, careless that she was getting soaked. The cool water was a relief after her exertions on this hot day. She danced about amidst the jets. As the water ran down her face, some of it dribbled into her laughing mouth. Salt. Salt water. She looked through the spouts of water at the high barrier and the towering sea. No change there. But this water...

All that sea out there, it must be really heavy, she thought. Water *was* heavy, she knew that. The higher the level of the sea, the heavier the weight at the bottom. All of that water, pressing down... Forcing its way through every crevice, forcing its way into the pipes, the subways, the channels which carried electricity and data. Forcing its way down... and then back up!

One of the paving stones next to her leapt high into the air with a wide geyser of water beneath it. The stone went clattering across the Plaza. Then another shot up.

Alarmed now, Amaya ran back to her skateboard, and started to scoot along as fast as she could. Through narrow streets, then the park, where the ducks and swans were long gone, and the pond was slopping over the footpath. Sloshing along her own street, leaving a wake behind her. Running up the stairs, one flight, two flights, three flights, to hammer on her apartment door.

Her father was there, his face ashen. Her mother was behind him, rosary clutched close.

"Thank God you're back," he said. "Quick, we're going up to the roof."

"The barriers..." her mother sobbed.

Grim, her father replied, "The barriers are safe, I told you that. It's just that... we didn't think... we hadn't taken into account... Oh hell. Just come, quickly."

Up the stairs they headed. Many people were following their example. Round and round, up and up, everyone went. Finally, standing out on the open roof, they saw the waters spouting up through their city, fountaining high, high, higher, until the jets peaked and the nearest splattered salty water over the watchers.

In the street, the waters rose and the rain continued to fall.

"'The same day,'" whispered Amaya's mother, "'were all the fountains of the great deep broken up, and the windows of heaven were opened...'"

For once, Amaya's father was silent in reply.

The Chisel's Sharp Edge

This was written for a prompt challenge to write a story in exactly one hundred words.

WITH ROUGH BLOWS HE FREES HER FROM THE STONE. Painstakingly, his delicate chisel cuts away all that is not her. Then the long last phase, as he grinds and polishes her smooth skin.

Finally, she stands, as perfect in marble as in his dreams. Almost as perfect. If only her flesh was warm, yielding to the touch. He would pay any price for that boon!

Kneeling, he prays as never before. At last the gods grant his wish. She moves!

At that moment, horrified, he feels his limbs stiffen into white marble.

He sees her pick up the chisel.

Killer Shot

photo by *Jordi Payà* on Flickr

DETECTIVE ARNOLD HELD A RECTANGULAR BOX HIGH in triumph as he came into the squad room. He spotted Mangiamele by the cooler and waved him over.

"The lab boys come through?" asked Mangiamele with interest.

"Yeah," Arnold said, "they did a good job. Getting that camera open in the pitch dark can't have been easy, considering the condition it's in. Let's see what we've got."

They went into one of the interview rooms, and Arnold put the box down on the table, then fished into his pocket and tossed the camera down. Already on the table was a small battered spiral notebook which they had been going through earlier.

Arnold opened the box and spread out the prints, making sure he kept them in chronological order.

Mangiamele picked up the first print. It was taken in the dining car of a train, and showed a couple seated at one of the narrow tables. The man had his back to the camera, but looked to be a bulky man in his mid-fifties, wearing a dark suit. The woman was young, blonde, and pretty, with dark lipstick. You couldn't tell the colour of course, in these black-and-white prints. The shot had been taken from a distance, probably from the doorway into the next carriage. Matt Evans, the private detective, wouldn't have wanted to be spotted.

The next was the reverse shot, this one a little blurry and from a funny angle. Maybe Evans had taken it while holding the camera at his side? Yes, the next few shots were repeats, all slightly different, some hopelessly out of focus or showing the back of one of the seats. But the best one was clear, showing the back of the blonde's head and the face of the man in the suit – Carl Studebaker, big business tycoon.

"I'll give Evans credit," said Mangiamele, "he wasn't afraid to take risks."

Arnold grunted. "Mrs Studebaker was paying him enough, he thought it was worth it to get the shots she wanted."

"These wouldn't be enough for the divorce case, though," said Mangiamele. "He needed to get something more explicit."

They skimmed through the next few prints. Evans must have bribed the train conductor to let him into Studebaker's first class compartment. First class was pretty good on a sleeper train, but the luxury was limited by necessity. There were shots of the folded-down single beds – the train was too small for a double bed – then some of the interiors of some of the drawers, one showing frilly underwear.

Arnold laughed. "Studebaker would have trouble explaining those to his wife!"

Mangiamele smiled too. "Maybe he could claim they were his? Mind you, that would probably be grounds for divorce too, hey?"

"Nah, I don't see a court buying that, not for such a big profile case as that would be. What do Evans' notes say?"

Mangiamele shrugged, leafing through the little notebook. "Sounds as if Evans was pretty frustrated on the train trip over here. No opportunity to get the kind of shot he needed. So he planned to wait until they got to L.A. and track Studebaker to his hotel. Which, of course, is what he did, poor sap."

The next few prints were indeed in the city. Some trailing shots, some showing the couple embracing as they came out of a restaurant. One showed them kissing.

Arnold tapped that one with his forefinger. "This one might have done the trick."

"Yeah," agreed Mangiamele, "but Evans was a pro. He would have wanted a clincher." He leafed through the next couple of prints. "Oh, oh!"

"What?"

Mangiamele spun the print over to Arnold. "I'd say this is where Studebaker started to cotton on that he was being followed."

The photo had been taken in a restaurant, and like the previous one showed Studebaker and his girlfriend at a table. But in this one, Studebaker was glaring at the camera, half-risen from his seat, his fist raised.

"Yeah," said Arnold, "that's an important one. It'll cut the heart from his defence. Could show evidence for premeditation."

"Explains why Studebaker had the gun handy, anyway. Do you think he'll get away with saying it was self-defence?"

"Dunno, he'll have some high-powered lawyers backing him. But I hear Mrs Studebaker is offering her money and resources to help the D.A."

And so they came to the final print. Evans must have bribed a hotel cleaner to give him a master key to the hotel bedrooms. Mangiamele reflected that Evans must have been pretty desperate to get a shot of the couple in bed together. Pretty risky, you'd only get one chance as you threw the door open. And what if the flash didn't go off? But it had, after all.

Arnold and Mangiamele both stared at the last photo. There were some patches of light spoiling the edges, but it was very clear, a great action shot, really.

After a while, Arnold nodded in satisfaction. "Yep, this is the shot that'll send him to the chair. Studebaker *must* have had time to recognize Evans and his camera."

Evans' final picture showed Studebaker, naked, sitting up on the bed, his girlfriend with her hands half-raised to try to cover her breasts. And in Studebaker's right hand, its barrel clearly pointing at the photographer, was the gun which had killed Evans a half-second later.

Mangiamele looked at the twisted remains of the little camera, its flash reflector flattened, its lens shattered.

When the hotel security had arrived, Studebaker had been trying to smash it to pieces under his naked heel, having been unable to quickly figure out how to get the back open to expose the reel of film inside. If he'd been wearing shoes he might have succeeded.

Displacement

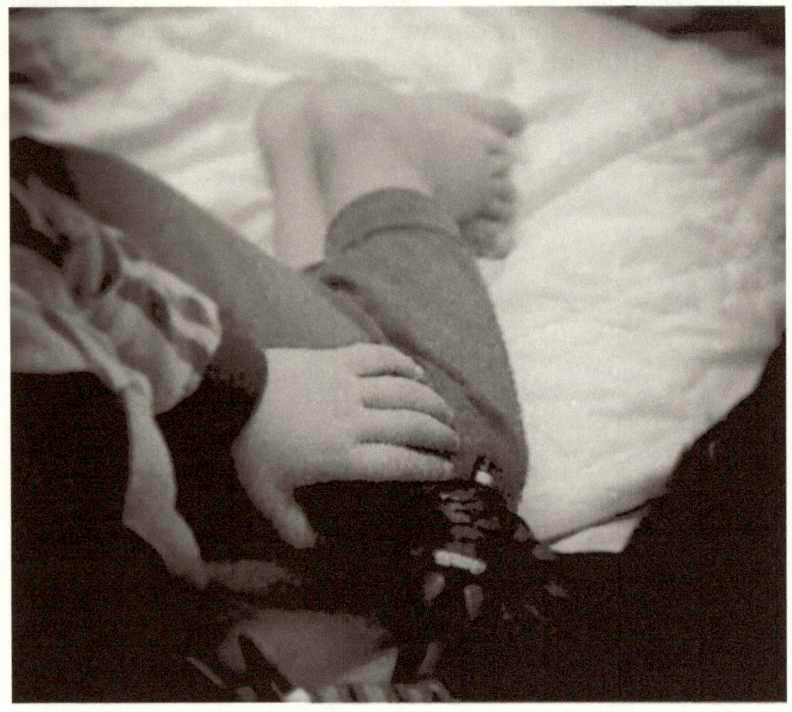

photo by roya_m on Flickr

Damian had fallen asleep at last, clutching his beloved Batman figurine. Jack Leavis gently eased it out of his son's hand and set it down on the wooden floor beside the stretcher bed. The little boy's hand twitched for a moment, but otherwise he didn't stir.

Maggie gave Jack a bitter look. Again. "I still can't believe that's all you grabbed out of his room," she muttered. Again. "Why couldn't you grab some nappies? Or his shoes, for God's sake?"

Jack sighed. "You know how little time we had. It's just what I spotted as I was picking him up. It was hard to think straight."

"You never think straight," she said, her face sour as she

looked around her at the crowded school gymnasium. The air-conditioning couldn't cope and the heat was oppressive. Hundreds of people were crammed in here. There were a few canvas beds like the one Damian was lying on, but many people were just sleeping on the hard wooden floor. A miserable soft babble, overlain by the plaintive cries of a few babies, filled the air.

Jack swallowed his anger. He was determined not to let Maggie start another argument. Back in their comfortable suburban home, there might have been time and space for such a dispute. But not here, not now. They had to stick together if they were going to get through this.

"They should given us more warning," his wife went on. "If we'd had time..."

That pushed him over the edge.

"There *were* warnings, Maggie," he said, mildly enough. "They kept telling us about the danger, said it would be a good idea to have an evacuation bag ready." *A bag you never packed*, he thought.

She folded her arms tightly, a surprisingly aggressive gesture. "That happens every year," she said. "Clear your gutters, cut down the dry grass, yada yada yada. But that's only for people living in the bush. Not for people like us, living in the middle of the city. *We* shouldn't have to worry about bushfires. Just those greenie nongs who live in wooden houses surrounded by trees they won't cut down because they love them so much. Then they bleat for help when their houses catch fire. No one could expect *us* to have to worry about all that stuff."

Jack contemplated Maggie for a long moment, during which he found himself seriously wondering whether he still loved this woman.

"And yet," he said, "we *did* have to worry. Every year it's been getting hotter and drier. The fire season has been starting earlier and earlier in the year. It's been harder and harder to keep the fires under control. And this year... well, they lost control. Once the houses on the outskirts started to burn, and the embers were driven into the city by the wind... Look, at least we got out alive."

Maggie's angry, set face twitched and then tears started and her mouth changed shape. "But we've lost *everything*, Jack. *Everything*."

"We're still alive," he repeated. "We can rebuild, start afresh. Think of how much unnecessary junk we had."

"*Junk* you call it? What about my clothes, my shoes, my jewellery? My... oh hell!" Her voice broke and she stared away from him, tears running down her face and dripping from her chin. He put a tentative arm around her shoulders, but she angrily shrugged it off.

That was when the school's PA system crackled to life. "Attention! Attention! I'm really sorry, folks, but we're going to have to move you all on."

A collective groan arose from the crowded hall. One man stood and started shouting angrily before his wife pulled him back down.

The announcement continued: "...the fire front is getting too close, and the brigade isn't confident of stopping it before it reaches here. We're trying to arrange some buses, but if you are able to walk we urge you to set off now. Head south towards the river. The Bank Street bridge is the closest river crossing. You should be safe on the other side." A pause, then: "God willing." The announcement finished with a final crackle.

"Oh, Christ!" Maggie said, her face ashen and despairing.

"Come on, love," Jack said. "I'll carry Damian. Let's hope he stays asleep."

He picked his son up gently and cradled him to his chest as Maggie, weeping, picked up the bags which now represented all that they owned in the world.

As the doors of the gymnasium were swung open, they saw an orange sky and could smell the smoke. People began to trudge outside with slow, heavy steps.

Still holding Damian close with one arm, Jack bent and picked up his son's Batman figurine with his free hand. He slipped it into his pocket. He couldn't have put into words why, but right now he felt as though the little plastic figure was their most precious possession.

They set off towards an uncertain future.

Not Drowning

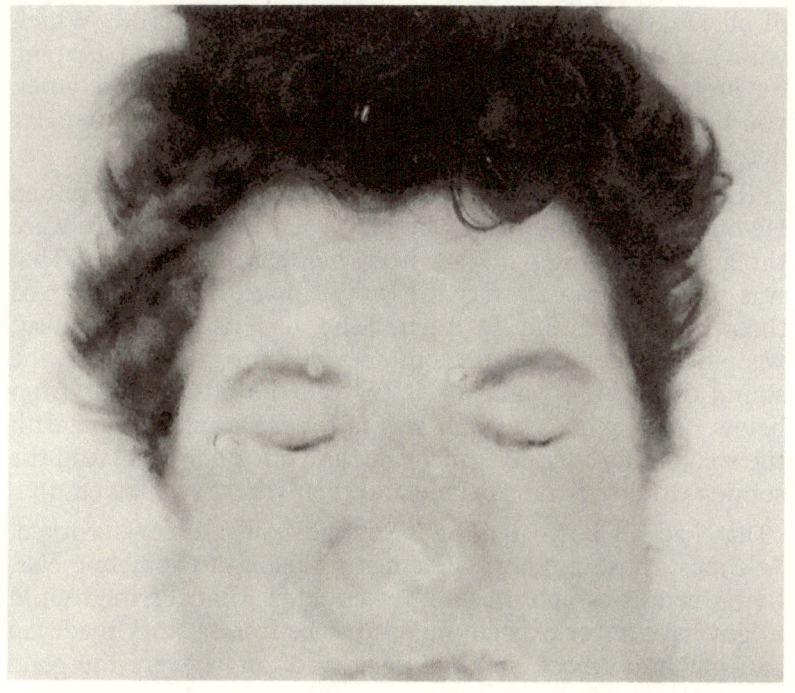

photo by roya_m on Flickr

ONCE MORE, ELISE DUCKED HER HEAD UNDER THE WATER. The bathwater was beginning to get cold, her fingers prune-wrinkled with long soaking. Soon enough she would have to get out and towel down, make herself ready for the visitors who were on the way. But not just yet. Not just yet.

Under the water, she thought back, remembering doing this when she was a child. However long ago that was. Take a deep breath and duck down into the welcoming water, to stay there as long as she could manage.

Every sound was changed down here. *She* was changed. What was that poem from the otherwise boring play she'd been forced to read at school? Something about your eyes turning into pearls, that was a nice thought. And your bones changing into coral, that was pretty, too. But Elise couldn't remember anything in the poem about what happened to your ears, and that was the important part.

Under the water, unwelcome sounds were shifted and masked into an echoing, distant gurgle, stripped of all meaning, stripped of all emotion. They became comic, almost cheerful. Which wasn't at all how they sounded when you were forced, gasping for breath, to pull your head out of the water. That was when you heard the real, ugly sounds coming from downstairs. Her parents, arguing. Over her, usually.

Elise never knew what he had done wrong to anger her father. He often seemed infuriated by her very existence. There were threats, and counter-threats from her harassed mother. That was when he would start throwing things, before he started throwing blows. But by then, Elise had usually run away, weeping, to lock the bathroom door and turn on the taps, the sound of gushing water drowning out the bitter words from below. Then, when the bath was full, Elise would slip beneath the welcoming surface of the water and duck her head. And the sounds would be transformed and their threat swallowed up.

That had all been long ago. Strange how memory worked. At times, those memories seemed to belong to someone else, living centuries ago, in another country. That terrified child might have never existed, might just be from a story made up and put into a book she had once read. Those were the good times.

But then there were the times when she felt the child very close to the surface, the girl's experiences raw and immediate. Perhaps Elise kept the child inside her somewhere, locked away, only every so often to escape and make herself heard?

No. Who was she fooling? She still *was* that child, that weeping child. Just wrapped up in a flimsy layer of years. A child, condemned to repeat the experiences which had shaped her mother's life.

She had to breathe. Gasping, Elise lifted her head from the water, which ran streaming from her face and her hair. Her newly shortened hair. She'd cut it short so that her husband could no longer grab it and hurl her to the floor. He'd enjoyed doing that. Just as he had enjoyed doing so many things which hurt and humiliated her.

But that was all over. She had ended it.

As the water cleared from her dripping ears, Elise could hear, as she had known that she would, the sound of approaching sirens.

The Right Direction

KATJA SPED DOWN THE ROAD ON HER BICYCLE. She was going to be late – again! – for her history tutorial.

Professor Carney would glare and make some cutting remark which would veer just this side of being so sexist that she could report him. Then he would continue with one of his typical monologues about the economic consequences of the Hundred Year's War.

Katja was really beginning to reconsider her choice of study. What use, after all, would an intimate knowledge of the household accounts of mad King Charles VI be in getting her a job? Well, a job which paid more than a pittance?

Whoops! Concentrating too hard on her miserable prospects, Katja had become distracted. She had to swerve suddenly to avoid colliding with a group of pedestrians who had begun to cross the road ahead of her. One of them, an elderly woman in black, shouted after in some foreign tongue. Katja blushed but went on. She steadied herself and applied herself to navigating safely.

She reached the university and spent time she didn't have in hunting for a spare bicycle rack. But they were all full. Another consequence of being late, which would make her later still. Finally in desperation she padlocked her bike to a nearby sign-post. The sign, in lettering of a regrettable shade of orange, warned against leaving bicycles anywhere other than in the officially-sanctioned racks. Too bad.

She might cop a fine, though. Which she wouldn't be able to pay. Katja worked in the evenings as a waitress at a small Armenian restaurant. It didn't pay very well, and Tigran the owner leered at her and had started to make unwelcome suggestions when his wife, the cook, wasn't within hearing. Not to mention the frequent bottom pinches from greasy middle-aged customers.

Honestly, she thought, *I don't know why I'm doing this.*

Grabbing up her heavy pile of textbooks, Katja stomped to the History building and up two flights of stone stairs. Down a long corridor, with an invisible but intense cloud of resentment trailing behind her.

At least she could gain some pleasure from the beautiful old building itself, with its fine stonework and the elegant carved lettering over the arched doorways. It dated back almost two hundred years, when people used to have some *taste*, she thought.

There was a piece of paper on the door of the tutorial room. Katja's orderly mind noted that it was stuck to the ancient oak at a distinct angle, affixed with grubby sticky-tape at its corners. It was printed in Comic Sans, a hanging offence in Katja's view.

"Professor Carney is unwell," it read. "No tutorials until futher notice." The word 'further' was misspelled.

It could have been worse, Katja supposed. The sign could have been printed in the faux-Gothic Old English font which one of the faculty secretaries was addicted to, apparently of the view that it was ideal for anything related to history. It was not.

Katja unstuck the paper and replaced it, perfectly level. Pity about the grubby sticky-tape, but there was nothing she could do about that.

She looked again at the words. "Professor Carney is unwell." Drunk, more likely, or hung-over, she thought.

She fumbled in her bag and selected a black fine-tip pen. With it, she carefully inserted a neat 'r' to correct the word 'further'.

Katja stood staring at the adjusted sign for a long time. A ridiculous time. And she made a decision. She marched back down the stairs, out of the lovely old building, and across the quad to the University Bookstore. She went up to the Second-Hand Counter and plomped down every textbook from her bag on to the desk.

"How much will you give me for these?" she asked.

The middle-aged woman behind the counter was startled. "It's mid-semester, dear. Are you giving up your course?"

"Yes," said Katja, folding her arms to keep tight her determination. "Can you tell me the way to the offices of the University Press? They're in this building, aren't they?"

"Yes, dear. Up those stairs."

"They're going to give me a job as a graphic designer."

"Oh. Are they?" said the woman as she began counting through the books in front of her.

"Yes. They just don't know it yet."

The Winter Garden

photo by Carbonnyc on Flickr

I WAS STANDING BY THE FROZEN LAKE when she came out of the mist, her head surrounded by a golden halo of hair, lit from behind by the lamplight.

How appropriate, I thought. My angel. Angelica. My father's third wife.

As she came closer, she moved into the light from a nearer lamp, and I could see her face for the first time. I made an attempt to smile, though the cold made my face feel stiff.

"Dominic," she said flatly. There was no accompanying smile, her mouth a thin line and her face grim. Her gaze was distant, distracted, but I felt a pulse of joy, knowing what it must mean.

We stood and looked at each other for long moments, our breath steaming in the chill air.

"Is it done, then?" I could hardly bring myself to ask.

She looked away from me then, over the icy lake surrounded by bare willow trees. "Yes. He's gone. But..."

My heart gave a skip. "But...?"

"But it wasn't as easy as you said it would be." She shivered, and pulled her coat around her. I thought briefly that she should be wearing a hat. But she had always hated wearing anything over her hair.

She turned to look at me directly for the first time. "That powder you gave me... what was it again?"

"I told you, some kind of neurotoxin. The chemist I paid for it said it would work instantly. And be undetectable."

"Work," she said in a bitter tone. "Such an easy word. You mean 'kill'."

"Yes," I said. "But it worked?"

She shivered again. "I'm so cold. Let's walk."

We started to amble around the lake. There were only a few other couples in the park that cold night, and I wondered whether we should have met somewhere else. But we had taken to meeting in the park months ago, when I first set out to charm Angelica.

Ever since my father had disowned me and thrown me out of his business, I had been convinced that he was having me watched and my phones tapped. The park was safe, no one could tail you without being seen. And I didn't want to be seen with Angelica, even now. Not for a while, at least.

"It worked?" I asked again, insistently.

"Not instantly," she said. "It was awful."

"Did you call the ambulance straight away, like I told you? The symptoms should have mimicked a heart attack. But the paramedics wouldn't be able to save him."

Angelica just nodded. I was a little puzzled by how she was responding, really. I had expected her to be happier. She had often told me how miserable she was married to my father, who was decades older than her. In fact, Angelica was a year younger than me. Still, I had to make allowances. The whole thing must have been quite traumatic, I supposed.

"And the will?" I asked. "You're quite sure he didn't get the chance to alter his will?" This was the really important question, of course.

"No, he hasn't changed it, I'm sure his most recent will is the one he made when I married him."

"Leaving the bulk of his assets to you. And a miserable allowance to me," I said bitterly.

"Not so miserable," she said. "Most people would say they could live comfortably on it."

"Well, it would be better than what I'm living on now," I conceded. "But I need to be back running the business. I've got a lot of plans. When we're married in a year or two..."

"Hush," she said. We were passing another couple slowly perambulating around the lake in the opposite direction. A tall man and a woman wrapped up in furs. For some reason I glanced back at them over my shoulder after they had passed us, and was startled to realise that yet another couple were following us several yards behind. Too far back to have overheard anything Angelica and I had said, I was sure.

"You can persuade the board to invite me back," I said. "And now you own the majority of the shares, they can't stop you anyway, if you insist. My father wouldn't have put anything down in writing about me, I'm sure, no matter what he felt. I'm his own flesh and blood, after all. Well, *was*," I ended lamely.

"And yet you wanted him dead," Angelica said. she looked away from me again, over the lake and at the mist-enshrouded lamps on the other side.

I stopped walking, startled by her tone. "Yes. But sweetheart, you know why. I told you that I couldn't stand seeing him pawing you, the way I feel about you."

"About me," she said, "or about the business?" Her eyes were fierce.

"Is that what's bothering you? Darling, I..."

Her face had changed now, changed in a way I couldn't comprehend.

"You really are a cold fish, aren't you?" she said in a stony tone. "I come here tonight and tell you that your father is dead, that I killed him for you, and you shed not a single tear, and offer me no comfort. You never really cared one iota about me, did you?"

I stood silent, barely comprehending her.

"And you were so sure of your ability to charm a woman,

weren't you, Dominic? Did you have a moment's doubt that I would fall for you?"

Suddenly I saw just in front of us one of the couples who had been walking around the lake. The man was holding up some kind of badge.

At the same moment a heavy hand fell on my right shoulder from behind and another hand tightly gripped my left wrist.

"Deceit can work both ways, Dominic," Angelica said, and from beneath her coat she pulled a microphone and recorder.

"Dominic Martin Chesterton," said the deep voice of the man with the badge, "I arrest you for the attempted murder of Charles Chesterton. You have the right to remain silent..."

Too late, I remembered that before she had married my father, Angelica Meadows had been an acclaimed stage actress.

Out from behind one of the willow trees stepped a heavy figure with a forbidding face. Angelica ran to him.

My father.

Did you enjoy this book?

If so, please visit *www.rightword.com.au/books* to purchase these other volumes of David's stories.